# Advance Praise for
## *Engraved on the Heart*

"A truly lovely debut novel. [Told] through the eyes of an unlikely heroine awakening to the injustices of slavery, *Engraved on the Heart* brings Savannah, Georgia, during the Civil War to life. Tara Johnson writes with honesty and compassion, undergirded with solid research. The characters are lovingly drawn, and Keziah's growth from sheltered weakness to faithful courage is simply radiant. A book to savor and an author to watch!"

SARAH SUNDIN, AWARD-WINNING AUTHOR OF *THE SEA BEFORE US* AND THE WAVES OF FREEDOM SERIES

"Set amid the beauty of Savannah, Georgia, at the onset of the Civil War, *Engraved on the Heart* is a story that is as spiritually profound as it is romantic, its heroine as memorable and unique as her lovely name. Johnson weaves a tale of secrets, selflessness, and service where love and truth triumph. A remarkable, memorable debut!"

LAURA FRANTZ, AUTHOR OF *THE LACEMAKER*

"Through the eyes of pop-off-the-page characters, readers are whisked into turbulent Confederate Savannah, from charming balls to the intrigue and danger of the Underground Railroad. Woven throughout this vibrant tale are strong spiritual threads sure to inspire. Lovers of

Civil War fiction will rejoice to add *Engraved on the Heart* to their collections. I'll be looking for more from Tara Johnson!"

"Blending realistic, relatable characters and the heartrending issue of slavery against a beautifully painted backdrop, Tara Johnson presents a debut novel that will leave you satisfied and yet still wanting more. Both major issues—living with an uncontrollable health issue and being trapped in servitude—could become oppressive or maudlin, but Johnson expertly handles both and weaves them so intricately into the story's fabric that a beautiful tapestry of overcoming hardship and experiencing freedom emerges. I highly recommend this engaging and intriguing historical novel."

"Tara Johnson delivers a stirring tale of danger and hope in *Engraved on the Heart.* I was invested in Micah and Kizzie's love story from the very first chapter—and fell more than a little in love with Micah myself."

# Engraved on the Heart

# Engraved on the Heart

## TARA JOHNSON

Tyndale House Publishers, Inc.
Carol Stream, Illinois

Visit Tyndale online at www.tyndale.com.

Visit Tara Johnson's website at www.tarajohnsonstories.com.

*TYNDALE* and Tyndale's quill logo are registered trademarks of Tyndale House Publishers, Inc.

*Engraved on the Heart*

Designed by Eva Winters

Edited by Danika King

Published in association with the literary agency of Books & Such Literary Management, 52 Mission Circle, Suite 122, PMB 170, Santa Rosa, CA 95409.

Scripture quotations are taken from the *Holy Bible*, King James Version.

*Engraved on the Heart* is a work of fiction. Where real people, events, establishments, organizations, or locales appear, they are used fictitiously. All other elements of the novel are drawn from the author's imagination.

For information about special discounts for bulk purchases, please contact Tyndale House Publishers at csresponse@tyndale.com or call 1-800-323-9400.

ISBN: 978-1-4964-2831-8

Printed in the United States of America

| 24 | 23 | 22 | 21 | 20 | 19 | 18 |
|----|----|----|----|----|----|----|
| 7  | 6  | 5  | 4  | 3  | 2  | 1  |

*For Jesus. All praise is yours alone.*
*Bless, break, and multiply.*

# CHAPTER 1

*Don't fail. Tonight of all nights, don't fail.*

Keziah Montgomery placed her gloved fingers into the waiting hand of the man smiling at her with confident expectation.

Taking a shallow breath against the corset threatening to crush her ribs in its unyielding grip, she willed her fluttering stomach to calm and allowed Mr. Watson to lead her onto the crowded dance floor. A colorful array of bright silks and lace flurried around her in circles. The thick, sticky air carried the weight of pomade and a nauseating mixture of shaving soaps and rice powder. The din of chatter and polite laughter choked her dizzying thoughts.

From across the room, she caught Mother's penetrating stare. Elsie Montgomery had been adamant Keziah be at her best. No one must know her shameful secret. The sooner she marry, the better . . . before her future husband realized what her parents were so desperate to keep hidden.

Looking up, she smiled into the youthful face of Tate Watson as he cupped his warm hand against her waist, keeping the proper distance between them as the musicians struck up the opening strains of "The Scenes of Our Childhood." She noted the golden stubble lining his jaw, his brown eyes bright. A flush of heat crept up her neck.

She blinked away the grit filming her vision. It was late into the festivities and the night seemed to drag. Still, she maintained her pasted-on smile and allowed him to sweep her through the whirling couples and blurring faces. If only it weren't so warm.

Mr. Watson's lips moved, but it took her several moments to focus on what he was saying. "Are you enjoying the ball?"

"Yes. The Ballingers throw an exquisite party."

"Indeed, although I fear all the talk of impending war may have dampened the festivities to a degree."

She nodded demurely, though she'd never admit conversing about the possibility of war was far more interesting than being forced to make polite niceties to the elite of Savannah's upper echelon. Her mother would faint if she allowed her tongue to spill the unladylike sentiment.

"If war is declared, will you go?"

His eyes glinted, his bearing stiff as he circled her past

potted palms, pulling her into the thick of the dancers. "Without hesitation. It's my sacred calling and duty to defend the freedoms Mr. Lincoln is attempting to rip from our way of life. No man worth his salt would dare flee his duty."

Keziah pressed her lips tight, unwilling to say anything further, knowing if she did, she would be unable to stop. The issues did not seem so starkly cut to her. Instead, she smiled and nodded again, praying her mother could understand the depths of her desire to please. Keziah would not mortify her. Not again.

The room suddenly dipped and twisted. Her breath thinned. *Stay upright. Focus.* Blinking hard, she realized Mr. Watson was asking her something, though she didn't understand what. Alarm flooded her, followed by a frisson of something indefinable tingling up her spine.

*No, God. Please, no. Not here. What will Mother think?*

The prayer had hardly crossed her thoughts before she plunged into the abyss, the spinning colors collapsing into merciful blackness.

Micah Greyson scoured the crowded ballroom as he sipped the too-sweet punch. He didn't belong.

Since returning home to Savannah from medical school in Philadelphia, he felt distant, removed. He had thought to open a practice and wanted to live near Mother. He owed her much. But now? He couldn't shake the unease gnawing his middle. The feeling was odd and altogether unsettling. Not just because there were new faces, nor because old classmates and neighbors had moved away. This was something else. As if society's values were different. The perspective on human life and dignity had altered.

No, Savannah hadn't changed. It was him. Too many abolitionist rallies. He'd seen and heard far too much to leave Philadelphia unchanged and unaffected. He felt as if he'd just awakened from a long, hazy dream, suddenly aware of how different life could be, only to find himself sucked back into the foggy nightmare once more.

And what to do with the knowledge of who he was in the midst of it all? He would never belong. Could never belong again.

He took another pull of his punch, rolling the syrupy taste of cherries over his tongue, and sighed. Some men feared death; others feared losing their loved ones. His fear was entirely different. He must not grow callous and indifferent to the plight of those suffering around him.

The raucous laughter of a man to his left grated his nerves. Placing the half-empty glass on a tray with a soft clink, he scowled. It was a mistake to have come. He'd only done so at his friend's pleading. Oliver was bursting to talk war with the other men, not to mention dance with the young debutantes. His friend could be quite convincing. But Micah was charmed by none of it. The music seemed at odds with his mood, the air too suffocating.

He had turned to make his apologies to the hostess when

a muffled cry rang out from the cluster of dancers clogging the floor. A male voice shouted amid the din.

"Is there a physician here?"

He stepped forward, eyeing the crush of people who had stopped moving. They swarmed around someone who had fallen. Man or woman? He couldn't tell. There was too much commotion. Too many people.

He shouted, "I'm a physician! Make way."

The crowd parted slowly to reveal a young man leaning over an unconscious woman crumpled on the glistening waxed floor. Pushing past the mob, he frowned.

"Please, give the poor woman some air."

As he knelt down to assess her condition, he sucked in a breath at the lovely form tangled in a swirl of blue silk, observing the way her fingers twitched sporadically, the soft muscles of her throat knotting as her head thrashed. His gaze landed on her face and his heart gave an odd lurch.

He couldn't believe it. After all these years. He cradled her head gently, stroking the soft skin of her cheek, and prayed.

Kizzie Montgomery.

Micah tugged Kizzie's slight weight closer to his chest as he struggled to carry her up the stairs of the Ballinger mansion, her voluminous skirts and hoops making his progress difficult. The murmurs of shock rippling through the room faded away as he followed the hostess to a guest bedroom.

"Here. This room should serve."

Mrs. Ballinger pushed aside the heavy door and hastened

to light a lamp as he laid Kizzie on the green-and-gold brocade-covered bed. He pressed his fingers to her slender neck, monitoring the thrum of her pulse. Steady.

"How can I be of help?" The concerned matron twisted her hands, looking out of place as a nursemaid in her glittering beads and filmy lavender gown. Lines deepened around her eyes.

"Could I trouble you for some clean cloths and a pitcher of cool water?"

With a nod, she breathed, "Of course. I'll send Minnie up straightaway."

"Thank you."

He smoothed Kizzie's strawberry-blonde curls away from her temples, her skin pale but warm. A slight spray of freckles on her delicate nose stood out in stark contrast to her creamy skin. She seemed to be sleeping peacefully. No more twitches or convulsions.

"Doctor, may I be so bold as to ask—" the hostess swallowed, still lingering in the room—"what malady has befallen this woman?"

Easing one of Kizzie's eyelids open, he nodded in satisfaction when the pupil in the center of her eye shrank against the light of the lamp. "I won't be sure until I've examined her more thoroughly, but I believe she's had an epileptic attack."

Mrs. Ballinger clucked her tongue. "The falling sickness."

"Yes, I believe so."

The poised woman held herself aloof as if unsure what to do. "Well, I'll fetch Minnie. She should be up shortly."

Micah barely heard himself murmur a response before leaning over Kizzie once more, admiring her long lashes, high cheekbones, and full lips. She was more beautiful than he remembered.

Beautiful and unconscious.

Troubled, he took her pulse again. Steady.

His breath froze when he saw her eyelids twitch, her lashes fluttering before her eyes opened, the walnut-and-cinnamon colors he remembered flaming to life yet filled with confusion. Her fingers roved over the silk of her bodice until he captured them between his own. He smiled and tried to keep his voice soft and calm, aware that she would be unlikely to remember this moment tomorrow.

"Kizzie, it's Micah Greyson. Do you remember me?"

She blinked and licked her lips. "Micah? From school?"

Nodding, he smiled. "From school."

Her chest rose and fell, her gaze flickering across his face. "What happened? Where am I?"

Micah squeezed her fingers, kept his voice soothing. "You're at the Ballinger house. You were dancing and collapsed."

Her eyes widened as a shadow of awareness crept over her face. "Was it . . . ?" She choked against the words forming. This had happened to her before.

"Yes. Epileptic attack."

She looked away. Her chin trembled. "Leave me, please."

"I'm a physician now. Please let me help you."

"There's nothing you can do. No one can."

"That's not true. Why, just last ye—"

She sucked in a tight breath. "No. Mother. She must have seen it." With a groan, she squeezed her eyes shut but did not release his hand. "She'll be mortified."

Micah frowned. "You can't help what happened."

Kizzie focused on his face, a sadness flickering in her expression. "My parents believe differently."

Cruel. Ignorant. Shaming their daughter for an ailment she had no control over? He ground his teeth as she relaxed against the soft down of the bed. Her eyelids drooped.

A murmur escaped her. "So tired."

"That's normal. Rest. I'll be right here."

Eyes sliding shut, she sighed softly, causing his heart to give an odd fillip. "Thank you . . . Micah . . ."

Asleep.

A raucous shout shook the floor under his feet. The crowd downstairs yelled and whooped. The glass globe of the oil lamp rattled. What was happening?

As the tumult below settled into a humming din, he watched the gentle rise and fall of her breath beneath her limp hand. Who could have imagined he'd run into her here, his first social gathering since returning? The one girl who'd managed to capture his heart as a boy.

Not that she would ever know. He wouldn't tell her. Couldn't tell anyone. They could never be together. He'd thought by now, with distance and the passing of time, the youthful feelings would have abated, but seeing her again had caused every old memory, every one of her sweet smiles, every dream, to roar back to life with frightening speed.

The bedroom door squeaked open as a petite woman with graying blonde hair and a stricken expression crossed the threshold.

He straightened, releasing Kizzie's hand. "Dr. Micah Greyson, ma'am."

Rushing to her side, the matron leaned over Kizzie and stroked her forehead before glancing toward him as if he were little more than a nuisance.

"Elsie Montgomery. I'm Keziah's mother. It took me several minutes to escape the melee."

"I heard the shouts. What happened?"

She straightened, her face somber.

"What we've known was imminent, Dr. Greyson. Fortunately for my daughter, her . . . *illness*—" Micah noted the distaste that pinched Mrs. Montgomery's mouth—"is the least of everyone's concern now."

"Why?"

Sighing deeply, the older woman furrowed her brow into deep lines. "War, Doctor. War has begun."

# CHAPTER 2

FROM THE FRONT PARLOR WINDOWS, Keziah eyed the passing forms of men and women strolling down the cobblestone street. The lace curtains hid her from their sight, but she could see them clearly enough. Resolute. Focused. Oblivious to the mortification that had filled her since awakening.

Her head pounded, but the embarrassment of last night's disaster bothered her far more.

She hadn't seen Mother since they had returned to the house just before dawn's persistent creep over the night sky. No doubt she had told Father the horrifying details. He would be irate, not only at the social ramifications but at the possible stain on his business relationships as well. She had destroyed her future, *their* future . . . and all of it in front of Savannah's most critical eyes.

Pushing away the thought, she sipped the tea cradled in her hands, inhaled the calming aroma of orange and cloves. She allowed her eyes to slide shut and her head to fall back against the stiff chair. Vague recollections of the evening nipped at her mind, all of them foggy after her collapse, except for the masculine strength in the hand that had gripped hers.

Why had Micah Greyson been there? She hadn't seen him in years. Not since his father had died, forcing him to leave the school they'd both attended.

She had always admired his outgoing nature and quick wit, a stark contrast to her own painful shyness. While the other boys teased her, calling her "Little Mouse" or "Shadow," Micah had been kind. When he'd teased, it had been with gentle affection, like a brother.

He had drawn her out with animated conversation or silly questions. His sky-blue eyes would light up and he'd pepper her with questions and dares.

*"Say, Kizzie, would you rather be a happy Indian living on the plains or a cranky miser in a mansion?"*

*"What do you think the fastest animal on earth is?"*

*"I bet I can run faster than you."*

The memories tugged her lips into a curve. As quickly as the smile came, it siphoned away. Five years since she'd seen him, and he'd found her in the most mortifying condition possible. Heat flushed her body, a heat she could not blame on the steaming tea in her hands.

Why had he been hovering over her?

The meager contents in her stomach soured and she placed her tea on the table in front of her chair, abandoning it the way she longed to abandon her shame.

A knock sounded on the front door, followed by the stiff rustle of skirts as Elizabeth, the house servant, shuffled past to answer. Likely one of Father's business associates coming to call. Keziah leaned back in her chair and watched a bird blithely hop on a limb outside the window.

A masculine voice drifted through the vestibule, followed by Elizabeth's warm tones in response.

"I'm sorry, sir, but Mr. and Mrs. Montgomery are away at the moment and Miss Montgomery is indisposed."

"Forgive me. I'm the physician who attended to Miss Montgomery last evening. I merely wanted to check her condition once more."

Keziah's ears pricked. Physician? She rubbed her temple. She remembered a man in the Ballingers' guest room, but the only face she recalled belonged to Micah.

Their voices dropped to indecipherable murmurs before a man's footfalls clicked against the polished wood floor outside the parlor.

Elizabeth's ebony face appeared, her expression apologetic. "Pardon me, miss, but you have a caller."

Elizabeth disappeared and a man's strong presence

appeared in the doorway. With a slight breath, Keziah stiffened her spine.

Tall, trim, but broad-shouldered. Dark hair and piercing eyes that stared back at her with an unreadable expression.

Micah.

He was no longer her childhood companion. No longer a boy but a man. Her fingers trembled, though why, she couldn't say.

Rising to her feet, she clasped her hands together and studied the handsome planes of his face carefully, unwilling to show any signs of weakness on her part. She would not be a helpless female again in his presence.

Elizabeth's soft voice jolted. "Would you prefer I stay, Miss Montgomery?"

Keziah swallowed. The thought of her entertaining a gentleman alone would have sent Father into an apoplexy, but this was not just any gentleman. It was Micah.

"We'll be fine, Elizabeth. You may leave the parlor door open and bring some tea if our guest would enjoy it."

Micah smiled. "Thank you, no. This is a business call, but I appreciate your hospitality."

The servant bobbed her head and slipped from the room, her skirts swishing behind her.

Keziah finally greeted him. "Dr. Greyson."

He crossed the distance between them, clutching his medical bag in one hand and his hat in the other. "Please, we're old friends. Call me Micah."

Dodging the familiarity, she offered a teasing grin, the

awkwardness melting away as it always had in his presence. "But then what would you call me?"

Tiny lines crinkled around his blue eyes. "Why, Kizzie, of course."

She felt her cheeks heat at the childhood nickname. She remembered the day the moniker had been coined. Billy Strauss and Charlie Holliday had teased Micah for treating "the shy mouse" with such tenderness.

Gap-toothed Charlie had called to Micah, *"Sweet on Keziah Montgomery, are you? Kissy, kissy!"*

Micah had turned and roughed Charlie up good before offering to carry her lunch pail with a wink. *"Pay no mind to what they say. They just wish they had the privilege of walking you home . . . Kizzie."*

She swallowed, the memory evoking a bittersweet angst. "No one has called me Kizzie since childhood."

"You'll always be Kizzie to me."

Her mouth dry, she offered him a seat in the rococo chair directly across from hers, thankful the tea table separated them. She suddenly felt as nervous as a frog on a hot rock. As he settled in, she took a deep breath. It was only Micah, yet her insides quivered like preserves all the same.

Smoothing the fabric of her green gown, she studied the bristle shading his angular jaw. "Tell me . . . where have you been the past several years? It feels like ages since I've seen you."

He sighed, regretful. "School in Philadelphia. I only recently returned to Savannah to begin practicing medicine and be near to my mother."

Keziah swallowed the hard knot in her throat. "Is she ill?"

He hesitated, the somber lines around his eyes deepening. "She is well overall, though not as strong as she once was. Her heart pains her from time to time."

"I should visit her. It's been far too long. When you said you needed to be near her, I feared her to be bedfast or suffering some serious malady."

He shook his head. "Nothing so dreadful as that. I was long overdue, however. And I've enjoyed reacquainting myself with my old chums." His eyes twinkled. "Like you."

Fumbling past the warmth in her cheeks, she laughed lightly. "Do you remember Lucy Kent? She married Daniel Lovelace last summer."

"I hadn't heard."

"I assume you've found Oliver King."

His white teeth flashed. "Indeed. In fact, he was the one who convinced me to attend the dance at the Ballingers' last evening."

The happy banter fled as Micah's eyes roved over her, concern flickering in his face. She felt exposed, knowing she could not hide what she was desperate to cover from his experienced gaze.

"Tell me truly, Kizzie, how are you feeling? Tired?"

She picked at imaginary lint clinging to her gown. "Some, yes. I'll be fine."

He sighed, his voice low. "How long have you been dealing with these episodes?"

She would give anything for an interruption to keep from having to answer his direct questions. It was too humiliating.

"I had them when I was just a child. By the age of ten they had all but disappeared, save for a few rare exceptions." Several of which she had hid from her parents. "That is, until I came down with a fever several years ago. They reappeared not long after."

Micah grunted under his breath and stroked his chin. "How often?"

"Every few months or so."

He nodded slowly. "Have you sought treatment?"

"Father called in our family physician. Dr. Kelsie told me not to read or exert myself to do anything beyond feminine pursuits like needlepoint or charitable endeavors."

"Rubbish, although I concede receiving enough rest is important. What else did he say?"

She stood, turning away from his probing stare to look through the sunlight-dappled window, hearing the pleading in her own voice. "Micah, I beg you, don't ask me anything more. It's something I've come to accept."

He moved to her side and forced her to look into his face. "But there are treatments that can address the symptoms. I promise I could help you."

Fearing he could see the despondency cloaking her, she shook her head. "Every time I have another episode, Father rants and raves about my inability to control myself. I shame him and Mother until I'm loath to leave the house."

He stared at her for a long moment, his face hard. "It's not your fault."

"Try to understand—they do love me. Truly. You know how most people view epileptic illness. Some would say I should be moved to an asylum and locked away." She forced a smile. "Mother and Father would rather cut off their arms than do such a thing." Emitting a tight laugh, she faced him once more. "I'm sure there are plenty of tongues wagging about my illness last evening as it is, even with the declaration of war."

His sudden chuckle startled her. "Indeed, but not the way you think."

"What do you mean?"

"From what I've heard, the ladies and gentlemen who attended think you're gifted, especially since news of the war reached the party ten minutes after your collapse."

She gasped.

"They are saying your moment of . . . *discomfort* was a glimmer of foreboding. A prophetic gift of some sort."

"I'll swan," Keziah said under her breath, amazement chasing away her shame. "It's rubbish, but at least I'm not being labeled a lunatic."

"Far from it, and I daresay anyone who would label you as such never knew you at all."

His compliment warmed her middle. She studied him, noting the serious glimmer behind his sweet concern and gentle humor. "What will you do, Micah, since war has been declared? Will you join and fight?"

He dropped his gaze and clasped his hands behind his back. "I—I'm not sure."

"Surely you know what people will say if you don't."

He took his turn staring out the window, though she knew he didn't truly see the flowers dancing in the gentle tug of the morning breeze.

"When this life is over, it is not my peers I'll stand before, is it?"

She offered no argument. He was correct.

Turning, he caught her gaze with his piercing blue one. "Come with me."

Her stomach flipped. "Where?"

"To a meeting. On Tuesday, three days from now, at the church on Brighton Street. Eight o'clock in the evening."

Words stalled on her tongue as she groped for a reply. "Why? What kind of meeting?"

His fingers grazed hers, and the breath thinned in her lungs when he squeezed ever so gently. His low voice coaxed her until she was helpless to refuse. "Please, Kizzie."

Father and Mother would never agree to such a thing, letting her leave the house unchaperoned with a gentleman, but she trusted Micah completely. An idea niggled. The Ladies' Aid Society would be meeting at her family's church on Tuesday evening. Her parents would think nothing of her absence from home if they believed her to be attending the regular charity meeting. And she wouldn't tell them a falsehood, exactly. She *would* be at a church.

She nodded, unsure of what had just happened or what

she had agreed to. He released her hand and she shivered against the loss of his warmth.

Scooping up his hat and bag, he smiled gently, his look communicating more than his words. "Eight o'clock. Meet me round the corner at half past seven."

She remained silent as he let himself out the front door and shut it behind him with a soft click.

Easing down onto the stiff cushion of her chair, she couldn't stop the smile curving her lips.

# CHAPTER 3

APRIL 16, 1861

Keziah cast a wary glance around the dim basement of the church, Micah at her side on the unforgiving bench. Soft murmurs and terse chatter filled the dank space as the small crowd waited for the meeting to begin. Did anyone recognize her? She prayed not. She needed no talebearers reporting her whereabouts to Father.

A mousy-looking man with a huge mustache and a spindly neck walked up and down the scant rows, handing out papers of some sort, as a beefy fellow hurriedly lit all the oil lamps lining the room. Within moments, the room brightened until she could read the paper thrust into her hand.

A CALL TO ARMS!

"Find out just what any people will quietly submit to
and you have found out the exact measure of injustice
and wrong which will be imposed upon them."
—Frederick Douglass

THE GREAT MORAL FIGHT CALLING TO ALL THOSE WHO
CHERISH THE GOD-GIVEN RIGHTS OF EVERY MAN:
ABOLITION OF SLAVERY

"I feel now that the time is come when even a woman
or a child who can speak a word for freedom and
humanity is bound to speak. . . . I hope every woman
who can write will not be silent."—Harriet Beecher
Stowe

Keziah blinked and snapped her eyes to Micah's, only to
find him watching her intently, hopeful, if perhaps sheepish.

Never so aware of listening ears, she hissed, "An abolitionist meeting?"

Micah reddened ever so slightly but rushed ahead. "Just
keep an open mind, Kizzie."

She glanced back to the stiff paper clenched between her
fingers. If Mother or Father discovered she'd attended . . .

He leaned close, the scent of bay rum wrapping around
her like an embrace. "Have you read Mrs. Stowe's story *Uncle
Tom's Cabin?*"

She shook her head. "You know it's banned here. I wouldn't even know where to find a copy. Not that it would matter. Mother forbade me to read it, proclaiming it dangerous libel."

"More's the pity. A thought-provoking piece of literature."

Biting her lip, she braved a question. "Do you have a copy?"

He smiled slowly and gave a nod.

"I said Mother forbade it. I didn't say I would obey."

Micah chuckled. "If you're certain, I'll lend you mine."

She cast a furtive glance around the basement. There were no familiar faces staring back at her. No one who would wag their tongue at her presence. Lifting her chin, she reminded herself that she'd done nothing wrong. It was only a meeting. Still, with the Confederate fervor pulsing through Savannah, news of an abolition meeting could be the spark that started an inferno.

The fever had only grown hotter since Confederates had fired the ominous shot at Fort Sumter. The entire town quivered with excitement. Each night she could hear the shouts of enthusiasm from the mobs of men crowding in clusters along Liberty Square. "God save the Confederacy!" Their shrieks of independence haunted her dreams, pounding like the dull thud of distant cannon fire. Yet she could not match their fervor. For some reason, she felt detached.

States' rights were well and good, but when people like sweet Hiriam were given no choice . . .

Her turbulent thoughts scattered as the wiry man who had passed out the pamphlets stood before the assembly.

"Ladies and gentlemen, thank you for coming to our meeting. Now, more than ever, the heaviness of the cause weighs upon us." He swallowed loudly, his Adam's apple bobbing like a cork on a pond. "War has only served to make the issue of freedom for all humanity a crucial tipping point. Some of you may be here from a zeal to serve. For some, it may be to understand the horrific plight of our Negro brothers and sisters." His nervous glance skittered over the small, silent crowd. "For others, you may have come out of mere curiosity."

Keziah squirmed in her seat, feeling as if he were singling her out somehow.

"Whatever the reason, we are delighted you're here. I have a very special friend with me tonight. A man who has endured much. A man whose bravery is matched by our great forefathers, who knew the risk they took by resisting King George but faced down tyranny with a bold stare and resplendent courage. Please welcome my friend Amos."

From the shadows hugging the walls, a large man stepped forward, his dark skin gleaming in the soft lights. His face was stern, his eyes hesitant yet unafraid. Moving to the orator's side, he offered a somber nod.

"My friends, for Amos's safety, I shall not tell you his last name nor where he has come from, but I can tell you this man was once a slave, shackled like a dog, whipped without mercy for the slightest infraction, and treated no better than an animal."

Murmurs rippled through the room, yet Keziah found

she could not tear her gaze from the man whose countenance held such silent pain.

The orator motioned for Amos to take a seat on a small stool. "Amos has come, knowing doing so could put him at peril but unwilling to sit idly by and watch his fellow man cruelly relegated to a life of bondage. He is a freedom fighter and wants to answer any questions you may have."

The room was eerily silent, no one willing to be the first to speak. Finally Micah cleared his throat, his voice strong. "Thank you for being willing to share your story, Amos. How long were you in slavery?"

The man spoke softly. "Nigh unto thirty years, best I can figure. I was taken from my home across the seas when I was just a wee one, ripped straight from my mama's arms while she screamed. A white man whipped her till she died for trying to protect me."

Nausea curdled Keziah's stomach at the thought of such horror.

"I's put on a boat right after and sold to a plantation down South."

Silence again. A voice drifted from the back of the room. "What were you bought to do?"

Amos's eyes glinted. "Field slave. I'm big. They save the big men for planting, harvesting, and hard labor."

"Were you ever treated with kindness?"

Amos stared hard, the intensity of it sending shivers down Keziah's spine.

"No, sir. My massa was a bad man. Filled with hate.

I know not every slave has it as bad as I did, but others have it even worse. No. There was times I wondered if Massa was the devil himself."

A soft female voice flitted over the somber gathering. "What kind of things did he do?"

"We was half-starved most of the time. Ate nothing but cornmeal, sometimes coosh, and whatever we could manage to eke out of the dirt on our own. Weren't much time to grow nothing, though. We worked from four in the morning until well after sundown each night. Every now and then I'd sneak some of the boiled corn they gave the hogs."

"Were only the men forced to work that hard?"

"No'm. We was all worked that way. Women and chillun too. The babies was cared for by our oldest women, who were too bent over and aged to do much in the fields. Our overseer was a mean man himself. Not just with the whip." Amos clenched his jaw, tightening his fists before visibly forcing himself to relax. "If he sensed we was resentful, overseer would bed our wives."

Gasps peppered the air. Keziah's face flamed at the scandalous topic.

Another man spoke, his voice laced with skepticism. "How do we know you're not making up these stories?"

Amos looked toward the orator who'd introduced him and sighed when the man nodded.

The orator spoke again. "We can prove the torture Amos endured. I ask your pardon now for what you are about to witness. Those with delicate sensibilities ought to look away."

Amos stood and slowly unbuttoned his white cotton shirt, turning his back to the audience, allowing the fabric to fall to the floor. Keziah felt the blood leach from her face as murmurs of utter shock punctuated the air. A woman in the last row released a cry.

His back was nothing but a hard crisscross of thick, grisly scars. Knotted tissue patched over other scars, some as thick as two fingers pinched together.

Never had she seen something so ghastly. Pressing her fist to her mouth, Keziah trembled, her eyes stinging with unshed tears, throat thick and stomach fisted.

Next to her, she heard Micah exhale a shaky breath and murmur, "Dear God in heaven . . ."

Turning back around, Amos picked up his shirt and slipped his arms into it once more, his face pleading. "I'm sorry you had to see that, but I ain't the only one who's suffered. There are still folks trapped just like I was, with no hope for them or their babies." He straightened. "Ain't right. God done said in the Good Book he made man in his image. He didn't say just the white man or the black or anyone else. He just said man."

He thumped his chest with a meaty fist. "I'm a man. I'm a man made in God's image. A man Jesus died for." He shook his head. "The whites tell everybody the Negroes are stupid. No different than animals. But it's only because those same whites denied us a chance to learn, to read, to make something of ourselves. We can learn—I'm learning to read right now. You know what I'm reading? The Good Book. And now I can read for myself how much Jesus loves me."

Warm tears streaked down Keziah's face. She felt every ounce of weight behind his impassioned plea.

"Every time you remember the scars on my back, let it make you think about all them folks still being whipped, still locked up or ripped from their families. Remember them and ask the Almighty what he would want you to do."

Micah walked beside Kizzie as they left the church. No, *Keziah*. Thinking of her with such a womanly name would take some getting used to, but a woman she was. He cut a sideways glance at her lovely form in the soft glow of gaslights dotting the darkened streets.

Had it been foolish to ask her to attend the meeting? Most likely so. Still, of all his old friends, he felt she would be the only one who might listen to the passionate pleas of those desperate for freedom. Not just listen, but understand. Understand the hurting. Understand *him*. And realize the choice he must make was far bigger than it appeared.

The normal beat of their booted heels was drowned by the late-night celebrations still erupting all over the city. When the *Daily Morning News* printed the headline "Our Flag Victorious," rejoicing and gleeful rallies sparked through every corner of Savannah. Celebrations that had yet to cease.

Just when Micah thought the exultation had died down, more guns would fire their booming victory shots, rattling glass windows and fraying his nerves. Even now, from the other side of the square, a group of men could be heard shouting, "Hurrah for the South! We stand together!"

Forcing the troublesome noise away, he pondered what would become of Keziah's younger brother. He was of age to enlist.

"What will Nathaniel do now that war has been begun?"

Her brows knit. "I'm not sure. He has been doing so well in his engineering studies at the College of Charleston, but now . . ." She let her voice trail off. "I fear war will change everything."

They walked along in comfortable silence. Even for a shy girl, Keziah was far too quiet, a marked contrast to the revelry buzzing through the city.

"Penny for your thoughts."

She sighed, her slim shoulders drooping. "I'm thinking how spoiled and ignorant I've been."

"That's exactly how I felt after attending my first meeting in Philadelphia. As if my eyes had finally been opened."

She nodded, staring at the ground before her as they strolled. "I will never be able to erase the image of his scars from my mind."

Giving her a sad smile, Micah yearned to grasp her hand but resisted. "Nor should you. Let his suffering teach you. Remembering will give you a greater compassion. A deeper love for those trapped in darkness."

She stopped and turned to face him, her large eyes filled with confusion. "But Father doesn't whip our slaves. They are not all treated with such hate."

He struggled to form words that would not cause her to rise in defensiveness. "You're correct. Some are treated quite well. But it still doesn't change the fact that they are given no choice. No individual pursuit of happiness." He stepped close, feeling his chest tighten. "Do you know almost none of them have any dreams? None! Because they've never been given the opportunity to think beyond what their masters demand. What kind of life is that?" He softened his tone. "We act as if God created them solely to bow to our own whims and desires."

"But what should be done, then?"

He heard the frustration thickening her voice. This time he didn't resist the desire to touch the soft skin of her hand. The contact of her cool fingers wrapped in his sent a ripple of awareness through him. He whispered, "You may never change all minds, but you can change one life. Pray. Ask God."

Keziah watched him intently, her eyes searching his. "This is why you cannot fight?"

He nodded and released her. "This is why." He held up his hands, studying their blunt contours. "God gave me these hands. Whatever happens, I will use them to heal."

Tenderly, she slipped her hands over his and squeezed. "I understand. Now better than ever before. You're a good man, Micah Joel Greyson."

He chuckled, unnerved by her soft touch and the sound of his full name slipping from her lips. "You sound like my mother when I'm preparing to be scolded."

At the sound of her light giggle, he lifted her fingers to his lips and pressed a kiss to her skin, wishing it could be so much more. *Careful, Micah . . .*

He walked her as close to her home as he dared, stopping a block away, his fingers wrapped around the iron fence lining the row of homes.

"Thank you, Micah. I shall never forget this night." She began to ask something but seemed to think better of it.

"What is it?"

Licking her rosebud lips, she emitted a timid question. "Will I see you again?"

How he wished it to be so. But he would not make a promise that could easily be broken by the severing lashes of war. "I pray so."

Hints of disappointment lined her face, and Micah couldn't resist the desire to stroke her feather-soft cheek with the pad of his thumb. He could never have more, so he would allow himself this one sweet moment. "Whatever God wills, he will accomplish. I give myself to him however he would have me serve."

Her breath hitched as he stepped closer. Yet a far greater barrier than this iron fence separated them. If she only knew . . .

No. She must never find out.

Micah drank in the contours of her delicate features in the shadowed dusk. "Discover what he wants you to do, Kizzie, and then give yourself to it with all your heart. I'm not sure what the future holds. An opportunity has been given to me that may take me away from here, but if Providence should bless us to meet again, I would be overjoyed to see you once more—" his voice grew hoarse as he rasped the hated words—"my friend." His breath hitched as he feared he might spill all the feelings he'd harbored inside since their youth. But he would not burden her with an attachment that would only bring pain.

Instead, he dropped his fingers. "May God shine over you in all you do."

Keziah slipped inside the foyer and shed the light shawl she'd carried to the meeting. As she looked for Elizabeth's helpful hands, the memory of Amos's scarred flesh seared her memory, and she clutched the shawl to her middle. She would take it to the proper place on her own. No longer would she demand anything from the staff that she could complete herself.

From the library down the hall, she could hear the scratch of Father's pen as he worked his ledgers. The aroma of his cherry tobacco drifted through the air. Mother was nowhere to be seen, likely upstairs writing letters or stitching her needlepoint. Feeling at loose ends, Keziah didn't want to retire for the night, not with the emotions swirling through her. Nor could she focus enough to read. Her thoughts were far too scattered. No, it was human companionship she craved.

She wandered into the parlor and stared at the glowing embers collapsed in the bottom of the fireplace. Hearing a thump beyond the kitchen, she hung the shawl in the closet Elizabeth used for wraps and picked her way through the silent kitchen to the steps descending beyond. Perhaps one of the servants was still awake.

The soft, honeyed glow beckoned her to the large workroom at the bottom of the stairs. She paused in her descent and watched Hiriam oiling an assortment of leather saddles and paraphernalia scattered across the worn table. Humming a jaunty tune, he rubbed the stained cloth into the hide of a saddlebag, his graying curls bent over his work.

Her heart softened as she watched the old driver and groom. He had been with the Montgomery family since before her memories were formed.

"Your voice is always so soothing."

He jerked his head up and smiled upon seeing her before patting the empty chair next to him.

"Miss Keziah, how did you know I was yearning for a bit of company this evening?"

She eased into the squeaky chair, arranging her ample skirts around her, wrinkling her nose against the sharp sting of oil and turpentine thickening the air. "I feel too flummoxed to rest."

His lithe hands never stopped moving, though his eyes lifted to study her, his curiosity unveiled. "Flummoxed? What's got the prettiest miss this side of the Mississippi so at odds tonight?"

Nothing. Everything. She didn't even know how to broach the topic of what she'd seen and heard, for truly, it changed everything. She watched his careworn hands with their thick calluses and wondered what his life had been like before he'd been purchased by Father. He'd never said. Never complained, and she loathed herself for not once asking.

"I suppose I'm feeling selfish."

His brows rose. "You? Selfish?" He shook his head. "Uh-uh. You're the most unselfish person I know."

She said nothing, content to watch the fluid motion of his hands, hear his gentle breath in the cellar's quiet.

Unable to quell the tide of not knowing, she heard herself blurt, "What was your life like?"

He froze, face turning to onyx as it rose to hers. "What do you mean?"

She swallowed, throat tight. "Before you came here. I just realized I've never asked. Never saw beyond my own needs and silly desires to ask you about your life. Where did you grow up?"

He resumed his work, his words slow as if he was weighing each one carefully in a balance. "Just a childhood. Nothing special to speak of."

"But you've always had such a gentle, calming way about you. Were you raised to be a driver?"

A spark of misgiving flickered in his eyes. "Why you asking all these questions?"

He knew her too well. Always had. She picked at the scarred table, keeping her gaze averted. "Just curious; that's all."

Grunting, he dropped the saddlebag from his hands and

reached for another, rubbing the oil-soaked cloth against it in smooth circles. "Some things is best left forgotten."

Forgotten. Were these "things" truly forgotten, or were they locked away? His refusal to speak of the past told her volumes.

Deciding to change tactics, she tucked her chin in her hands just as she had when she was a child in pinafores, watching him work in this very room.

"What about now? What are your dreams?"

Hiriam chuckled. "Ain't got no dreams, missy."

His words so closely echoed Micah's, she could do nothing more than blink. "But surely you have something you'd like to do before your life is over. Some place you'd like to visit or family you'd like to see."

Sadness etched heavy lines down his face. "No, missy. I don't."

"You don't have family?"

He stilled and looked off into nothingness for a long moment. So long, she feared she'd been forgotten completely. Finally he spoke.

"I did once. But my wife and daughter was sold away. Ain't seen or heard of them since." His voice grew hoarse. "Don't even know if either of them is alive or in glory."

"I'm so sorry. I didn't know."

He shook away the sorrow around him with a gentle smile. "Ain't your fault, Miss Keziah. Life is a bread eaten with sorrow, but there is good things too. Like you." His dark eyes twinkled. "I got to see you sprout up from a little 'un to the beautiful lady you are now. Master Montgomery lets me keep watch over the horses I admire. I'm content."

Forcing a smile, she nodded, though she couldn't shake the sense that her family had wrought a huge injustice on Hiriam and the rest of the house slaves. Contentment was admirable. Or was it resignation? Could it be that the less painful path was to never dream at all?

"Go on now. Get yourself up to bed. Rest."

She rose and turned to leave before tossing him a pleading look over her shoulder. "You're sure you don't want to tell me about your past? I truly would like to hear it."

He frowned, gave a short shake of his head, his voice sad. "It'll serve no good purpose. Go on now."

Lifting the hem of her skirt, she made her way up the stairs, but instead of heading to her room, she meandered through the kitchen and found herself slipping outside into the cool of the night. The perfumed scent of irises and jonquils drifted on the air. She stopped and leaned against the balustrade, staring up at the sliver of moon surrounded by twinkling stars. Amos's scarred, mangled flesh invaded once again.

*"Let his suffering teach you. Remembering will give you a greater compassion. A deeper love for those trapped in darkness."*

Micah's gentle admonition wrapped around her, flooding her with purpose. She felt as if she must do something. *Anything.*

Studying the moon, she let its serene glow light her face as she prayed.

*Father God, I want to help. Forgive me for my apathy. I've never truly seen the horrors inflicted upon your children, have been content to turn away as long as my own home was happy. No longer. I want to be of service to you. Whatever talents or abilities I have, use them. I give myself to you. Lord, I want to make a difference.*

*Help me make a difference. . . .*

# CHAPTER 4

APRIL 23, 1861

"Must the rallies be so loud?"

Mother's exasperated complaint was far shriller than the dull shouts erupting across the square. Though over a week had passed since war first commenced, Savannah continued to pulse with ribald excitement. It seemed the rallies proclaiming Confederate freedom never waned. From the midmorning hours until late into the night, the entire town quivered in anticipation, punctuated by war-thirsty men rallying those less inclined to take up arms and fight. Brass bands blasted their message at odd hours throughout the day.

Keziah was perturbed in mind and body.

Father took another sip of his coffee and replaced the delicate cup in the saucer with a soft clink, snapping open the stiff pages of the *Daily Morning News* with a smug smile of satisfaction.

"Look here. The paper declares the recent display of Georgia's brave militia companies was the most imposing and gratifying military display ever seen in Savannah." He chuckled, chest puffing out. "We'll show those Yanks yet."

Keziah picked at the fluffy eggs cooling on her breakfast plate. "But what of our ports?"

Lowering the paper, Father stared at her over the brim of his spectacles, his expression shrewd. "What of them?"

She leaned forward with unfettered curiosity. "What defenses have been made for our ports? The Federal Navy will surely attack, seeing as how so much more damage could be inflicted by sea rather than land."

Father grunted and continued perusing the ink-smudged paper held aloft in his fingers. "You might be right at that. Ah! See here. Governor Brown is calling for volunteers to join the Confederate Navy."

"But what if there's a blockade? No doubt Georgia will be ill-equipped to defend itself against the Federal Navy."

Mother cut in, a frown marring her refined features. "Don't tire yourself over worries of war, dear. It's not healthy. Not in your condition." Her eyes sharpened, displeasure evident.

Keziah's face flamed. She was nearing the age of twenty and yet continued to be coddled like a child. Impertinence would get her nowhere, though, so she held her tongue and lifted a forkful of eggs to her lips to restrain the words longing to bubble forth.

Father nodded, oblivious to her ire. "Quite right. We need no more of the displays you mortified us with at the Ballingers' party. Why, the very next day, Mr. Ballinger showed up at my office, peppering me with all kinds of questions about your condition. I might as well have been a lawyer for all the fancy talking I did that morning to convince him you weren't a lunatic."

Keziah lowered her head, the cold, dark wash of shame dousing her earlier irritation as he continued.

"As far as concerning yourself about the war, I wouldn't let it tax you overly much. It shouldn't last more than a few months at most anyway. The Union has yet to see the Confederates in all our military glory. And don't forget—" he smiled over his spectacles, his side-whiskers tipping upward—"we have God on our side."

*Do we?* Amos flitted through her mind once more, just as he had a thousand times since last week when Micah had opened her eyes to the harsh truth.

Laying aside the paper, Father plucked the spectacles from his nose and steepled his thick fingers. "I wholeheartedly agree with Stephens's report in the paper several weeks back. He said the fundamental flaw in the old government was that it built its foundation on an error—the equality of the races. The Union declares that what God has clearly made unequal are equal. The old government was built on a lie, and so it fell."

Mother daintily dabbed her mouth with the linen napkin. "Precisely. Doesn't the Good Book say, 'Be ye not unequally yoked together with unbelievers: for what fellowship hath righteousness with unrighteousness? and what communion hath light with darkness?'"

Keziah interjected, "But wasn't the apostle speaking of marriage between the children of God and heathens? Not the races."

Father frowned. "The Negro is not our equal. The verse applies either way."

Biting back a retort, Keziah pushed away her plate, her appetite suddenly spoiled. Elizabeth continued to serve meekly, her head bowed. What did the house servant think of such talk? Keziah tried to catch her eye but to no avail.

Sickened by her parents' callousness, she started to rise but stopped when a loud rapping reverberated on the front door. Elizabeth scurried out only to return a moment later, her face apologetic.

"A gentleman is here to see you, Master Montgomery. A Dr. Micah Greyson."

Keziah's heart gave a thump, a reaction that surprised her.

Father dropped his napkin on the table with a frown. "It's a bit early for visitors, but I'll see the man."

Elizabeth meekly trailed him out of the dining room as Mother sipped her morning coffee.

Why was Micah here? She hadn't expected to see him again, not since the night they'd said their tentative good-byes.

Tamping down the flicker of anticipation quivering in

her chest, she reached for the discarded newspaper only to be stopped by Mother's biting tone.

"You shouldn't be reading the paper, darling. Remember what Dr. Kelsie told you. You shouldn't exert yourself in any way, whether that be physical work or mental fatigue."

Her excitement wilted as she struggled not to retort. So she couldn't even be trusted to read the paper? She was a prisoner, trapped in her own home. In her own body.

"Besides, war discussion and political intrigue are not a fit use of time for a lady of good breeding. Wouldn't you say?"

Before Keziah could formulate a reply, masculine shouting sounded from the parlor. She jumped to her feet, her gaze colliding with the rounded eyes of her mother as she lifted her pale-blue skirt and hurried as fast as a lady dared toward the parlor door. The shouts grew in volume as she approached, her mother following her every step.

Throwing caution aside, Keziah cracked open the door to hear her father bellow, "How dare you lecture me on how to treat my daughter!"

Blood draining from her face, she peeked inside to see her graying, stocky father squaring off against a scowling Micah. Heaving a huff of frustration, Micah continued, both men oblivious to their audience.

"Sir, please believe me, this would help your daughter! Medical science has made great strides in finding new, better solutions for epilepsy and—"

"We already have a family physician, thank you."

Thunder built on Micah's handsome face. "A physician

who told her not to use her mind or lift a finger. It's poppy-cock! Keziah is exceptionally bright. Treating her like glass is unfair. There are treatments that would help and yet allow her to live a fulfilling life."

Father's whiskered jowls turned a startling shade of red. "'Keziah'? How dare you speak my daughter's name in such a familiar manner!"

Stepping into the fray, Keziah placed a calming hand on her father's arm, afraid he might strike Micah in his rage. "Father, please, Dr. Greyson is only trying to help—"

He swung toward her with a glare that made her tremble. "Why do you defend this charlatan? And why does he refer to you in such a forward way? Have you been courting him without my knowledge?"

Appalled at the sharp-tongued accusations, she shook her head. "Nothing improper has happened between us. Dr. Greyson was the physician who attended to me the night of my collapse at the Ballingers' home. He and I were at school together."

Micah stepped forward, his tone conciliatory. "Miss Montgomery is quite correct. My only purpose in coming here was to offer other alternatives to treat her health."

Father narrowed his eyes to slits, turning slowly back to Micah, a knowing spark lighting his face. "Wait . . . Micah Greyson. I remember you. Was your father Samuel Greyson?"

Micah regarded him warily, seeming to brace himself, though Keziah was helpless to know why.

Father smiled, though it resembled more of a sneer. "Oh

yes, I know all about you and your kind. Your father was a disgrace."

Keziah gasped as Mother lurched toward Father with a whispered plea to stop. He ignored her, his glare taking on an odd malice.

"Samuel Greyson was nothing more than a troublemaker, telling anybody who would listen to his drivel about the merits of John Brown." He scowled. "At least your father died before he could watch his beloved hero die the fool after Harper's Ferry."

Keziah rushed to Micah's side. "Father, stop! Dr. Greyson is my friend!"

Father's glare flashed fire, daring Micah to deny the poisonous claims.

She looked to Micah. A muscle ticked in his cheek. His jaw appeared to be carved out of marble. Though he spoke calmly, his voice was edged in steel. "My apologies for interrupting your morning, sir. I'll not be back."

Father nodded stiffly, his mouth a hard line. "Please. We don't welcome Yankee lovers here."

Mother attempted to shush him as Keziah's face burned.

Micah's gaze softened, landing on her. "Peony root and mugwort, Kizzie. Try peony root and mugwort."

Before she could reply, he strode out of the parlor, through the foyer, and out the door, slamming it with a forcible bang.

Shaken, she slowly turned to her father, his behavior leaving her too mortified for words. Not that it mattered. His ire was still up as he railed at poor Elizabeth.

"If you ever see that Yankee lover's son lurking around this house again, you get Hiriam and have him toss the man into the street."

"Yes, sir."

Keziah's ears buzzed so loudly, she could do nothing more than stand dumbly in the middle of the parlor. Mother scolded Father, begging him to calm down, as Elizabeth hustled out of the room. The activity barely registered as Keziah watched the closed front door.

Micah was gone. For good.

# CHAPTER 5

JULY 24, 1861

Keziah's breath caught, snagging against her bodice as the cheers and whistles piercing the early morning air drifted through her open bedroom window, the sticky air little deterrent to the morning's commotion.

Father's early trip to the office had left them all with a reprieve from their normal breakfast downstairs. She didn't mind. When such mornings occurred, Elizabeth would sneak her a copy of the newspaper along with her breakfast tray, leaving her to read at her desk to her heart's content.

She scanned the thick, black headline of the *Daily Morning News*.

VICTORY AT MANASSAS: UNION SCATTERS IN THE FACE
OF CONFEDERATE RESOLVE

Gripping the edges of the oily paper, she read swiftly.

The Confederates chased the yellow-backed Yankees,
crushing them in a decisive blow. The Union
retreated. . . .

What would this news do to abolitionist fervor? Would
it dampen their spirits? More importantly, what would such
a sound defeat mean to men like Amos, those desperate for
a taste of freedom?

She shook aside the thought and dropped the paper back
on the tray, rattling the flower-trimmed china plate. She
couldn't eat. She wouldn't be able to taste it.

Unbidden, her tumultuous thoughts returned to Micah.
Where was he? She hadn't seen him since the disastrous meeting with her father several months back. Had he maintained
his resolve not to enlist? What if he had joined up after all
and been injured or even killed at Manassas? Nausea curdled
her stomach. She stood and leaned against her bedpost, wishing she were still in her nightclothes and not the constrictions
of her whalebone corset.

The dull thump of timpani pounded through the floor,
unsettling her heart. She should be concerned for the safety
of her neighbors who had valiantly marched to defend their
Georgia soil. Old classmates and cousins, acquaintances and
friends. Yet it was Micah's face that swam in her vision.

The pounding of drums grew louder, more insistent.
With a start, she realized someone was knocking on the

front door with sharp raps. Had there been news of casualties already? Lifting her gown, she descended the stairs as quickly as she dared just in time to see Elizabeth open the door. When her brother's smiling face greeted her, she nearly squealed in delight.

"Nathaniel!"

He stepped over the threshold, grabbed her hands, and brushed his lips across her cheek. "You look as beautiful as ever."

Squeezing his hands, she looked into his face. The softness of youth had given way to more mature angles; the blond whiskers faintly lining his jaw testified to his arrival at manhood. That, and the glow of pride in his brown eyes.

"Thank you. And you—" she smiled—"have grown into a man."

He chuckled and released her. "Not completely grown. I imagine we could still manage to get into a bit of mischief if we put our minds to it."

"Remember the time you brought a toad into the house and it jumped out of your shirt pocket during dinner? When it landed in the soup tureen, Mother shrieked so loudly I feared she would faint."

His laughter rolled over her like an embrace. "Or the time you took all my toy soldiers because I scalped your doll?"

She propped her hands on her hips. "That was cruel and you know it. I had to tell Father what you'd done. Smoking his pipe?"

Nathaniel winced at the memory. "I couldn't sit down for

a week." His grimace melted into a grin. "And now look at you. Forcing me to return home before the term ends just to keep the suitors away."

Her joy suddenly dropped to the bottom of her stomach as something cold swept through her.

"What is it, Nathaniel? Why *did* you come home? Aren't you in the middle of your summer studies?"

His eyes searched hers with a seriousness that frightened her. "I've come home to enlist."

Micah eyed the fresh mound of dirt with an aching heart. The oppressive heat clung to his body like paste, plastering his shirt to his back. This cemetery was far too quiet, one of Savannah's smaller, less frequented resting places, blessedly secluded from the hustle of clopping hooves, noisy peddlers, and buzzing businessmen.

Quiet. Still. Not even a breeze stirred to cool his heated face.

A fly buzzed near his ear and he swatted it away. Poor Oliver. So vibrant and full of life. Cut down in the bloom of youth. Such waste.

Releasing a warm breath, Micah dropped the cluster of daisies onto the fresh-churned mound of dirt. Despite their differing views on slavery, Oliver King had been a true friend, loyal and jovial, even during grammar school. He'd faced his destiny with courage.

Unlike Micah, at least according to Savannah's standards.

Something unwelcome tightened in his chest as he recalled the box that had been delivered to his door mere weeks after war had been declared. He'd opened the brown-paper parcel only to find it filled with ladies' unmentionables—frilly crinolines with a scrawled message attached. *Wear these or volunteer.*

That very day he'd traveled to New York. Within the week, he had enlisted as a physician for the Relief Commission, as had several of his colleagues from Philadelphia. His convictions would not let him fight for the South, but his heart couldn't bear the thought of picking up arms against his Southern friends either. He was stuck, unwelcome in both worlds . . . especially among those who remembered his father's contentious leanings.

A soft voice intruded. "I wondered if you'd heard."

He sucked in a breath as the scent of lilacs drifted toward him. *Kizzie.* He could never think of her as Keziah for long.

Her cinnamon eyes tugged at him, pulling him in before her focus shifted to study the flower-strewn grave. Sunlight pierced her glossy hair, turning the strawberry-blonde tresses into fiery gold. Every curve of her lips, her chin, was perfection.

He looked away, content to stand side by side with her in the silence. Funny how stifling the quiet had seemed until she arrived. Now he didn't mind it so much.

After a long moment, she sighed. "Poor Oliver. Gone so swiftly. His first battle of the war."

"Some thought it would be over by now." He kept his eyes trained on the marker that would keep vigil over Oliver's resting place until the headstone was cut. How many more graves would fill the small cemetery over the next months? "I'll miss him."

He felt rather than saw her nod of agreement. "I have such fond memories of him." A sudden giggle escaped and he turned to see a smile flit across her face. "Remember what he did to Lucy Kent when she tattled on him for hiding Jimmy's lunch pail?"

He chuckled. "Dipped the tips of her braids in the inkwell while she worked. Lucy was furious."

Kizzie's presence soothed a frayed place inside as sweet memories washed over him. "Do you remember the time he bet Paul North his best aggie that he could eat more green apples than Paul could?"

Throwing back her head, she laughed again. "I'd forgotten. Oliver was as green as a pickle. I don't think he ate anything for a week afterward."

"And he lost his aggie to boot."

Their mirth drifted away as a somber silence invaded. Kizzie's voice shifted, her tone melancholy. "Oliver's poor mother. I don't know if she'll ever recover."

"Not doing well, I take it?"

"No. She was so consumed with grief, she was almost unable to attend the burial. She managed but collapsed on the way home. Word is she hasn't risen from her bed since."

He felt sick. "I wish I would have known. I would have returned immediately."

"I know." She glanced at him and her curious stare snagged his attention. "Have you been in Philadelphia?"

Had she been wondering about him? His heart thudded faster before he remembered how deeply her father detested him. It seemed that most in Savannah did.

Forcing his eyes from hers, he blinked against the sun's bright glare. "No. I was in New York." He tried to form the words clearly, but his throat constricted. What if she hated him as much as everyone else appeared to?

Her sweet face paled. "D-did you enlist?"

Her fear was palpable, and he longed to soothe her worry. Instead, he forced himself to remain still. "No. I joined the Relief Commission as a physician."

"What does that mean?"

"I'll be providing medical care to Union troops. My particular job will involve going into Confederate prisoner of war camps and caring for the Union soldiers kept inside. That is, when I'm so allowed. It takes much negotiating."

"I see." The heaviness in her voice spoke volumes. Some might view his voluntary service as an act of Christian compassion. Some would consider it treason to the Confederacy. But he had spent five years in the North, and Philadelphia had begun to feel as much like home as Savannah ever had.

Longing to escape the stifling heat and chase away the morose mood that had suddenly settled, he managed a smile. "Say, the school is only just around the bend. Let's take a stroll, shall we? Revisit old memories?"

The clouds lifted from her face, and he was rewarded with her sunny smile. Tucking her hand into the crook of his arm, he led her through the iron gate toward their old haunt.

Sunlight dappled through thick clusters of trees, bringing blessed relief from the glare, leaving shadows of dancing lace across the grassy path. Bees buzzed in their hives overhead, their hums drowning out the soft crunch of pebbles and twigs beneath booted footfalls.

"Have you heard from your brother lately?"

Keziah bit her lip. "Nathaniel arrived yesterday."

"Oh? I assumed he would be staying at the College of Charleston for the summer."

Her profile spoke of a deep, aching sadness. "He was, but no longer. He came home to enlist. He leaves in a fortnight."

Would there be one soul unaffected by the war? Not likely, unless it was over as quickly as the Confederacy claimed it would be.

"I'm sorry. I know you're proud of him for his bravery, but the worry does not lessen."

"I will be anxious for him, and in truth, I'm just as worried about Mother. She thought it might be coming, but his decision seems to have lowered her spirits just the same. But me—" she paused, tugging him to a gentle stop beside her— "how do I reconcile praying for my brother who is fighting for a cause I no longer believe in?"

Micah's heart pricked at the honest admission, as well as the turmoil swirling in her words. "You do not support the Confederacy?"

She shook her head and dropped her voice to a whisper. "How can I after hearing Amos's story and seeing his scars? I feel as if I've had blinders removed from my eyes."

Her sentiments so closely echoed his own that he fell silent for a long moment.

"I know. Your heart is divided."

Sighing, she resumed their stroll and he noted the trickle of sweat darkening her curls, held aloft in their snood. "Exactly. I dare not speak my mind. Nor can I lift a finger to help without feeling like I'm betraying my own brother, not to mention friends like poor Oliver."

Micah felt her turmoil all the more. "That's why I joined the Relief Commission. It gives me an opportunity to help without picking up arms. I want to use the talents God loaned me to bind up. Not destroy."

Keziah tightened her grip on Micah's strong arm, feeling the pull of muscle beneath the cotton of his shirt. Sweat rolled down the middle of her back, gluing her bodice to her skin, but the heat was no bother. Not compared to the war of emotions struggling within her.

Micah led her the two blocks down the cobbled road as she noted the straggly grass poking up between the uneven stones. He stopped abruptly and pointed, the angular planes of his face creasing into a smile.

"Look any different to you?"

Keziah drank in the sight of the charming schoolhouse, noting the peeling paint around its edges, yet somehow comforted by the sight. It was still there, still used, still sheathed with memories.

It had been a warm, sunny morning, just like this very day, when she'd realized with startling clarity there was something wrong with her. She and Lucy Kent had been picking flowers during the lunch break, and suddenly there was nothing. Nothing but fuzzy blackness. A hole where time should be. She was standing still, not understanding. Why couldn't she think? Why couldn't she remember what had just happened? Where had the past gone? Had she disappeared for mere seconds? It felt more like years, yet Lucy looked the same.

Her friend stared at her, her dark brows creased. "Keziah? What's the matter? And why did you drop your flowers?"

Lucy's voice sounded far away as if she called from across a wide, yawning meadow. Yet she was standing right in front of Keziah. Then they were surrounded by others. Charlie and John. Micah. Lottie.

Sensation slowly began to return. She felt the warm, wet fabric of her undergarments and knew what she had done when time had mysteriously been erased from her mind. Heat licked up her neck and into her face.

Charlie took one look at her and laughed. "Look at the mouse! She's blushing like a red-hot stove! And standing there like an idiot! Whatsa matter, little mouse? Cat got your tongue?"

With a growl, gangly Micah had picked up the taunting Charlie and thrown him to the ground in a puff of dirt. He stood over the bully, chest heaving and fists clenched. "Don't you dare say another ugly word, or I'll knock your teeth out!"

Face mottled red, Charlie had slunk away, as had the other children. When Micah gathered up the discarded flowers and held them out to her with a shy smile and a "Here you go," a friendship had formed. From that day forward, Micah had been her defender, confidant, and dearest friend.

Now Keziah peered up at his handsome face. Did he remember it as clearly as she? Or perhaps she'd been so desperate for companionship she had dramatized things in her mind. The thought stung.

Breaking away from his side, she moved toward a fallen log. "I can't believe this is still here."

Shoving his hands in his pockets, he grinned. "I wonder how many lunches have been eaten on this spot."

"And how many secrets exchanged."

He nodded toward a cluster of trees behind the small schoolhouse. "Not as many as were exchanged around the Kissing Tree, I'd wager."

The Kissing Tree . . .

A pang pinched her as she roamed toward the grove, noting the multiple knife cuts carved into one particular tree's thick flesh. She ran her finger over the deep gashes—letters, crudely etched names. She'd nearly forgotten about the Kissing Tree, but at the sight of it, the rush of shame spilled through her just as it always had.

Micah's strong presence behind her jerked her out of the bitter memories.

"Did you keep any secrets here?"

His voice, so low near her ear, caused shivers of awareness

to traverse her spine. She kept herself facing away from him, content to bury her thoughts where he couldn't see them.

"No, not me."

He moved to her side and traced a name with his own fingers. "Really?" He turned to her, his face lined with surprise. "I find that hard to believe."

She felt a flicker of stark pain. "I never took you to be cruel, Micah."

At once, his expression sobered. "What are you talking about?"

She nearly tripped over her tongue, desperate to keep the pain from leaking out—but this was Micah. What she refused to speak he would easily enough ferret out. "You know what I was like in school."

"Yes." He spoke slowly, studying her. "Pretty. Sweet—"

"Stop." She wrapped her arms around her middle. "Don't tell me what I want to hear. I was skinny and backward, too shy to even scare a fly—to say nothing of my condition. I had few friends and certainly no boy ever took a fleeting interest in me." She shook her head, pushing away the old pain. "No, there were no secrets, no sweet romances."

He was silent at her side, and she allowed herself to touch the battered, gnarled tree once more, enjoying the feel of the scratchy bark against her fingertips. "I longed for some fellow to carve my name into the tree, but no one ever did," she whispered. Instead of allowing the grimace she would normally permit, she chose to smile. "It used to bother me.

Not as much anymore. After all, few—if any—of these pairings lasted longer than a week or two."

Micah was so silent, she braved a glance to find him staring at her, his breath visibly shallow. He looked as if he wanted to speak but could not.

She'd made him uncomfortable. Surely he pitied her.

Dropping her fingers from the old tree, she carefully began to pick her way across the yard. She didn't want his pity. For whatever reason, no one had ever looked beyond her paralyzing shyness to see the girl longing to break free. And now, with her illness as unpredictable as ever, it was unlikely anyone would.

Some days the thought made her sad, but most times she was content. That was, until Micah had appeared in her life once more.

Refusing to analyze the wayward thought, she quickened her step upon spying the old tree swing on the far side of the school. "Push me?"

"Kizzie—"

The earnest plea in his voice stopped her. Turning, she noted the somber cast of his features. "Yes?"

"I—" He swallowed hard. "I'm leaving tomorrow."

"Oh." A hollowness consumed her. "Where will you be sent?"

He refused to meet her eyes. "I don't know. But I just wanted to tell you because . . ." He swallowed again and lifted his gaze.

Fear, excitement, uncertainty—all wrapped around her

heart. Before he could finish, she jumped in. "Your friend-ship means much to me."

He opened his mouth to say something before snapping it shut once more. Nodding slowly, he murmured, "Yes. Friends."

"I'll pray for you every day."

He made no move to touch her, yet the way his gaze caressed her face felt more real than if it had been his fingers. "As I will you." His mood lifted and he nodded toward the swing. "One last ride?"

Grinning, she bit her lip. "Only if you push."

# CHAPTER 6

"Make sure you don't dawdle, Keziah. Remember, Mrs. Ward is coming to call later today. I want you back before she arrives."

"Yes, ma'am." Keziah kept back the retort threatening to tear from her throat. She was no longer a child yet was treated as such, instead of a woman rapidly approaching spinsterhood.

Mother clucked her tongue, looking over the crates of rolled bandages and packed lint. "Dearest, are you sure you can manage such a load? Perhaps it's too much for you."

Repressing a sigh, Keziah grabbed the wrap offered by Elizabeth's sturdy hands and settled it around her shoulders, intent that this November afternoon would provide freedom—freedom from Mother's suffocating attentiveness and

Father's too-watchful looks. He eyed her strangely of late, a glimmer of something altogether unsettling in his expression.

She looked up and caught Elizabeth's amused expression. Only yesterday the servant had whispered to Keziah, "If Mrs. Montgomery don't have nothing to worry about, she finds something and then frets because she didn't have anything to worry about to begin with . . . a sure sign her memory must be failing. Just another thing to fret over." Keziah smothered a smile at the memory.

"I shall be fine. Don't be anxious. Hiriam will be doing the majority of the lifting, after all."

"Of course, of course. Please tell Reverend Elliott the Ladies of Savannah are continuing efforts for the charity bazaar. We should have a location determined within a fortnight."

Nodding, she could barely restrain herself from bolting out the door and running as swiftly as her feet would carry her. Freedom . . . if only for an hour or two.

Instead, she forced herself to glide gracefully down the front walkway, ignoring Mother's reprimands to be careful as Hiriam deftly loaded each crate into the waiting wagon.

The late-autumn air swirled around her in a sudden burst, causing her to wrap the woolen shawl tighter around her shoulders. The cold blast of wind slithered up her skirts. In truth, she didn't care. It was brisk and clean and a blessed reminder she was momentarily free from Mother's demands.

Hiriam extended his hand, assisting her into the wagon groaning with supplies before easing his way into the driver's seat. No longer did the aging slave leap into place with the energetic step of yesteryear. He was slowing down—his smile just as easy, his eyes twinkling with familiar merriment, but his body no longer nimble. His gentle movements reminded her more and more of a clock slowly winding down.

With a flick of the reins and soft click of his tongue, the sleek black mares clopped pertly down the cobblestone road. For the first time in weeks, she felt the tightness ease from her shoulders. She could not often escape Mother's incessant worries for her health, nor the grim news of war pummeling them from every side. Most of all, she couldn't escape the haunting thoughts of Nathaniel in continued peril, nor of Micah's welfare as he helped the wounded.

Surely the Relief Commission wouldn't change his assignment and allow him to treat soldiers in the heat of battle, would they? A stab of fear pricked her heart. What if he were injured or even killed trying to help those in need?

*Stop it!* Shoving the clawing panic back down, she stiffened her spine. Heavens, she didn't want to become a worrisome, fretful woman like Mother, did she?

The dreadful thought caused her to lift her chin. She would not stew. She would trust God. She had no alternative.

*Heavenly Father, please protect both Micah and Nathaniel. Give your angels charge over them. Hide them in the shadow of your wings.*

Praying for two men's safety on opposing sides of the war. How strange.

The waning afternoon sun kissed her cheeks as the wagon

turned down the lane. Living just beyond Washington Square as she did, she had to traverse the heart of the port town to get to Christ Church. As the wagon stalled in the crush of people scurrying up and down Bryan Street, she heard a man's strong voice booming from the corner of Reynolds Square.

"Brave men wanted for the navy of the Confederate States! Wages ranging from twelve to eighteen dollars a month, plus four cents per day allowed for grog. Both able-bodied seamen and land men are needed. Who will step up to defend our Georgia soil?"

Keziah eyed the red-faced man with his thick side-whiskers and gleaming brass buttons. If the navy were as confident in their skill as Father had declared them to be over the past several months, why were they still desperately calling for any able men to volunteer?

A shiver coursed through her. She feared Father's fervor for the Confederacy was based on blind enthusiasm and little else.

Flicking away the dark musing, she straightened as Hiriam turned the wagon onto Bull Street. The gleaming white columns of Christ Church lay just beyond.

As he pulled the mares to a gentle stop, she stood and stepped down from the rocking wagon. The old driver frowned and shook his head.

"Sure wish you'd let me assist you, you being a proper lady and all."

Giving him an impish smile, she smoothed her skirt and

laughed. "You've been saying the same thing since I was in braids and pinafores."

He chuckled and reached over to lift a crate from the back of the wagon bed. "And ever since you was in braids and pinafores, you've been fighting your way to independence." His teeth gleamed. "Strong-willed and sassy. You ain't gonna worry me none, though. Uh-uh."

So he'd noticed her silent scream for freedom, the continual urge to wiggle loose of the smothering forces keeping her trapped.

Desperate to have a carefree afternoon, she pushed yet another thought down and reached to carry one of the lighter crates, picking her way to the intimidating doors of the stately building. Hiriam pushed them open with a grunt of effort.

She had barely taken two steps inside the door when a portly man crossed the vestibule, his puffy white sleeves adding volume to his already-cumbersome appearance. Thinning gray hair and spectacles perched on his nose made him appear severe, but his smile was wide enough to put her at ease.

"May I help you, miss?"

Adjusting the crate in her arms, she offered a smile. "Yes, I'm looking for the Right Reverend Stephen Elliott. I have a donation from the Ladies of Savannah Charity League to be used for the war effort."

"Ah, yes! How very kind." The lines around his face relaxed, causing his bulging paunch to stick farther out, straining against his vest buttons. "Christ Church is overseeing this particular effort, and we can use all the talents and resources available to aid our boys fighting for freedom."

*Whose freedom?* The caustic remark nearly burst from her lips, but she caught the wayward thought before it could escape. Instead, she passed the crate into the reverend's waiting arms while he conferred with Hiriam about unloading the rest of the donations.

As Keziah glanced about the cavernous room and its gleaming white columns, the jaundiced eye of a sainted statue arrested her attention. His haughty gaze bored through her and she shivered, wrapping her cloak tighter about her shoulders. She had always wondered what the inside of the prestigious church looked like. Now, however, she was grateful for her own smaller, less pretentious church building far away from the saint's probing stare and hard jaw.

Shaking away the absurd unease, she walked out the doors, where a crisp wind stole the breath from her mouth. Hiriam and the reverend rounded the corner, their arms full of crates and supplies, delivering the bulging packages to some unseen storage room around the far side of the building. Ushering herself down the steep steps, she edged her way to peer over the wagon bed, looking for any stray crates or supplies that still needed to be unloaded.

Instead of the supplies she expected to see, she was startled to observe small fingers yanking the canvas tarp down before slipping inside the dark confines of the covering, disappearing from view.

Her breath froze. A stowaway. And if the quick flash of

dark skin she saw continued past the small fingers, it was a slave who'd found shelter in their wagon bed.

Heart hammering, she gave a soft gasp when the reverend's soothing voice lifted on the November wind as he spoke with Hiriam. They were making their way back to the empty wagon. Well, nearly empty.

The memory of a scarred, mangled back prodded her into silence. *Don't speak.*

Something was restraining her. Providence, perhaps? She composed herself before turning toward the approaching men with a sunny smile.

"Here I come to help unload, and I discover you two strong men have already done the work. Well-timed on my part, I'd say."

With a light chuckle, the reverend peered into the wagon bed, his eyes searching. "Did we manage the entire delivery?" He reached for the tarp.

"No need!" The urgent reprimand sounded far harsher than Keziah intended, causing Reverend Elliott to stop abruptly and stare at her, blinking slowly behind his spectacles. Desperate to keep the stowaway hidden, she softened the sharp comment with another smile. "No need to overexert yourself, sir. I already checked. I pray our brave soldiers will find a measure of comfort and mercy from the goods our ladies' society was able to provide."

The bulbous man smiled and nodded, adjusting his spectacles with pudgy fingers. "Indeed. It is I who thank you and all our admirable ladies who have given so generously for the cause. May the Almighty bless your endeavors."

Nodding demurely under the praise, she allowed Hiriam to hand her into the wagon and settled her skirts, every nerve in her body buzzing with the knowledge she possessed. The clip-clop of horse hooves against the cobblestones drowned out the thrumming staccato of her heart, though it could not cover her racing thoughts.

*What am I to do with a runaway?*

Picking her way across the yard in the fading evening light, Keziah headed toward the stable, glancing over her shoulder for curious eyes. Nothing greeted her but the solemn stillness of twilight. Brown leaves crunched underfoot as she moved. At least the majority of the crimson and gold leaves still clung to the branches overhead, providing a perfect canopy to keep her hidden.

She pushed into the stable, cringing as the doors squeaked under her hand. The smell of leather, the sharp tang of oil, and the sweet aroma of hay mingled with the oddly comforting scent of horseflesh. No human voices greeted her, no bright lanterns. Good.

The pale light of dusk cut slats across the hay-strewn floor as she tiptoed past the nickering mares, running her fingers along the wooden stalls until she reached the yawning area where the wagon was kept. She braved a whisper in the quiet of the space. "Hello?"

Silence.

Keziah bit her lip. Had she only imagined the hand grasping the tarp? Perhaps she was addled. Releasing a warm breath, she wavered in uncertainty.

She felt the heavy cylinder of wax in her dress pocket and decided it was worth the risk. At least it wouldn't cast as much light as an oil lantern. Hiriam might see the light and come exploring, but she wouldn't be able to rest unless she knew whether the apparition belonged to flesh and blood or was only a mirage.

She pulled the sticky candle free and reached in her other pocket for the single match she'd stashed. Striking it, she blinked as it sizzled to life and thirstily licked up the waiting wick.

Keziah hunkered down and eased her way along the wagon bed, carrying the candle to the far side to obscure as much of the light as possible. "Are you there? It's all right. You're safe."

Not a trace of human presence greeted her ears. Unable to put her mind at ease, she reached for the crumpled tarp and yanked it free. A soft gasp sounded in the quiet. She stepped back in surprise as two frightened eyes blinked at her from the darkness of the wagon bed.

Taking a step closer, she whispered, "Don't worry. You're safe here."

The waif was still for a long moment and then lunged, scurrying out of the wagon bed like a cornered animal. Keziah grabbed the skinny, wiggling body and snuffed out the candle before she unwittingly started a fire. Hefting the wiry little form onto the edge of the wagon, she panted against her stays as he stilled. A pale shaft of early moonlight threaded through the shuttered window on the other side of the room. Not much light, but hopefully enough for the tyke to make out some of her form.

"Please don't run. I promise I won't hurt you."

The boy's frantic breathing cut a path through her heart. Did the poor thing think she was the sort to whip a terrified child? The frantic thrum of the runaway's pulse felt like the flutter of hummingbird wings against her fingers.

"Are you hurt?"

A sniffle. "No'm."

"Who are you?"

The trembling mite wiped his nose, his small voice shaky. "My name is Solomon."

Relaxing her grip ever so slightly, Keziah nodded, though she doubted the boy could see the movement in the faint light. "A pleasure to meet you, Mr. Solomon. What, may I ask, caused you to seek refuge in my wagon?"

She could hear the indecision thickening the air around the boy. Finally he spoke. "I can't say, ma'am. You might try to send me back."

"Send you back where?"

Solomon's thin frame shuddered under her touch. "To my massa."

"You're a runaway then?"

Solomon snapped his mouth shut, refusing to utter another incriminating word.

Knowing he would decline to say anything further, she tried another tactic. "Are you hungry?"

If the featherlight arm she clutched was any indication, the poor child was starving.

"Yes'm."

"Perhaps if you tell me why you're running and what I can do to help, I could get you some food."

Although his features were hidden in the shadows, the skepticism dripping from his voice was unmistakable. "How's I know you won't give me to a paddy roller?"

She opened her mouth and closed it again. He was correct, of course. How could she prove she meant him no harm?

"I suppose you'll have to trust me, Solomon. If not me, then God. I saw you earlier after you snuck into the wagon— don't you think that if I intended to relinquish you to the authorities I would have done so already?"

His voice drawled, "Well . . ."

"I suggest a compromise. I'll go get you something to eat first. It's your choice if you decide to run away in the meantime. But if you wait for me here, you'll have a full stomach and my solemn oath to help you if there is any possible way that I can. Agreed?"

His faint outline nodded, causing her to smile and release him. He would very likely run while she scraped together a meal for him, but there was little else she could do. He would have to trust her and she him.

A difficult task since neither of them knew the intent of the other.

---

Keziah watched Solomon shove another piece of corn bread into his mouth. In the silver patch of moonlight painting the stable walls, she could see yellow crumbs dotting the nearly threadbare shirt covering his thin chest. What she had managed to sneak from the kitchen wasn't much—the corn bread, a slice of ham, a wedge of cheese, a jar of canned peaches, and some water—but for this starving boy, it was a feast. With one hand, he continued to cram in bite after bite.

Spreading her skirts around her, she studied the child, surprised he had not run when given the chance. He must have decided to trust her after all. Either that, or the prospect of a full stomach was a greater enticement than freedom.

"So, Solomon, tell me how you happened to find yourself in my carriage."

With a loud swallow, he hunched his shoulders, his face solemn. "I got separated from my group."

"What group?"

"The other slaves."

Her heart pricked. "So you ran away from your master with a whole group of slaves?"

"Yes'm." He sounded resigned as if he already knew what she would do with him and had accepted his fate. "We was told to meet the next engineer at a church. Said he would have a wagon waiting for us and that we should hide in the back." He sighed. "I fell behind and had to guess which church we was supposed to go to. I musta been wrong."

She tried to puzzle out what he was saying—and not say-ing—but her thoughts were in a jumble. "Wait, you said something about an engineer. What does that mean?"

He blinked, the shaft of silver light reflecting off his mahogany eyes. "It's a person to help us get from place to place until we cross into free land."

The picture was slowly beginning to sharpen in focus. "So it's a secret association of people to help runaway slaves find freedom?"

"Yes'm."

Something stirred in her chest. A longing. A flicker of that need to *do*. She leaned forward, dropping her voice even lower. "How can I help you, Solomon?"

His breath hitched, his face slack. "You mean you wanna help me escape?"

"Yes. Unless you'd rather return to your master."

He shook his head vehemently. "No'm. I sure don't. He a mean man. The other slaves talked about his cruel streak, but he was always nice to me, especially when he learned I have a gift with the fiddle. He loved me playing fiddle for the parties he threw. Massa always puffed up with pride when other white folks would say what a good fiddler I was. That is, until . . ." He grew silent, and she nearly trembled at the stark fear lining the silver traces of his face.

"Until?"

"Massa had some folks to the house. Important folks, I guess. He called me to come and play the fiddle for them, but I couldn't. I'd done cut my fingers up but good in the fields that morning. I tried to play, but . . ." Solomon shrugged his scrawny shoulders. "Massa got mad. Powerful mad."

"What did he do?"

Solomon looked down and clutched the cold slice of ham. "Don't remember much. I got a whipping, I guess. When I came to, my right hand was smashed up and bleeding bad."

"Let me see."

Wordlessly, he lifted the small hand he'd kept tucked away, the pale shaft of moonlight illuminating a deformed gnarl of twisted fingers and mutilated flesh. Nausea bubbled up her throat. How could anyone be so cruel? And to a child?

She reached out with trembling fingers, grasping Solomon's deformed hand and giving it a light squeeze, enough contact to let him know she was not repulsed by him but easy enough not to hurt his still-healing injuries.

"Returning to your master is not an option then. How do I help get you back to the others?"

Nibbling slowly on his victuals, he swallowed and puzzled out the predicament, his eyebrows pinching in thought. "Don't know. We ain't told what to do next until we get to each station. The only thing I was told was to go to a church."

"Think, Solomon. Do you remember anything else? Any names, either of a person or the church itself?"

Solomon closed his eyes in concentration. "All's I heard 'em say was it was a church for the slaves."

*A church for the slaves?* Keziah's mind struggled to latch on to what the phrase might mean. With a start and a gasp, she murmured, "First African Baptist." It had to be. It was the only church she knew of in that part of Savannah that might be described as "a church for the slaves." Its congregation was completely Negro, the majority consisting of slaves from nearby homes who were allowed to attend their own house of worship on Sundays. But would the congregants be so bold as to smuggle their own in such a manner?

No, most people wouldn't believe the meek, obedient slaves who attended there would have the intellect or capacity to do such a thing. Keziah suddenly smiled. She knew such a thing was possible. But she couldn't just drop Solomon off at the door.

She searched his face. "Keep thinking, Solomon. Anything else. A person mentioned, perhaps?"

Wiping the ham grease from his lips with the back of his good hand, the boy wrinkled his nose. "Don't recall a name. I did hear some talk about a blacksmith, but no one told me his name."

She frowned. There were any number of such men in Savannah.

Solomon took a nibble of the cheese and murmured, "The man told us this blacksmith was a friend to slaves."

A friend . . .

Giddy relief danced through her chest. Friends and Brothers—the blacksmith and farrier's shop. Marcus Brothers. She'd never met the man but had heard her father praise him. A good craftsman.

Grasping Solomon's arms, she moved closer and looked him directly in the eyes, an attempt to press the importance of her plea into his child soul. "I think I know where the church is, but going there will take some planning. It's not safe to keep you here through the night. There's no secure hiding place, but I'll figure out how to get you away. Do not leave this stable for any reason. Please."

He nodded solemnly. "Yes'm."

She stood and brushed the dirt from her skirts. "Drink the jug of water while you wait for me to return."

The poor boy would likely fall into a sleep, exhausted as he was. Now for the more daunting task. How was she to sneak him all the way across town without being discovered?

Keziah knocked as loudly as she dared on the house settled next to the blacksmith shop. She bit her lip. Past midnight already, and the chance of Mr. Brothers hearing her timid knock was remote.

She glanced back to where Hiriam stood waiting in the darkness, holding the reins to Molasses with a gussied-up Solomon perched in the saddle. Not that anyone would suspect it was a young slave boy nestled atop the nickering mare, clothed as he was in a small dress, complete with pinafore and bonnet.

She knocked lightly again, trembling under her own racing heart. She felt Hiriam's disapproving frown on her back as she impatiently shifted her weight from foot to foot. Back at the house, he'd caught her trying to hitch up Molasses and demanded to know what she was doing leaving so long after dark. She had no choice but to spill the whole awful truth.

At first, he'd stubbornly refused to involve himself, insisting the foolhardy plan would put her in grave danger, and even threatening to tell Father. But when she'd pulled Solomon from the darkness, forcing Hiriam to look into the solemn eyes of the boy so thirsty to be free, something in the old slave's expression changed. With a weary sigh, the driver reluctantly agreed to help . . . just this once.

She frowned. Why his initial reluctance? His vehemence had surprised her. Shouldn't Hiriam be burning to take action, even more than she was? It didn't make sense.

Even though she had initially put on a brave face, insisting she would go with or without him, she was relieved he'd acquiesced. His wisdom and quiet strength were the only things holding her in place at the moment. She shook like a brittle autumn leaf.

The door jerked open and she gasped, peering into the face of a very large, very grouchy-looking, bearded giant of a man. He held no lantern, no candle, but squinted at her through the inky blackness of night.

"May I help you?"

She tried to speak, sucking in a sharp breath, but her tongue cleaved to the roof of her mouth.

"Miss?" His dark brows furrowed, eyes snapping. "Did you knock on my door simply for the joy of rousing me from a decent night's rest?"

Stung by his barb, she straightened her shoulders. "Absolutely not. I'm here because my horse threw a shoe and we are desperate to be on our way."

He shook his head and stepped back from the door. "Sorry, miss. I don't do that kind of work until the sun is up."

"Please." A burst of courage propelled her forward, and she wedged her boot in front of the doorjamb before he could shut her out. "I don't know who else to turn to." She enunciated each word slowly, desperate to convey a message rife with double meaning. "I have a package I've promised to deliver tonight and cannot without your help. I was told you were a *friend* to be trusted." She arched a brow, praying that if he was the man she sought, he would catch on. "Perhaps I was mistaken."

He stared at her, his gaze discerning, taking her measure. She refused to cower or look away.

After a long moment, he gave a curt nod. "Very well. Bring your animal into the livery next door. I'll meet you over there shortly. And don't forget your package. It would be a shame to lose it while I work."

A surge akin to euphoria sliced through her veins. He understood. Stepping back, she slunk into the shadows and motioned to Hiriam. "Come. Follow me."

The hopefulness in Solomon's faint whisper pierced her heart. "Will this man help me?"

She patted his knee. "Yes, Solomon. Very soon, you'll be on your way to freedom."

She paced in the dark confines of the livery, impatient for Mr. Brothers to appear. Solomon watched her with a sense of calm that belied his age, but Hiriam looked as nervous as a worm on a hot rock. Just when she thought she could stand it no longer, the door creaked open and the giant Mr. Brothers approached.

"That was a mighty foolish thing you did, miss."

Taken off guard by the rebuke, she arched her back like a riled cat. "Pardon? I'm merely trying to help this child who came to me for assistance."

Mr. Brothers came close, and she took a hesitant step backward, even as Hiriam moved to stand beside her. The giant's expression was fierce, but his voice held no anger, only concern. "If you want this post to continue operating, you must follow the rules. Lives are counting on it."

Her shoulders slumped. Feeling like a foolish child, she could do nothing more than nod, chastised by the enormity and recklessness of what she'd undertaken.

"Forgive me. I wasn't thinking. This has never happened before."

His bushy black eyebrows shot up. "This is your first time conducting?"

*Conducting?* "I—yes. That is, I suppose so," she stammered.

The fierceness lining his face relaxed a degree, though his eyes gave a warning. "Don't fret. I'll take the boy to the next station. But in the future, don't knock on my door in the dead of night. It might arouse suspicion. Next time find a way to pass me a note during business hours. Be discreet. Wise as serpents, harmless as doves."

She nodded wordlessly, gave a parting squeeze to little Solomon, and slipped back out into the street, Hiriam and Molasses two steps behind.

Would the boy be safe? Had she done the right thing trusting a stranger, a cranky giant who could very well be an impostor? How would Solomon find his group? What if danger befell him?

Feeling like a mother abandoning her child, she joined Hiriam on the mare. They hurried as fast as they dared through the streets of Savannah, Keziah's mind racing with every step. When they arrived home, Hiriam gave her a look that conveyed a dozen meanings before quietly slipping Molasses back into the stable.

She tiptoed into the house and escaped to her room without incident, kicked off her boots, and shed her dress. Squirming into her nightgown, she slid between the cold covers, her body buzzing with exhaustion yet pumping wildly with purpose.

Eyes gritty, it wasn't until she heard the grandfather clock downstairs chime four times that she recalled Mr. Brothers's admonition. *"Next time find a way to pass me a note during business hours. Be discreet. Wise as serpents, harmless as doves. . . ."*

Next time.

She feared Mr. Brothers was all too correct. She'd unwittingly opened a door that could never be shut.

# CHAPTER 7

"Two letters came for you, missy."

Offering Elizabeth a smile, Keziah set her cup of steaming coffee on the parlor table and took the wrinkled letters from the servant's outstretched hand. Sleepiness tugged at her, though it was ten in the morning. A yawn escaped and she tried to cover it with the back of her hand.

Elizabeth frowned. "You been doing a powerful lot of yawning lately. Are you patrolling the city during the night watch?"

Unsettled by how accurate the jest was, she gave the curious woman a weak smile and prayed Elizabeth would change the subject. Keziah was indeed tired, but she couldn't say why. For indeed, she *was* roaming the streets of Savannah in the dead of night.

Somehow the underground network of people working to lead escaped slaves to freedom had been alerted to Keziah's sympathy for the cause. Perhaps it was through Mr. Brothers's instruction. She didn't know. All she knew was that since delivering Solomon to the blacksmith a week ago, two more escaped slaves had been routed to her, both of them hiding in the stable on separate occasions.

After the escapade with Solomon, Hiriam had steadfastly refused to help her anymore, saying she was playing with fire and he would not be responsible for encouraging her to risk her life. She'd reminded him that Solomon's appearance was an accident, purely providential, and that she'd only helped him out of compassion. But the look the old servant gave her forced her to admit, if only to herself, that such a decision had already put her in the thick of danger.

Instead of beseeching him further, she'd smuggled the terrified slaves to the blacksmith herself. Alone.

She suppressed another yawn and blinked hard. She must get more sleep. Dr. Kelsie and Micah had both pressed the importance of sufficient rest. The last thing she wanted to deal with was another epileptic attack.

The breath froze in her lungs. What if she had an attack while transporting slaves to their next stop? A brick settled in her stomach. No, that couldn't happen. *Please, God. Protect us from such a disaster.*

But Elizabeth was watching her carefully, so Keziah forced a brightness she didn't feel despite the sudden worry. Even though her body was tired, she'd never felt more vibrant or alive. God would protect her if she was doing his work, wouldn't he?

Waving a hand in dismissal, she chuckled. "Too many late nights reading, I suppose." Guilt pricked her for the ease with which the lie slid from her lips.

The housekeeper clucked her tongue, but her smile was all affection. "Well, you best be sleeping tonight."

Keziah smiled. "I'll do that."

As the servant swept out the door, Keziah studied the letters in her fingers. The bold, masculine script slapped her awake. Nathaniel. She would know his penmanship anywhere.

A pang of longing pinched, and she glanced at the other letter, her hopes crashing into disappointment when she saw the loopy handwriting: her cousin's in Port Royal. Not Micah's. Again.

She wanted to kick herself for being so ridiculous. He'd never promised to write, nor had she imposed such a demand. He owed her nothing. They were childhood companions. That was it. Nothing more.

Yet why did her heart crave even one word from his hand?

Angry at herself for the desire, she shook her head. She was only concerned for his safety, after all. It would have been nice to know that he hadn't been blown into tinder while treating the wounded. Was the decency of a line or two to let her know he lived too preposterous a thing to ask?

Forcing herself to breathe calmly, she uncurled her

clenched fingers and opened the letter from her cousin, saving her brother's message for last. Like savory roast and creamed potatoes after a sip of too-sweet lemonade.

As she unfolded the stiff paper, Cousin Jennie's flamboyant scrawl greeted her. Memories of her larger-than-life cousin danced across her mind, eliciting a smile at her silly antics and wild personality.

*My dearest Keziah,*

*I am certain by now you've heard of our terrible ordeal, and as one well aware of her own propensity for exaggeration, I say this with level certainty: I never dreamed I would behold the hideous sight of the Stars and Stripes flying over our own forts. The Yankees have taken our beautiful town, as I am sure the papers have reported.*

*I praise Providence that the battle was largely naval, most of the fighting retained to our port ships, but my heart nearly fainted for fear when the reports came—the Yanks took both Fort Walker and Fort Beauregard. Father is livid, as you can well imagine. There are some reports of Yankee misdeeds throughout Port Royal, primarily theft and destruction of property, but for the most part they are keeping to themselves. Still, I shall never become accustomed to the sight of those lecherous villains strolling through my lovely town wearing their mocking blue and snide superiority. Save me, dear Cousin!*

*Could you take me into your home for a chummy visit? Father staunchly refuses to leave the house, fearing*

*it will fall into Union hands, but does not like me*
*surrounded by our dreadful enemies. I feel stifled here.*
*There are no parties, no silks or laces, no fun to be had.*
*Rescue me, dearest. I long for your beautiful smile and*
*the dazzling charm and innocence of Savannah.*

   *Please write posthaste. I shall wait, be it ever so*
*impatiently, for word.*

*Your cousin,*
*Jennie*

Keziah felt an odd mix of emotions as she lowered the letter. She yearned to see her unpredictable, jovial cousin, whose ability to brighten any occasion would be a boon during the drudgery and anxiety of war, albeit sometimes a tad obnoxious. But one more person in the house meant one more person she would have to hide her clandestine activities from, provided she continued to be trusted to transport passengers to Mr. Brothers.

She laid Jennie's message aside and unfolded Nathaniel's missive. His clean, blunt letters were a sharp contrast to her cousin's.

*Dear Keziah,*

   *I pray you, Mother, and Father are all faring well.*
*I am as well as can be expected. Daily food rations*
*are monotonous, sometimes inedible. We feast mainly*
*on hardtack, beans, coffee, and occasionally a bit of*
*meat that looks too blue to eat. Imagine our delight to*

*see a delivery of vegetables last week, only to have our hopes plummet when they were, as my friend declared them, desecrated. It could be worse. At least we have something to fill our bellies.*

*We drill and march, drill and march again. I shall not tell you more of war itself. Such things no lady should ever hear. Do not despair, for we have fun sometimes too. A favorite among the fellows is a game I had heard of, yet never played, called baseball. We divide up into two teams and fashion a small ball as best we can out of items in our knapsacks: rolled-up socks, strips of leather, and the like. We lay three sacks out in a diamond pattern. They are called the bases. The hurler throws the ball toward a man on the opposing team who tries to hit the ball with a long stick. If the striker whacks it far enough, sometimes he can manage to run around all three bases and still make it back home, ensuring a point for his team. We have great fun with this when moments allow, though the competition is fierce. I hear the Yankees are great hands at this particular game and were the ones who introduced it. Perhaps they do have one merit after all.*

*Give Mother a kiss, and on Father bestow a hearty handshake that will suffice until I am able to do so. It needs be a manly one, Keziah. I must strive to let him think the best of me.*

*Sincerely,*
*Nathaniel*

She folded the letter, wishing it were Nathaniel who would be coming home, not Jennie. She pushed away the uncharitable thought. Nathaniel was doing what he thought he must. Jennie couldn't help that she had been pampered her entire life. When the spoiled met with discomfort, everyone suffered.

She rose with a sigh, stretching her stiff limbs, and walked resolutely toward her father's study. She would inform him of Jennie's request and the decision would be in his hands, just as it always was. And she would have to deal with the repercussions, just as she always did.

Late that evening, Keziah clamped her jaw tight to keep her teeth from chattering as she huddled deeper into the recesses of the wool shawl covering her head and torso. Tonight's cold snap was an unwelcome change. Behind the cover of thick-waisted tree trunks and brittle bushes, she left the quaking Negro couple to hunker for warmth while she traversed the small distance between the line of trees and the secret door of Brothers's shop. She exhaled a puff of frosty air and pushed against the concealed latch, expecting it to give way to the dark warmth waiting inside. It didn't budge.

Odd. She frowned and pushed again, giving the stubborn door a more forceful shove, but it stayed firm. Immovable. Glancing around, she saw no lights, the lantern Mr. Brothers usually kept lit in his southern window black as pitch. Something was wrong. Was he ill? Or perhaps he was being watched.

The thought pricked her heart with alarm and she hurried back to the cover of trees, feeling the meager heat of the couple in the bushes. The moon was bright. Far too bright for her to attempt entering the front, exposed as it was to curious eyes. But where could she take the shivering couple?

The church. First African Baptist. That's where Brothers took them, after all. But how would she get in? There must be some kind of hidden entrance. Perhaps a trapdoor? Or a secret tunnel?

She felt a tug on her sleeve, and the slave woman's bony, frigid fingers brushed her skin. Keziah wrapped the woman's hands within her own, trying to impart whatever heat she could. Keeping her voice barely audible, she murmured, "Something is wrong. I'll have to take you to the church myself."

The husband's low voice whispered, "We trust you."

Keziah swallowed hard. What if she failed? What if something happened? What if bounty hunters and retrievers were watching them even now?

*I will not live in the land of what-ifs. God's not there. He is I am.*

The thought bolstered her waning confidence. She plucked up her courage, patted the woman's hand, and took the first step toward the church. Another precarious footfall to their freedom.

She prayed with all her heart it truly was the pathway to freedom and not a trap.

When they were finally just a stone's throw from the

church, Keziah surveyed the building from the thick bushes, sucking in a bitter pull of air. The side entrance was not an option, bathed as it was in the moon's silver luminescence. She squinted, trying to see if there were any doors near the back of the church. Not from what she could tell.

Motioning the couple to follow, she wordlessly crept around to the rear of the large building. There! In the darkness she could barely distinguish the outline of a small window near the bottom. To the basement, perhaps? It had to be. If there was another entrance, she wasn't aware of it. This would have to do. At least it would get the weary slaves ushered into warmth.

Breaking away from the seclusion of the comforting shadows, she crossed to the basement window and felt its cold edges as best she could with her stiff fingers. Surely there must be a latch of some sort. . . .

She hissed in pain as something sharp sliced through her index finger. She put the burning finger in her mouth and tasted blood.

There was nothing to be done for it. The slaves were all that mattered now.

She eased her throbbing finger from her lips with a grimace and kept searching for a way to open the window. Four corners and two diagonal nails. Suppressing a growl of frustration, she yanked at the first nail and her heart froze when it wiggled. It was loose! She jerked it back and forth, nearly squealing with relief when it pulled free.

Now if only the other nail would slide out as easily.

Tugging, she exhaled a whoosh of air when the nail gave way. Her fingers were sticky with smears of warm blood from her cut, but she didn't care. She rose on shaking legs and darted back into the bushes, grasping the woman's hand and guiding her along, the man on their heels. As they approached the church, she pointed to the open window, and in the darkness she felt rather than saw the man nod.

He knelt, helping his petite wife through the window. She slid through the small space easily, but Keziah still held her breath, fearing the muscular slave would have a more difficult time. He offered to help Keziah through first, but she shook her head and murmured, "Go with your wife. I will follow."

With another curt nod, he lowered himself through the window without so much as a grunt, though squeezing through took considerably more effort than it did for his wife. Once he was safe, Keziah lifted the hem of her skirt, thankful it was devoid of hoops for this midnight excursion. She could see nothing but inky blackness but prepared to dangle her foot inside when a hand clamped over her mouth, cutting off her scream of terror. A strong arm snaked around her waist, pulling her backward.

Clawing at the iron arms encircling her, she tried to scream but a low, masculine voice hissed near her ear.

"Not a sound or I'll knock you out cold."

Micah tightened his grip around the soft slimness of the woman in his arms, though her body had grown still at his harsh whisper. Guilt stabbed him. He had no intention of hurting her, whoever she was, but lives were counting on him. If she was an informant, this entire line of the Railroad would be compromised.

It wasn't until he began dragging her into the cover of the trees that she stiffened once more. She arched her back, fighting with a strength that surprised him. He drew her farther, clenching his jaw when her boot landed a well-placed blow to his shin.

Sucking in a breath, he lost his hold for a moment. The woman whirled around, pummeled his chest with her fists. He grabbed her wrists and pushed her against the trunk of a wide tree, his breath erratic. The woman he held fared no better, panting and squirming against his hold.

"Please, please let me go."

The frantic whisper pierced him and he froze. It couldn't be.

But he'd know her voice anywhere. He swallowed hard. *Please, Lord, no.*

"Kizzie?"

# CHAPTER 8

KEZIAH'S HEART HAMMERED, pounding like the soldiering drummers' relentless strikes as they paraded through the streets each week. Her breath stuck in her throat. Surely not . . .

The anguished whisper from the man's lips shredded her as he spoke her name once more. "Kizzie, please tell me—"

"Micah?"

The stranger gentled his hold, though it never had been cruel, only firm. "What in blue blazes are you doing here?"

She didn't know whether to hug him or strangle him, cling to him or scream at him. So she scalded him with a hot whisper. "I could ask the same of you. And I'd be remiss if I didn't tell you to watch your language!"

Not knowing any way out of her predicament, she turned in an attempt to flee, but his hand clamped down on her wrist. She attempted to break free, but he held fast.

"Let me go!"

He pulled her roughly to him, and she collided with the solid muscle of his chest. His warm breath tickled her ear. "You're in danger here. Follow me and stop fussing. Paddy rollers are nearby even as we speak."

Paddy rollers? Terror snaked through her. Horrible men. Nothing more than bounty hunters with a fondness for violence and an insatiable thirst for money. What would they do with her, an unmarried, unarmed woman alone? She licked her lips as blood pulsed in her temples. What about the frightened couple she'd just sent into the church? If they were to be captured . . .

Her stomach constricted. They would be whipped, probably to the point of death. The responsibility she'd so easily embraced suddenly pressed into her chest like a hot iron. She'd presumed too much. How could someone like her possibly help? Now her foolishness might cost those poor souls their hope, their freedom. Maybe even their lives.

Sliding his fingers down to grasp hers, Micah tugged her forward with an urgent whisper. "Come."

Cold nipped at her nose and fingers, but she nodded silently as they hurried across the street and crept their way through the brittle leaves littering the the square. Micah's hand swallowed hers and his warmth took away the tightness in her jaw.

Moments later, he froze and squeezed her hand tightly, issuing a silent command for quiet. Her breath hitched as they listened. Waiting.

Muttered curses. The nicker of a horse. Someone was out there, looking. For her? For the slaves?

Micah ushered her into a grove of trees, easing her to the ground as he sat down beside her, his body rigid. She nearly gasped when his finger brushed across her lips. She knew. No talking. If it were possible, no breathing.

The sound of crunching leaves grew louder, closer.

The hiss of a sneering masculine voice caused her pulse to hitch.

"Come out, come out wherever you are . . ."

A soft chuckle sounded farther away but no less menacing. Squeezing her eyes shut, she tried to calm her racing heart. At least she heard no baying dogs in pursuit, a mercy for which she was most thankful.

Agonizing minutes ticked by, thick moments when she dared not draw a deep breath for fear of being discovered. Micah's solid, warm presence beside her kept her grounded. Her fingers and toes grew numb, and a nagging sleepiness crept over her as the voices moved away and the air became silent.

She startled when Micah shifted beside her, his soft voice propelling her stiff muscles into submission. "They're gone. For now." Wrapping his fingers around hers, he led her forward. "Follow me."

"Where?" The frigid air burning her lungs nearly caused her to choke on the strangled whisper.

"To safety."

Micah bit back a growl at the smirk Ma Linnie gave him when he ushered a shuddering Kizzie into the older matron's dingy pub in the dead of night. No one else seemed to notice their entrance. A boisterous group of bearded men occupied the center table, engaged in their pasteboards and cider. Groans rose up as four queens were laid down on the worn table, ending the game with growls of frustration. Another man lay facedown on a lone table in the corner, his grizzled beard bunched up under him as his loud snores punctuated the dank air. No other patrons could be seen.

Moving to grasp Kizzie's elbow, Micah steered her gently to the scarred oak bar, noting how her eyes seemed too large, her face too pale. What on earth was she doing outside the church in the middle of the night? There were only two reasons he could fathom, and neither was good.

And now she'd seen him. It was far too risky for her to be anywhere near him, let alone clinging to his arm in the Cold Oyster Pub. He pushed down the panic clawing up his middle. His concern was to ensure her safe return home. She had no business associating with him. None. But how could he now protect her and keep his distance at the same time?

Ma Linnie's round face creased into a wide smile, her gray eyes twinkling. "The Lord be praised. Doc Greyson went and claimed himself a wife!"

Micah glared at the meddlesome, albeit kindhearted,

older woman as she snickered under her tight mobcap. Kizzie stiffened at his side.

Ma Linnie gave him a teasing wink and patted Kizzie's hands. "And what a beauty she is too! Mercy, her hands are cold as Lincoln's heart." Motioning around the bar, the plump woman tittered and ushered them to the back. "Come with me, dearie, and I'll get you all warmed up by the kitchen fire. You'll at least gain a reprieve from these coarse menfolk."

Micah followed behind and through the swinging door to the warm comfort of the dim kitchen. A lone tallow candle danced and flickered on the worktable. Ma Linnie ushered Kizzie into a rickety spindle chair and whirled, dropping the pretense she'd maintained in the front room.

"Land o' Goshen, this poor thing is half-frozen. What happened out there, Micah?"

He rubbed his palm against the back of his neck, trying to knead the tight muscles. "I was near the church when I heard a couple of paddy rollers. I was sneaking around, trying to lose them, when I ran into Miss Montgomery here."

Ma Linnie grunted and poured steaming chicory coffee into a tin cup, pressing it into Kizzie's fingers. "Take this, dearie. It will warm your insides."

She blinked rapidly but sipped the brew, wrinkling her nose against the taste.

Ma continued probing Micah as she scurried to stoke the fire in the woodstove. "Were you followed?"

"I don't think so. It was mighty close, though. Too close."

Straightening from her stooped position, Ma banged the

stove door shut and rubbed the ash from the poker off her hands. "What was the girl doing at the church?"

He shook his head. "I don't know."

Kizzie stood from her chair with an exasperated sigh and placed the cup on the table. "Pardon me, but I'm present. I can answer your questions." She raised her face to Micah's. Her expression was guarded. "But first you must tell me what *you* were doing, Micah. What's going on?"

Keziah lifted her chin as she watched Micah glance toward the robust woman. Something was most definitely wrong. Why was he acting in such a baffling way?

She pressed him further. "I thought you were working with the Relief Commission. I even wrote you a letter." Guilt flashed across his face and she nearly recoiled, hurt and disbelief washing over her in waves. "Did you lie to me?"

He shook his head, a streak of crimson climbing up his neck. "No, Kizzie. I didn't lie. I *am* with the Relief Commission."

"Then why were you snooping around the church in the middle of the night?"

His countenance darkened as he set his jaw stubbornly. "I could ask you the same."

She stalled. She would not betray the runaways she'd led into the basement. She set her own jaw and pressed her lips into a hard line.

Micah raised a dark brow. "I see." His tone was clipped.

"Three in the wee sma's is too early to be stewing." The older woman plopped her plump hands on her ample hips and gave them both a motherly glare. "Something happened out there or you both wouldn't be sitting here in my kitchen."

Three in the morning? Keziah gasped and slid the hood of her cloak over her head. "Thank you for the coffee, ma'am, but I must take my leave."

Micah stepped in front of her with a frown. "Where do you think you're going?"

"Home, of course." She cinched the ties of her cloak, preparing to brush past him, but the hands he placed on her shoulders stopped her.

"By yourself? Are you daft?"

Why did everyone think her a dullard? Giving in to vexation, she snapped, "I think I can manage my way back."

"I'll accompany you."

"That won't be necessary, sir."

"I'll either walk by your side or follow from a distance, but I'll not allow you to travel home unescorted."

"Whatever suits you, *Doctor*." She knew she sounded churlish but was helpless to keep the disdain from leaking into her voice.

Micah's eyes narrowed, but he remained silent as he buttoned his wool coat. "Thank you for the protection, Ma."

Ma Linnie barely suppressed a chuckle. "I've no doubt I'll be seeing both of you again. And soon."

Unable to sort out the cryptic remark, Keziah gave her a weak smile and slipped out into the harsh air, Micah on her heels. She was blessedly free of the stale atmosphere in the pub but carried a larger burden instead. How could she explain what she was doing?

Micah watched from the shadows as Kizzie slipped through the servants' entrance, praying the house servants had not yet awakened. He blew warm breath into his cupped fingers. Dawn would soon turn the sky a streaked pink. Lifting a hasty prayer for her safety, he stepped farther into his hiding place among the trees lining the Montgomery home.

Judging by Kizzie's expression when she realized the late hour back at the pub, her family was unaware of her clandestine activities. No surprise there. No man in his right mind would allow his beautiful daughter to traipse all over Savannah in the dead of night. So what was she up to?

She'd spoken not a word to him the entire way back. Nor he to her. Her icy silence was far more chilling than the night air. She thought the worst of him. Thought him to be a liar or, heaven forbid, a coward. How could he possibly explain his work without dragging her into the subterfuge with him? No, she was too precious to live in such danger. He'd rather she think him an ogre than place her in harm's way.

Heart heavy, he turned away from the imposing house. Whatever Kizzie was involved in, she was playing a dangerous game. Of course, he was too. Still, he'd always sensed from a young age that the shy little foal held the heart of a wild Arabian horse inside, caged and desperate to be loosed. Perhaps the Arabian had found a way to run free.

But was it a taste for freedom that drove her to recklessness? Or perhaps something altogether different? She had been at the church, a primary point along the Railroad. A suspicion niggled. Was Kizzie a conductor?

As quickly as the idea formed, he shoved it away. No. She would never entangle herself in something so precarious. Likely she didn't even know about it.

Regardless of the reason for her late-night wanderings, Kizzie needed a keeper. He steeled his rapidly softening heart.

No matter the situation, her keeper could not be him.

# CHAPTER 9

"Darling, you look frightfully tired."

Keziah pasted on a smile and looked across the dining table to meet her mother's eyes. They were far too astute. Picking at the potatoes cooling on her plate, she forced her exhaustion away as best she could. "Nothing to worry about."

More rest. She must get more sleep. But how could she when there were runaways hiding in their stable, waiting for someone to lead them from misery and chains? She must do something. She couldn't ignore them. Not ever again.

But if she were to collapse en route . . .

And what of Micah? She had tossed and turned for hours wondering what he'd seen, if he suspected anything, and worse yet, if he planned to tell anyone of her clandestine activities. Dread stalked every waking moment.

"You've not been getting enough rest. That's plain to see."

She straightened, swallowing a bite of peas. "I didn't sleep well enough last night. That's all. Too much on my mind."

Father frowned. "I pray you're not wearying yourself with thoughts of your brother. Nathaniel is holding up well, judging by his letters."

Mother's gaze flitted between them. "Was that the reason for your unrest?"

Keziah pressed down her guilt. "Yes, ma'am." The lie slipped out easily enough. An exaggeration about her concern for Nathaniel was far less destructive than admitting she'd been helping lead escaped slaves across town.

Father took a sip of his coffee and grimaced. "Dreadful. Where is the sugar? I cannot drink my coffee black."

Mother shook her head, daintily lifting a forkful of potatoes to her lips. "The price of sugar is rising drastically. I thought it a frivolity we could do without."

Yanking off his spectacles, Father glowered. "Cursed Yankees. It's bad enough they want to destroy our lives, strip us of our freedom—and are snarling to snuff out our children. Must they take our sugar as well?"

Mother shot him a warning glance pregnant with some unspoken message Keziah was helpless to understand. Father cooled his tirade and visibly relaxed before turning toward Keziah with a soft smile. Her gaze flickered between her parents. What was going on?

Father leaned back, his chair squeaking. "Keziah, I have something to tell you."

She placed her fork on her plate with a clink. His expression was congenial enough, but his eyes . . . something serious and unwanted lurked in their depths.

"Yes?"

"You are a lovely young woman, and you have known for quite a while that your mother and I long to see you in a good match, though we've faced certain obstacles."

She sighed. "Father, please—"

He held up a silencing hand, and she stopped the protest.

"You are past the age when many of your peers married, and it's high time you settle down and prepare for a family of your own. Particularly as it seems your condition has been . . . less prevalent in recent months. That is why I've decided you should court and eventually wed—illness or no."

Her breath grew shallow. "I see." She fought against unwelcome sensations within and tried to stay calm. "And where should I find such a suitor? All the men we know are away fighting."

Father nodded but did not look concerned. Her panic heightened. "That is true, at least if one were looking for a suitor among young men. But a different opportunity has presented itself." He smiled and her blood grew cold. "A gentleman of our acquaintance seeks your attentions. I believe you're familiar with him. Mr. Lyman Hill."

Her eyes slid shut. Yes, she knew of Lyman Hill. A stern-faced, middle-aged man with gray-streaked hair. A widower, if memory served her correctly. She remembered him watching her at a soiree, his dark stare intense, much like a hawk's. She could still recall the shivers when his eyes locked with hers.

She did not care for Lyman Hill.

Her stomach churned and she feared she might cast up her accounts. "I do not wish to be courted by Mr. Hill."

Father growled, banging his fist on the table. "Keziah Grace Montgomery, this is not up for discussion."

She lowered her chin and bit her lip. His uncharacteristic use of her full name was all that was needed to capture her silence.

"Mr. Hill is quite smitten with you and has sought my permission to court you properly. I've granted him this request. He will come to sup with us this evening, and you will receive him graciously. He appears to be blissfully unaware of your illness, and I think it best he remain so as long as possible. I don't need to remind you that a woman with your infirmity should feel nothing short of grateful for a chance like this."

Feeling as if she were smothering, Keziah stood on wooden legs and moved to leave the dining room before she said something she would regret. She stumbled to her room with blurry vision, only allowing the tears to fall once she was safely ensconced inside.

Courted by Lyman Hill? Her world had narrowed further, into a more suffocating prison from which she feared there was no escape.

—◦⟨∞⟩◦—

"It was a splendid dinner, Mrs. Montgomery. I haven't eaten stuffed chicken so delectable in years, and now you offer my favorite cookies as well?" Mr. Hill's oily chuckle reminded Keziah of something serpentine. "If you continue to spoil me so, I fear I may never leave."

Keziah felt ill watching Lyman Hill grovel at her parents' feet. He hadn't stopped since he'd arrived at their door more than two hours ago. And now, with supper finished, the four of them sat in the parlor, sipping tea and nibbling on Elizabeth's butter cookies.

Keziah perched stiffly on her chair, wishing she could end this silly charade. The rest of the evening still yawned ahead, promising an agonizing display of false flattery and inane chatter over topics of no consequence. She'd rather be reading or visiting the stable . . . or sleeping.

Mother beamed. "It was our pleasure, Mr. Hill. Would you care for some entertainment? Our Keziah plays a lovely tune on the pianoforte." Mother sent her a knowing look, and she inwardly sighed, rising to move toward the instrument.

Mr. Hill lifted his slim hand. "Thank you, but no. I actually don't care much for music."

Mother blinked. "Oh, but of course."

Keziah resumed her seat. He didn't care for music? What sort of a man didn't care for music?

Mr. Hill took another sip of tea. "It gives me frightful

headaches. All the banging." He shook his head. "No, I never could tolerate it. Singing either."

She bit back a retort. Banging indeed!

Father chuckled. "I take it you're not a fan of the opera, then?"

"Ach, a more torturous display was never invented. I say if our Confederate generals want to really let the Yankee prisoners of war suffer, they need only take them to Mozart's *Don Giovanni*. The screeching from the soprano alone should suffice to torment their souls for all eternity."

Mother's trilling laughter grated over Keziah's nerves. Rather than let his criticism go unchallenged, she picked up her teacup and forced herself to take a sip before staring directly into his gray eyes.

"You seem rather harsh in your criticism, sir. I found *Don Giovanni* to be a sweeping masterpiece. A bit lush, perhaps, but a transcendent work of art. Any man who could craft such beauty is nothing short of a genius."

Mr. Hill quickly masked his evident displeasure. "I'm glad someone can appreciate such noise. Unfortunately, I cannot."

Something itched between her shoulder blades. "What of church music? Hymns and sacred songs?"

He took another sip and sighed. "To be honest, I find the music itself dreadfully dull. I'd much rather just read the words and contemplate the meaning."

Father cleared his throat. "I daresay others share the same opinion, judging by the number of men I've witnessed dozing in the back pew from time to time."

The two men chuckled, but Keziah was not amused. A person who did not like music was a person who could not be trusted.

Mother stood. "Forgive me, Mr. Hill, but it appears Elizabeth has forgotten the cream, and I'd like to inquire if she also has some of her famous cinnamon squares to serve. I'll return shortly."

Father hastened to her side. "I'll help you, my dear. You may have trouble managing all that if Elizabeth is occupied."

Keziah stared into her cup of tea as they retreated. Father had never offered to help Mother carry food before. Their scheming to leave her alone with Lyman Hill was thinly disguised at best. How humiliating.

The clock on the fireplace mantel ticked slowly, the sound far too loud in the strained atmosphere. She should make conversation, be a stimulating hostess, but she had no desire. Each click from the timepiece felt like a minuscule pull on an ever-tightening noose.

"So, Miss Montgomery." Mr. Hill cleared his throat, forcing her attention away from her cooling tea. "You have an usual name. Keziah. Wherever did you acquire it?"

She arched her brow. "Why, from my parents."

A muscle ticked in his cheek. "Of course, but where did they discover such a name?"

Something about the way he worded the question made her think he found the name distasteful. As a child, she'd loathed the moniker, wishing her parents had named her something sweet and simple like Kate or Rose. But she would never concede such a thing to the likes of Lyman Hill.

"I was named after my paternal grandmother. Keziah is a biblical name."

"Really? I don't recall it."

She offered a thin smile. "Job chapter 42, verse 14. It was the name he gave one of his daughters after he endured his trial and emerged victorious."

"Interesting. Still, it's rather odd. Didn't you ever wish for a name more ordinary?"

She lifted her chin. "As I've grown older, I've begun to see the tremendous value in being able to stand apart from the crowd."

His eyes narrowed. "I always took you for a shy soul, Miss Montgomery."

"When I was younger, I was painfully shy. But I find I'm growing less so all the time." She allowed her face to form a more sincere expression. "Never mistake quietness for weakness, nor meekness for timidity."

He opened his mouth, but she was saved from his reply as Mother and Father swept back into the room, carrying a small pitcher of cream and a serving tray heaped with cinnamon squares.

"There we are. Elizabeth's cinnamon squares will melt in your mouth." Mother offered one to Mr. Hill, who took it with a gleaming light in his eyes. She settled back in her chair and smiled. "And how are we getting along?"

Keziah forced a civil response. "Just fine."

"Splendid," Father boomed. "Tell me what you've heard concerning the war, Mr. Hill. I've been devouring the newspapers. It appears we have the Yankees on the run in Virginia."

Mr. Hill bit into the pastry and nodded. "Of course. Was there any doubt? We have Providence on our side."

She could stand that argument no longer. With a sigh, she placed her cup in its saucer. "But isn't that the problem?"

Father frowned. "What do you mean?"

"We believe we have Providence on our side. The Union soldiers no doubt believe the same. We cannot both be right."

"Keziah." Mother's whispered rebuke caused her to fall silent.

Mr. Hill lifted his brows. "Do you believe the Confederacy will lose, Miss Montgomery?"

She shook her head. "I'm not saying that."

"Then what *is* your point?" Father cut in.

"I believe perhaps political fervor might be more optimistic than the reality of our resources. The Yankees have us outmanned and outgunned. Their artillery factories are far more numerous than ours. Not to mention the force of the Federal Navy—"

"Keziah, please," her mother scolded. "You know you're not to be reading those newspapers."

"I just think perhaps people might be riding a wave of emotion at the moment and not seeing the bigger picture."

Mr. Hill leaned forward. "Which is?"

"The war will surely last longer than a few more months.

In April, everyone thought it would only last one month. But it's November now."

"Keziah, that's quite enough," Father snapped.

Mr. Hill ignored him, keeping his gaze fixed on her. "How long, do tell, will the war last then?"

She swallowed. "I pray I'm wrong, but I fear it could last for years."

Mother gasped. "Surely not!"

Mr. Hill's lips pinched into a tight, condescending smirk. "A woman's grasp of politics and warfare. How charming."

Father glowered. "Indeed."

The two men shifted the conversation to business, effectively blocking her from further input. Judging by the sharp looks from Mother, and Father's occasional scowl in her direction, she knew she had disappointed them once more. But it would be a worthwhile disappointment if it prevented Mr. Hill from visiting her again.

# CHAPTER 10

"PLEASE DROP ME OFF HERE, Hiriam. Mother wanted me to peruse the newest hats to see if one might be suitable for the upcoming Christmas bazaar."

"Yes, missy."

Keziah clutched her reticule in trembling fingers and stared at the millinery shop as Hiriam gently pulled the carriage to a stop. The horses nickered softly as they slowed, tossing their heads with haughty disdain as Hiriam set the brake and turned to offer her a hand down. As her boots touched the cobblestone walk, she turned to him with a smile.

"There's no need to wait. I may be here for quite some time. You know how exacting Mother can be when it comes to our apparel."

Hiriam scratched his thick, graying curls. "I did promise to take some papers to your father's office. He sent a messenger boy asking me to retrieve them, and he's mighty particular about his accounts . . ."

She bit back a cry of relief and nodded instead. "That should be fine. If I finish early, I'll stroll down to the dry goods store and wait for you there."

He tipped his hat and clucked his tongue, urging the pawing mares back into motion. She watched his departure before pressing a hand to her quaking stomach. She hated deceiving sweet Hiriam but could see no way around it.

Skirting the millinery shop, she walked as fast as she dared to Mr. Brothers's blacksmith shop. She pushed through the door, grateful for the blast of heat emanating from the glowing furnace. The November air was uncharacteristically cool for midday. Mr. Brothers, busy pounding a hammer against a horseshoe glowing red with trapped heat, did not so much as spare her a glance as his massive fingers clutched his tools. Two older men stood in the corner, tugging their bushy beards and chatting about axles and wheels, topics of no interest to her. A younger man stood in front of an array of iron goods—fire tongs, ax blades, and spades—lost in thought as he decided on his purchase. All the men ignored her entrance, a situation not much different from Lyman Hill's conversation with her father the evening before. After she'd spilled her sentiments about the war, he'd ignored her the rest of the evening, save the leering glance he'd given her when her parents were occupied with other matters. Shudders that had little to do with the heat of the blacksmith's shop slipped down her back.

She approached the long table that served as Mr. Brothers's transaction space, opened her reticule, and pulled out the money she'd folded up before leaving. Guilt twisted. Her only recourse had been to pluck it from the allowance Elizabeth had been given to take to market that morning. But she would replace it. Even if she need sell a bauble or piece of jewelry, she would.

Pinching the paper money with white fingers, she prayed the message she'd secured inside would not fall out.

She cleared her throat, playacting a bravado she didn't feel. "Pardon, sir, but are you the proprietor of this establishment?"

Brothers raised his head from his work and narrowed his eyes before dropping the hammer onto his worktable with a dull clunk. "Aye. May I help you?"

She stood straighter. "Yes. My father has sent me with our payment for the work you recently performed."

Without missing a beat, Brothers nodded and snatched the bill from her hand, stuffing it into the pocket of his thick apron. "'Twas a pleasure. I trust your horse is no longer limping then?"

"She's in fine form now. Thank you."

"Tell your father to find me if the shoe troubles you anymore." He dismissed her abruptly and returned to his work, giving her a view of his broad back as he pounded the glowing iron once more.

She hesitated, anxious not to blurt out something foolish.

She'd struggled far too long penning the simple message folded within the currency.

*Should I continue to procure your business as my*
*smithy?*

She'd neither addressed him by name nor left a mark as to her own identity in case the slip of paper fell into calculating hands. Surely Mr. Brothers would understand the cryptic message, but she must find some way to receive his answer. Considering the disaster that could have occurred night before last when she'd been locked out, she desperately needed to know if she should continue to lead fugitives to his shop.

Searching for a way to get immediate information from him, she swallowed and called out, "Oh, I nearly forgot. Father wanted to know when his other order might be ready."

Without turning, the giant blacksmith called over his shoulder. "Three days' time, I'd imagine."

Nearly laughing with relief, she schooled her features into casual disinterest. He understood the reason for her visit.

"Very well. Someone from the family will return in three days."

Her legs trembled as she stepped back out into the swirling cool, but she couldn't suppress the rush of victory. She'd sent her first secret message without mishap. Now to wait three days for Brothers's answer.

For surely more runaways would arrive soon, and her part

in their freedom hinged on the blacksmith's willingness to trust her.

———⁕———

Micah lifted the sleeping infant and studied his color in the dim light of the church's musty basement. The single window had been boarded shut after he'd discovered Keziah snooping near it not two nights before. If she was somehow involved in all of this . . .

He forced the nagging thought away, just as he'd done a thousand times since he pulled her into the shelter of Ma Linnie's pub. She was no longer his concern. But these poor slaves were.

Easing back the dingy flannel blanket covering the small body, he roved his fingers over the infant's stomach, feeling for any protrusions or abdominal swelling. His touch roused the little fellow from his slumber, and the baby's nose wrinkled in irritation as he pinched his eyes even tighter, puckering his tiny mouth into a pout. Micah tucked the blanket back around him and returned him to his mother's waiting arms with a smile.

"Is my boy healthy?"

Micah gently reassured the weary mother. "He looks perfectly healthy. You've done a good job with him. My only concern now is you." The woman looked down at the baby in her arms, her face lined with a sadness he'd seen far too often among the runaways. "You must find some way to eat more. Your son depends on your nourishment."

She nodded but frowned. "Mighty hard to find sust'nance when you're running from paddy rollers and bloodhounds."

The bleakness of her situation hit him again, and he felt helpless to offer anything useful. "You're correct, of course. Once you're in Canada, things will be better." He forced a bright smile. "We just need to keep you both healthy until then. Someone will be bringing you some buttermilk and food soon. Eat every bite." He reached into his black bag and pulled out a vial, placing it in her gaunt hand. "Here. Liquid vitamins. Take a drop or two each day. It will help."

"Thank you, sir. May the Almighty bless you for this kindness."

Patting her hand, he stood in the cramped space and ducked under a beam to study the woman's husband, who lay on the lumpy cot. He pulled the steady glow of the oil lamp closer and knelt. "I hear you got caught in a trap a while back."

"Yessir." The brawny fellow's face gleamed in the warm light. "Animal trap clamped around my leg while we was creeping through the swamps."

"Hm. I see. May I take a look?"

With a nod, the man drew back the blanket covering his thick form. Micah tried not to show alarm at the festering cut bulging from the man's calf.

"Does it pain you much?"

"Yes, sir."

Pulling some clean cloths, salve, and a small bottle of whiskey from his bag, Micah set them aside for later use and went to work cleaning the cut with tepid water from a basin. "Yet you traveled with this nasty cut for how many miles?"

Cold sweat beaded the man's forehead as the water touched the fevered skin of his leg. "Forty miles, best I can figure."

Micah dribbled more clean water over the wound. Forty miles on foot through swamps and woods while injured this badly? "You're very strong, I'd say."

The man winced when the first application of whiskey met the infection. Hissing through his teeth, he shook his head. "No, sir, I'm not the strong one. That'd be my wife. Traveling all this way with our son nothing more than a wee thing." The fellow captured his wife's gaze, and a smile broke through his pained expression. "That woman's my hero."

Micah dropped his eyes, feeling as if he were intruding on a private moment, and instead focused his attention on applying salve to the cut marring the fugitive's flesh.

No doubt desperate for distraction, the man spoke into the quiet, his upper lip dotted with perspiration. "What about you, Doc? You got a woman?"

Micah unrolled the clean white bandages and began wrapping them carefully around the infected leg. "No. Can't say as I do."

"Kind fellow like you ain't got a girl to call your own?" He grunted. "A shame, that."

Micah raised a brow. "Now how could I possibly find time to court a lady while I'm bandaging legs and easing fevers?"

The man grunted deep in his throat as Micah tied off the bandage. "If there's one thing being a slave has taught me, it's that life is short. Too short to do nothing but work. Love and freedom—those the only things that matter. The only things that will last."

Unbidden, Kizzie's beautiful smile flashed before his eyes, and his heart twisted with sharp longing. Why did she continue to haunt him so? He had done better engrossed in his studies in Philadelphia, only thinking of her every few days instead of this continual stream of yearning. Seeing her once again as he had upon his return to Savannah had ignited embers that he'd managed to keep from burning him in the past.

No longer. He was consumed by her already.

Yet he was not fit for her. Truly, he was not fit for any woman, not involved as he was in the cause.

And just when he thought he'd said his final good-bye, their lives collided once more.

But what still gnawed him was the reason Kizzie was sneaking around the church that night. Surely there was a reasonable explanation.

Until he knew the answer, peace would elude him.

# CHAPTER 11

"THERE'S MY DARLING COUSIN!"

Keziah's smile faltered as Jennie smothered her in a bone-crushing embrace. Jennie finally released her and stepped back, her green eyes sparkling.

Keziah had come home from her errands with Hiriam and was surprised to see her vivacious cousin just arriving, her hack bulging with trunks crammed full of clothes, hats, and who knew what else.

"Keziah dear, you grow lovelier with every passing year."

Jennie's mirth was palpable, and now that she was able to draw a breath, Keziah resumed her smile. "As do you. I pray you had an easy trip. Did you run into any trouble leaving Port Royal?"

As she smoothed her fiery-red curls with a dainty hand,

Jennie's lips curved into a mischievous smirk. "Nothing that a bit of honeyed talking couldn't fix. Those Yankee vermin have a hard time saying no to friendly Southern ladies. And of course, I had Aunt Ollie travel with me as far as Levy."

"Oh? Did she not want to venture this far?"

"Aunt Ollie?" Jennie trilled a laugh. "Heavens, no. The poor dear is afraid of her own shadow. I was required to give her smelling salts upon the top of every hour for some silly thing or the other. No, her daughter lives in Levy and Aunt Ollie is most happily settled there now for the duration of the war. Doubtless I would be too if my home boasted as much brandy as her daughter's husband seems to enjoy."

Keziah coughed, trying to smother the laughter that threatened to bubble out. If Mother heard Jennie's outrageous talk, she'd have been scandalized.

Cousin Jennie twirled in her navy traveling suit and tossed her wrap to Elizabeth with a dismissive air. "See to my things. And mind how you care for my gowns. I can't abide wrinkles."

Elizabeth dropped her eyes and mumbled an obedient reply as Jennie turned to Hiriam, who was struggling to carry one of her many enormous trunks through the foyer.

"Be careful with that! That trunk is worth more than you've ever dreamed of."

Hiriam nodded. "Yes, Miss Jennie. My apologies."

Unable to refrain, Keziah touched Hiriam gently on the arm. "Are you certain you can manage? I'm sure one of the neighbors' servants wouldn't mind assisting if we asked."

Jennie intruded with a sharp reprimand. "Don't coddle him, Cousin. He should know how to manage a trunk, for pity's sake."

Burning with embarrassment for Hiriam, Keziah straightened as the old groom heaved the cumbersome load toward the staircase. She turned to Jennie with a frown. "Hiriam is an old man. Toting such a load might prove too much for him."

Jennie waved her hand. "My, my. Have you gone soft on me, dear? Mark my word," she scolded with her finger extended, "you don't want to let your Negroes think they are in charge. They must remember their place." Her brows lowered into a heavy scowl. "We learned that quickly enough when the Yankees came. We thought Sarah, George, and Cook were so faithful, but the minute they saw Union blue, they left us." She sniffed in derision. "Can you imagine such ingratitude?"

Keziah was taken aback. It had been some time since she'd seen Jennie, and she did not remember her being so high-handed with the servants, nor her tongue so sharp. Had she always been so? Perhaps Keziah had never noticed before.

Mother's cultured voice broke up Keziah's tumbling thoughts as she glided into the room. "Oh, Jennie, how beautiful you look."

"Auntie!"

The two women squeezed hands and exchanged kisses on the cheek. Slipping her arm through Jennie's, Mother led her into the parlor. "Come now, you must be exhausted from your trip. Your uncle will be home soon and we'll enjoy a nice supper. So I take it you were unsuccessful convincing your father to visit as well?"

Jennie lowered herself onto a parlor chair with a melodramatic sigh, fluffing her skirt around her as if she were a Russian princess at court. "Alas, I was. Father is unrelenting. He says he will not leave the house while Yankees prowl about our town."

Mother clasped her niece's hand. "Of course. I daresay I would feel the same."

Jennie feigned wiping away a stray tear. "I pray you will never suffer as we have."

Keziah took her own chair and stifled a smile. For all her theatrics, Jennie looked hale and hearty, hardly the victim of famine or ill treatment.

Mother, oblivious to her niece's dramatic rendering, patted her hand. "There, there. You are in Savannah now, and we promise to help you forget your troubles."

Jennie brightened, straightening in her seat. "Do tell. What festivities are occurring in fair Savannah? Soirees? Balls?"

"Oh, my dear, no. Nothing so grand as that." Mother sobered her tone. "War dampens such events, you know. The expense alone is far too much with rising prices, and many feel parties are too frivolous while our men are away fighting for our protection."

Jennie's exuberant face drooped. "This foul war. Is there no fun to be had anywhere?"

Keziah managed to keep her lips pressed together. Jennie

acted as if the world existed merely for her amusement. Wasn't she aware that men and women were facing death each day for one taste of the freedom she so blindly took for granted? But then Keziah herself hadn't been aware of that until quite recently. Had she been as self-absorbed as Jennie? Self-loathing coated her tongue.

"But I forgot!" Mother faced Keziah with a hopeful smile. "There is an event just before Christmas. We received the invitation yesterday." She turned back to Jennie. "A holiday benefit for our brave soldiers, held at the great hall in Liberty Square. All proceeds will provide blankets, shoes, and other necessities for our defenders."

"A benefit?" Jennie wilted. "A social gathering, I admit, but not much fun."

Mother leaned forward, pleased with herself. "Ah, but there is to be dancing. It's a costume benefit, at that."

Clapping her hands together, Jennie bounced like an eager child. "Oh, how splendid!" She fixed her gaze on Keziah, eyes shining. "Do say you're going, Keziah dear. We'll have such a grand time. And we can design our costumes together!"

Keziah opened her mouth to speak, but Mother interrupted. "Certainly Keziah will be attending. Her beau has already requested permission to escort her."

Unable to stop the displeasure that coursed through her, Keziah frowned. "Mr. Hill made no such request of me."

Mother waved a hand. "There was no need for him to ask you. He already spoke with your father. Don't look so glum. You'll have a splendid time."

Jennie's shrill giggle grated on her. "Cousin Keziah has a beau? Do tell."

A blush filled Keziah's face as she plucked at the knee of her rose-colored skirt. "I've only met him formally once."

Mother frowned in her direction and turned to Jennie. "Such a handsome man, and he's quite taken with our Keziah." She shook her head. "He's a relief from that horrid doctor who was poking about."

Jennie leaned in, no doubt sensing a titillating morsel. "What's this about a doctor?" Her teasing grin rankled, though Keziah resisted the urge to explore why.

Mother chattered rapidly. "Nothing to worry about. He seemed unusually interested in your cousin, and your uncle Benjamin insisted he leave." She dropped her voice to a whisper. "His father was an abolitionist, you know."

"How odd that he would show such interest in Keziah, then." Jennie pursed her lips.

Heat seared the back of Keziah's neck, but she forced herself to stay calm. "The doctor was an old schoolmate of mine, Mother. Nothing more."

She harrumphed. "He had more on his mind than your health, darling. In any event, I'm relieved he moved on."

"Yes, he's gone." She was suddenly assaulted with the remembrance of his strong hands struggling to hold her in the night's cold darkness. The scent of bay rum that always clung to his clothes. His secrets that kept her awake long after the rest of the house was rocked in slumber. Micah was gone yet more present with her than anyone else.

She lifted her eyes to see her cousin staring at her in a disconcerting way, her gaze radiating a shrewdness that left Keziah feeling undone.

---

NOVEMBER 16, 1861

"Oh, look at that one, Keziah dear."

Keziah moved to Jennie's side to study the lavish confection in the millinery shop. "That hat is lovely indeed. But how would it aid as a costume?"

Jennie giggled behind her hand. "Why, pair it with a cream-colored eye mask, maybe something covered in seed pearls. With those gorgeous feathers adorning the top, I could be a regal swan."

At times like this, her cousin's laughter was infectious, and Keziah couldn't resist giggling along. "You would make a lovely swan."

Jennie flashed her straight white teeth. "I would, wouldn't I? Perhaps I should consider it."

Keziah reached out to touch one of the delicate, silky feathers. "It is quite a hat, but the price . . ." She sighed. "Goods are becoming dear, aren't they?"

"I shan't be deterred by something as vulgar as cost," Jennie pouted. "Father would want me pampered in his absence. He sent me plenty of coinage to do with as I please."

Keziah dropped her fingers from the exquisite hat. Had her cousin not noticed the soaring food prices? Sugar, bacon, coffee, flour . . . all of it draining bank accounts throughout the city. If sugar and coffee could be considered a frivolity, how much more so a silly frippery like a hat?

Before she could respond, she sensed a presence behind her. Turning, she saw a gangly youth of no more than fifteen, his straw-colored hair sticking out wildly from under his cap. He held a small crate in his hands.

"Yes? May I help you?"

His freckled cheeks reddened ever so slightly. "Pardon my intrusion, Miss Montgomery, but I work for the smithy, and upon seeing you on the boardwalk, he remembered he'd completed an order for your father." He raised the crate in his hands. "Mr. Brothers sent me over here straightaway. Thought it might save your groom a trip back."

"That's very thoughtful." Keziah's heart quickened as she reached out for the parcel, which was surprisingly light. It took all her willpower to keep from prying it open immediately. "Fortuitous that he spotted us. I'm sure Father will be pleased."

The youth tipped his hat, donning a winsome smile as he slipped back through the door.

"How odd that a delivery would be made in such a fashion." Jennie's suspicious tone caused Keziah's hackles to rise, but she schooled her features.

"Oh, not at all. Not for Savannah, at least. You'll see it's still a very friendly town, and Father is well-known. At any rate, at least it will spare Hiriam from inquiring about the order later. Come." She nodded toward the ostentatious hat, praying the distraction would work. "We have a hat to buy."

The ploy was successful, and Jennie's face lit up. She chattered happily about her new finery all the way home, but Keziah could contemplate nothing but the mysterious contents calling to her from inside the crate.

⸎

NOVEMBER 23, 1861

Keziah exhaled heavily from her perch within the darkened grove, as she peered to see if the thick clouds were moving to cover the shimmering silver light bathing the path to the blacksmith shop.

*Please, Lord, it has been weeks since my last efforts to transport. Be with me. Be with them. Lead them safely to their Canaan land. And keep my body from failing me.*

Jennie's arrival had greatly cramped her ability to move about at will. Her nightly excursions to the stable to check for new arrivals had aroused Jennie's curiosity, though she seemed to believe that the jaunts were Keziah's way to relax each evening before retiring—a story made plausible by her claim that she loved to brush down her mare, Magnolia. Still, Keziah felt as if she were being watched all hours of the day and night.

Even after destroying the blacksmith's cryptic note, she felt ill at ease. The comforting message she had committed to memory was lost on her tightly wound nerves.

*Thank you for your patience as I recovered from the croup. I am managing to fulfill all orders in a prompt manner and would welcome any business your family might request from me.*

It had been a full week after receiving his note before any more passengers had arrived, and she'd feared her work as conductor had been compromised. But not this night. When she'd searched the wagon housed on the far side of the dark stable, three exhausted men met her.

The moonbeams were suddenly snuffed out in inky blackness as the clouds passed overhead. Keziah's muscles tightened in response, her whisper terse. "Now. Come."

Silently, the three men followed her every step as they crept with haste to the secret entrance at the back of the shop. As she felt along the wall, her cold fingers found the notch easily and she pushed the door open just far enough to allow them to slip through. Wordlessly, the last one turned to her, the darkness almost completely obscuring her view of his face. Still, she saw the nod of gratitude he gave her before disappearing inside.

Easing the door closed, she crept back into the cover of trees and attempted to calm herself. This night's work was nearly complete . . . as long as her curious cousin remained asleep in the room directly across from Keziah's own.

Micah felt as if he'd been punched in the stomach.

When a trusted agent sought him out earlier in the day at Ma Linnie's pub, saying little more than, "It appears a wind's coming up from the South today," he knew passengers were arriving, likely at Brothers's shop. How could he have prepared himself for seeing not a male, but a female conducting a group of fugitives?

And not just any female. Kizzie.

The hood of her cloak had slipped ever so slightly as she passed him, unaware he was watching her from the thick bramble. His heart had dropped to his feet upon viewing her profile.

His worst suspicions about why she'd been outside the church were correct after all.

A sudden rush of cold washed over him. This was all his fault. He was the one who had taken her to the abolitionist meeting. He was the one who had opened her eyes. Though he didn't regret his part in showing her the truth, he had inadvertently unlocked a door that would bring her harm. She had no idea what she had undertaken. She was playing at life and death as though they were nothing more than a game of chess.

Running his fingers through his hair, he wanted to scream with the frustration of it. All these months he'd kept away, fearing any association with him would put her at the mercy of those who wanted to destroy him. How could he have known she'd beckon retribution right to her own door?

And retribution it would be, with certainty, if anyone were to discover her clandestine activities. He must find a way to talk with her. Reason with her.

There was little time to spare. Indeed, she might have already dug too deep.

# CHAPTER 12

DECEMBER 14, 1861

Keziah's vision blurred as the colorful silks and laces spun past her, a throng of whirling dancers and thick air.

She tried to keep her gaze focused on Mr. Hill's black lapel, but she felt dangerously close to being overwhelmed just the same. She must not let it happen again.

"Are you quite all right, my dear?"

Feigning interest in her austere beau was just another facade she must maintain. The entire evening had pressed her nearly beyond her ability to cope.

When they had arrived at the costume benefit earlier in the evening, Keziah was immediately enchanted with the great hall's boughs of Christmas greenery trimmed with jaunty red ribbons. The multitude of glowing candles and the lively orchestra music had chased away her exhaustion . . . for a few moments, anyway.

With a polite smile, she looked into her escort's stern face. "Yes. Just a bit winded." She fought the urge to sigh. The black mask Mr. Hill had donned for the masquerade, despite covering the upper half of his face, could not hide his perpetually dour expression.

His eyes narrowed, studying her as one would examine a scientific specimen of plant or animal. "You seem fatigued."

Apparently her own delicate mask could not entirely hide her expression either.

Ire bloomed hot in her chest and she steadied herself, determined to endure. "I don't feel tired in the least." The lie tasted bitter, for she *was* tired. Dreadfully so. Two consecutive midnight deliveries of passengers had left her dangerously sleep-deprived. Of course, she could never tell him what she'd been doing. Could never tell a living soul.

The thought left her feeling even more limp than before.

Mustering her grit, she threw herself more heartily into the dance's spirited steps. As long as she had no epileptic falls, all would be well. It had to be. Too many people were depending on her.

Unable to squelch a sauciness born of irritation, she asked, "Do you find my appearance lacking, then?"

Lyman Hill's mustached lips formed an odd smile. "Hardly that. You outshine every other lady in attendance." He shot her a reproving look. "Though coyness is not necessary to evoke a compliment from me."

The man's condescension was unbearable. When the dance ended, she found relief in knowing he could not dance with her again this evening, not without causing tongues to wag. They were not yet betrothed.

Instead she took a moment to catch her breath and study the festive room, smoothing her shimmering pale-blue dress and adjusting the mask covering her forehead, nose, and cheeks. Only her lips and chin peeked out from under the disguise, a costume in which she felt a certain amount of pride. The gown's glittering fabric held traces of silver, and the thought made her smile inwardly.

Every person in attendance wore a mask of some sort, all featuring a wide array of colors and fabrics. Some, like Jennie, wore disguises reminiscent of noble animals. Judging by the inordinate amount of attention her cousin was receiving from admirers, her swan costume was a success.

Keziah's own design was a bit more obscure.

The sight of somber-faced women in the corner of the room collecting donations for the soldiers brought Keziah a measure of melancholy. These women all wore widows' weeds, the black fabric telling the same story.

She'd seen far too many black gowns this night.

Though the women in mourning were not allowed to dance or partake in the merriment, they could enjoy the music and participate by collecting donations. A noble endeavor and one that took much courage, considering their losses must be fresh.

A low voice near her ear caused her heart to skip. "May I have this dance?"

She turned to see a man studying her intently, his face obscured by the white mask he wore. His chestnut hair was wavy and his mouth unsmiling. He cut a dashing figure in his black coat, with broad shoulders and trim waist. He held out his gloved hand, and she assented demurely before slipping her own gloved fingers into his. Something about his bearing, the way he moved, reminded her of someone. . . .

Holding her loosely as propriety demanded, he swept her into the crush of dancers. She kept her eyes trained on his lapel, just as she'd done with Mr. Hill. Her nerves always held her tongue captive when she danced with strangers. The easiest course was to avoid eye contact and pray the dance would soon pass without incident.

"May I be so bold as to brave a guess at what your costume represents?"

This man was brash, to be sure. Uncertain how to refuse him, she nodded. "You may."

"You are quite breathtaking in pale blue and silver. Might you be an ocean wave?"

His gentle teasing pried a smile from her lips. "No, but your guess is admirable."

A dark brow arched above his white mask. "A blue lagoon then?"

She shook her head. "You flatter me, but no."

He laughed low, and her skin tingled. There was something so familiar . . .

"A falling star?"

Giving him a smile, she acquiesced. "You are close. The North Star."

His masked face melted into somber reflection. "Ah, of course. The North Star. A beacon. The path to freedom, some might say."

She gasped and felt her feet stumble ever so slightly. The man's hand tightened on her waist. He knew.

Heart hammering, she lifted her gaze to meet his. From behind the man's disguise, sky-blue eyes collided with hers and her knees nearly buckled.

Micah.

Micah tightened his grip on Kizzie's waist. The revelation startled her, just as he knew it would. They had not spoken since that night he'd discovered her outside the church. No doubt she thought him an apparition—materializing on obscure occasions only to vanish once more.

The soft skin of her jaw had paled beneath the silver eye mask she wore, and she drew shallow breaths. Her pained whisper tugged at him. "Micah?"

"You play a dangerous game."

Her cinnamon eyes darkened. "I play no games, sir."

"I disagree." Looking for an escape among the swirling couples, he maneuvered her lightly to the side. "Come. Follow me. I'll dance you out of the circle. We need to talk."

Micah artfully wove her through the spinning costumes

and the cloying scent of thick perfume, breathing a sigh of relief as they approached the outer circle. He released her waist and tucked her hand into the crook of his arm, then escorted her through the open doors leading to the gardens outside. Cold air stung his exposed jaw, but he refused to slow a single step.

At least the bite of December would ensure they could speak without listening ears.

Silver moonglow dappled through naked tree branches overhead, leaving patterns of light and dark spots along the ground. He intended to lead Kizzie farther into the darkness, but she suddenly stopped short, pulling her arm free of his hold.

"This is quite far enough. Whatever is wrong with you?"

"I saw you. That's what is bothering me."

She furrowed her brow. "Saw me? Saw me where?"

He came so close, he could feel the warmth of her body. She stepped back and grunted softly when she bumped against the rough bark of a tree. Dropping his voice to an urgent whisper, he answered, "At the blacksmith shop."

He heard her sharp intake of breath and removed his mask, watching the moonlight glitter across her face. Lifting his hand, he cupped her jaw in his fingers and drew her downcast eyes to meet his. "If I'm wrong, tell me."

She trembled under his touch, and his fears solidified. "You're not wrong."

"Kizzie," he groaned, stroking her jaw, "what you're doing is so dangerous."

She drew back from his touch, her eyes flashing. "And what exactly are you accusing me of?"

Micah gave her an incredulous look. "I *saw* you, you know . . . North Star."

She winced, and he couldn't keep a small smile from escaping. "Only those of us involved in—" he searched for a proper word—"*transportation* would know the double meaning behind your costume."

Her eyes widened and she yanked off her mask. "You? Is that why you were outside the church that night?"

"Yes. I saw you and was afraid you might find passengers I had just delivered to the church." He chuckled mirthlessly. "Little did I know you were conducting your own cargo."

She shook her head. "But that night you told me you truly had joined the Relief Commission."

"I did. I—" He rubbed the back of his neck, dropped his voice another notch. "It's not safe to talk here. But I'll explain it all to you. Someday. I only sought you out to beg you to reconsider your participation. Think of what might happen if you fail."

Her beautiful face sharpened, steeling into a stubborn look of determination. A look he knew all too well.

"I assure you, I'm quite capable of my duties."

He leaned in, placing his palms against the roughened bark of the tree, effectively trapping her between his arms without the luxury of touching her soft skin. "Why, Kizzie? Are you attempting to prove something to yourself?"

"Of course not."

"Your parents are not correct about your medical condition, you know. You are fully capable of doing whatever you set your mind to accomplish. There's no need to risk your life nor face dangerous escapades to prove it."

"How dare you!" Her harsh whisper struck him as hard as a slap. "You presume to think I'm helping the cause out of some kind of selfish need to prove my own worth?" She shook her head, and he felt the full force of her anger. "I do not need to justify myself to you or anyone else."

"And have you considered what might happen if you were to have a falling spell while transporting? The danger you might put innocent men and women in?"

"Stop!" She rubbed her temple with trembling fingers.

"Please, Kizzie, I'm only concerned. You could be killed. Or worse." He swallowed, the thought of losing her filling him with something dark. His chest tightened.

Her face contained a sadness that made his heart ache. "Do you really think so little of me, Micah? Do you believe I would willingly risk the lives of passengers to puff up my own pride?" Her chin trembled. "I thought you knew me better than that. God has protected us on all counts, both myself and the fugitives. I trust he will continue."

This wasn't going at all as he'd hoped. "It's not that. I'm just—"

Her tone hardened once more. "You have an awful lot of pluck, you know. Lying and running away, ignoring my letters, choosing instead to let me think you dead or wounded." Her gloved finger jabbed him in the middle of his chest, and he dropped his arms, fearing she might strike him across the face. "All the while snooping and working for the very same ideals you condemn me for."

Her accusations stung. Locking his hand around her wrist, he glowered in the waning moonlight. "Pardon me, my dear Miss Keziah, but there is a difference between us. I'm a man. You're a young woman. I can defend myself against attackers. Can you physically ward off angry paddy rollers or suspicious men or snarling dogs?"

Her eyes glittered like dark ice as she spoke through clenched teeth. "I've done fine thus far."

He pressed on, desperate to make her understand the fire she was dabbling with. "Do you think the authorities—or even your own neighbors—will show any mercy if you're arrested? You'll be a traitor to the Confederacy. Imprisoned. Possibly even hanged." His breath hitched at the thought of losing her.

"And why would my fate matter to you so much, Micah?" Something raw lay beneath her words.

Everything in him screamed to declare his feelings, and the burning confession nearly burst from his lips. Quenching the flames, he heaved a sigh and released her, his taut muscles relaxing a measure. "We're friends. I care."

"I see." Her whisper sounded pained. Tight.

How to make her understand? "You are a lovely woman and deserve the best life has to offer. A husband. Children. Happiness." He shook his head, regret and longing flooding him. "You'll experience none of those joys if you continue on this path."

She laughed distantly. "Your worry may be in vain. If Father has his way, continuing to aid the cause may become nearly impossible for me."

"What do you mean?"

Ignoring the question, she pulled her mask into place and stepped close, her breath warm against his face. "Thank you for your concern, but this is something I have to do. Something I feel called by God to do . . . for whatever length of time he gives me." She looked into his face. Could she see the turmoil ripping him to shreds? "Perhaps our paths will cross again."

His heart thudded erratically. "Perhaps. If God ordains."

She nodded and offered a small smile. A truce of sorts. "If God ordains."

And then she was gone.

Keziah shivered, her skin tingling as she walked back into the warmth and chaos of the great hall. She pasted on a smile when Jennie caught her eye from across the room, but her mind fogged with thoughts of Micah, her heart constricting until it felt like a block of lead.

He'd judged her and found her lacking. Tears clogged her throat, but she would not give in to them.

Who was he to accuse her? It was his invitation to the abolitionist meeting that had prodded her to think beyond herself and the life she'd always known. He'd ignited a compassion, a yearning to do something, anything, to help. And now he condemned her for it?

She mentally shook herself as she glided through the mass of costumes. Perhaps *condemned* was too strong a word. Micah hadn't seemed so much condemning as . . . concerned.

The thought had no more than formed when Jennie found her, her delicate gown appearing to float amid its adornments of plumage and lace.

"Where have you been? I've been desperate for you!"

Keziah forced a light laugh. "Desperate for me? Why the theatrics?"

Jennie giggled behind her feathered fan and leaned in. "I was held hostage by the most fascinating gentleman. He claims to be a blockade runner. One of the few men in attendance who is young, healthy, and hale."

"Then why seek to part from his company?"

Jennie's lips pushed out into a pout. "I couldn't bear his mustache. Most hideous apparition. It curled up on the ends in such a way, it made him look like he was smiling while talking about morose topics like war and death." Jennie straightened and shook her russet head. "No, I simply couldn't abide it."

"Life with you is never dull."

"Indeed." Jennie nodded toward an approaching man. "Here comes your escort. And he does not look pleased."

Keziah turned just as Mr. Hill stopped before her, his face devoid of the mask he'd worn upon arriving. His scowl darkened the air between them.

"Miss Montgomery, I would be remiss in my duties if I did not ask where you've been this past half hour."

She blinked, taken aback by the ire lacing his hard tone. "I've been here, sir. I strolled outside for a bit of fresh air and was most recently conversing with my cousin."

Grasping Keziah by the arm, he pulled her away from a gaping Jennie and ushered her into the closest corner, eyes flashing as he muttered through clenched teeth. "Don't ever humiliate me like that again."

Yanking her arm free, she longed to give in to the urge to slam her slippered foot into his knee. "Pardon?"

He straightened and gave his vest a quick yank. "I am your escort. Your beau. You cannot ignore me all evening and prance about as if I were nothing more to you than a trite inconvenience."

Her mouth dropped open. "We are not betrothed, sir. You know as well as I that for me to dance with a man, any man, more than once would be scandalous."

His lips curved into an insolent smile. "Ah, I see. Desperate for my proposal of marriage, are you?"

Outrage licked her insides. "I am desperate for no such thing."

The infuriating man's look of anger turned to coy understanding. "Obviously a lady of distinction could claim no such desire without appearing overly forward. Not to fret, my dear. It will happen soon."

Sickened at the thought, she rubbed her temple. "Please, I'm not feeling well. I must leave."

"Of course. I admit to being bored with this whole bene-fit anyway. Seems a childish way to raise funds for our sol-diers. Playing dress-up like a bunch of children."

The headache blooming in her skull pulsed with increas-ing pain. "I shall fetch my cousin, then."

Turning from him, she breathed a sigh of relief even as her headache increased. She pulled Jennie from her throng of admirers, leaned in, and whispered, "Forgive me, but we must leave."

Jennie's eyes rounded in surprise. "Are you feeling quite well? You're as pale as a ghost."

"Truthfully, I'm not well. I've been tired of late, and now my head feels as if it might burst."

Shooing away the older men gathered behind her, Jennie slipped her arm through Keziah's and strolled through the great hall. "You're not about to have one of your episodes, are you?"

Keziah felt heat warm her face, along with the cold, dark shame that slithered through her every time her condition was mentioned. "You know about those?"

"Yes. That is, Auntie Elsie told me a little. Come. We shall take you home and put you to bed. I'll have Mr. Hill summon the carriage."

Unable to do anything more than nod, Keziah followed Jennie into the December night's air. She prayed the harsh temperature would chase away her headache.

Just as the carriage arrived and she prepared to step inside, a too-familiar tingle shot up her spine. She groped for Jennie's hand.

"Jennie, I—"

A cry of panic slipped from her lips as the world crashed into darkness.

# CHAPTER 13

"HAVE YOU HEARD THE LATEST?"

Within the confines of the Cold Oyster Pub later that night, Micah rested his elbows on the battered, sticky table of Ma Linnie's simple kitchen. The smell of fried onions and potatoes saturated the stale air. Beyond the kitchen doors, men smoked fat cigars and spoke of war as they discarded pasteboards in spirited games of poker and twenty-one.

Ma dropped the daily paper before his eyes with a ruffled thud. "Blockade at Tybee has tightened up. Prices on food-stuffs are only going to rise." She huffed and wiped her hands on her stained apron. "Salt is up to a dollar and twenty-five cents a sack, and bacon is thirty cents a pound. Now you tell me, how on earth am I supposed to feed hungry men day after day with those prices?"

Micah leaned back in his chair. "Do they honestly think a group of untrained men can stand up against the Federal Navy?"

Ma pursed her lips, causing the spectacles perched on her button nose to tilt. "Some of our commanders think the war will come to a head on land here in Savannah." She looked over the top of the crooked spectacles. "But mark my words: as sure as my hair is gray, the Yankees are going to cut the Confederate Navy into ribbons."

Micah stared off into the distance, his thoughts on Kizzie, just as they had been since she'd left him at the benefit two hours before.

Ma plucked off her spectacles and speared him with a sharp glance. "Who put a bee in your bonnet? Ain't said more than two words since you came in here an hour ago, dressed in your fancy duds and acting like someone shot your dog."

Giving her a sour look, he grunted.

"Does this have anything to do with the pretty miss you brought in here a couple weeks back?"

Micah nearly growled when Ma's smug smile stretched from one side of her face to the other.

"Let's drop it."

Ma leaned her considerable girth forward. "So what's her story? You never did tell me why you brought her in here. Does she know what you do?"

He kneaded the skin above his eyes. "Only in part. I didn't

say much that night because we had paddy rollers on our tail, and I wasn't sure what she was doing."

"And?"

"She's a conductor."

Ma sat back in her chair, her voice soft. "I'll be. She's one of us. Plucky little thing."

He slammed his fist down, causing the oil lamp resting in the middle of the table to rattle with an unnerving clatter. "She doesn't know what she's gotten herself into. You and I, we know the danger and have taken measures to ensure we have a fighting shot. But Kizzie—" Unease gnawed his middle. "She's inexperienced. I've got half a mind to write William Still and request that the Railroad sever their connection with her, to find a different route. I don't know how to make such a message clear, though. At least not without putting her at risk."

Ma slapped her plump fingers against the table. "You would really try to manipulate that sweet girl in such a way?"

"How else can I protect her?" Micah dropped his head into his hands.

Ma suddenly cackled, causing him to lift his head with a glare.

"I fail to see the amusement."

"You love her."

"I care for her. Yes."

"No." Ma shook her head, her jowls swaying as her eyes twinkled. "It's more than that. Admit it."

He wanted to deny it but was weary of doing so. Ma

would see through his feeble protests anyway. Resting his head in his hands again, he murmured, "Yes, I love her."

Ma squeezed his arm and leaned close. "Bless you, you stubborn dolt. Love doesn't manipulate. And it doesn't control. Love gives, even if it costs the giver everything."

"But if something happens to her—"

"It's her decision. You can't take that away from her. Not if you really love her. Free will, and all that. Would you deny her a passion Providence laid on her heart because you're afraid of losing her?"

He had no ready reply. No argument. Ma was correct. Still . . .

He scraped his fingers against his scalp. "Is it so wrong to want to shield her from pain?"

Ma stood and toddled over to the stove, grabbing the coffeepot. "There can be no growth without pain, Doc. You should know that better than anyone. Even nature tells us that."

He huffed. "Sometimes treatment of a wound involves pain before healing occurs. That's true enough. But how much better not to have the wound in the first place."

Ma slipped back to the table, a gray curl springing free from under her dingy mobcap. "Ain't what I'm speaking of. Have you ever slit open a butterfly's cocoon?"

Odd change of topic. "Can't say that I have."

She poured him a cup and plunked it down in front of him before filling her own mug with black brew. The steam fogged her spectacles, once more balanced at the end of her nose. "Nor should you. Did you know that if you try to help a butterfly out of its cocoon, if you slit its house open, the butterfly will die?"

"No, I didn't know that."

She took a sip of the coffee and grimaced. "I must say, I'm not much particular about my coffee, but this chicory is a poor substitute." Giving him a long look, she abandoned her cup on the weathered table. "Part of what enables that butterfly to soar is the struggle it takes to break free."

The analogy struck him hard. Was that what he was doing with Kizzie? Trying to slit open her cocoon?

"So what should I do then, Ma? Stop fretting? Stop caring?" He shook his head. "I can't do that."

"It ain't that easy, is it? No. You do what the Good Book says. Perfect love casts out fear. If you fully understand how much the Almighty loves that little lady, how he has a plan for her life, whether you like the plan or not, you trust him with it. That perfect love of God will grab fear by the throat and toss it out the door."

"Yield her up to God." Peace settled through his soul at the thought. "I think I can do that."

She chuckled. "God knows what's best anyhow. Not you. And if you don't want to lose her, you ought to try encouraging her, not bossing her 'bout what she should or shouldn't be doing."

He narrowed his eyes. "Isn't that what you're doing to me right now?"

Ma watched him, a smile playing about her mouth.

"Someday when the two of you young'uns are married, you'll look back on this moment and say old Ma was right."

Barking a dry laugh, Micah scrubbed his fingers down his face, trying to rub away the exhaustion. "Married? What kind of life could I possibly offer her? I'm not in one spot long enough to leave a mark. Always scurrying between here and wherever the Relief Commission or the Railroad tells me to go. And you know my own history." He sighed. "She would never want me if she knew."

"Seems to me you don't give her much credit. And it's true enough that you're busy now, but the war won't last forever. With the good Lord's aid, slavery will be abolished altogether. Then there won't be a need for sneaking and running all over kingdom come."

Weariness caused his shoulders to slump as he voiced the fear lurking in the back of his mind. "But what if we don't win?"

She frowned, her voice heavy. "We must. We win or die trying."

We are troubled on every side, yet not distressed;
we are perplexed, but not in despair; persecuted,
but not forsaken; cast down, but not destroyed;
always bearing about in the body the dying of the
Lord Jesus, that the life also of Jesus might be made
manifest in our body.

Keziah shifted her weight against the pillows cushioning her back. Since suffering the seizure at the costume benefit two nights before, she'd done little more than sleep, rest, and read her Bible. For some reason, she had settled on 2 Corinthians chapter 4, and the apostle's words continued to roll around in her mind. There was truth contained inside, something indefinable she tried to grasp, but it eluded her still.

She needed to muster her courage. For every day that passed with the stable light extinguished and the back door padlocked shut was another day helpless men, women, and children groped through the cold alone.

A sharp rap sounded on her bedroom door, and she closed the worn book with a sigh. Laying it aside, she smoothed her dressing gown. "Come in."

Her cousin peeped around the edge of the open door. "How are you feeling, Keziah dear? If you despise the thought of company, I shall leave."

"Don't be silly. I welcome your visit." She patted the edge of the bed. "Truthfully, I need to rise and join the family. I plan to be at supper tonight."

"You may want to reconsider that notion. At least until Auntie Elsie is in a more affable frame of mind." Jennie wrinkled her nose and perched on the soft bed.

Groaning, Keziah eased back against the pillows. "Is Mother upset with me for having another spell?"

Jennie shook her head, red curls bouncing despite the pins holding up her locks. "No, your condition is not the source of her ire. With Christmas coming next week, she's fretting about the high food prices. The blockade has her in a tizzy." Jennie giggled. "Though no more so than Uncle Benjamin."

Keziah offered a lopsided smile. "I can imagine. And Father was so sure the blockade would be dissolved within three days' time."

Rising once more, Jennie picked up a brush from the bedside table and studied the delicately carved handle. "Little chance of that. At least, not before Christmas. What did you dine on for Christmas dinner last year?"

"Mother's standard holiday fare: duck soup, French chicken pie, veal olives, fried artichokes, pineapple pudding . . ."

Jennie groaned and dropped the brush onto the bed, clutching her stomach instead. "Stop or I shall faint from want! I haven't had such delicacies in ages."

Keziah tossed a pillow at her melodramatic cousin. "Hardly that long. Still, I imagine we should be thankful to have anything to eat at all. The poor are in much more dire straits."

"Pshaw! I have no desire to think of the downtrodden. Not so close to Christmas." She crossed her arms. "I'm much more upset that I have no beau to invite to our Christmas meal."

Pushing the covers back, Keziah scooted to the side of the bed. "Do you ever think of anything other than men?"

Jennie smiled coyly. "Naturally! I think of clothing and jewelry too."

With a laugh, Keziah stood on wobbly legs. The last episode had knocked the stuffing right out of her. Still, after two days of rest, she felt stronger. She looked up when she sensed her cousin's gaze boring into her.

"Do you think it's wise to be up yet?"

Keziah blinked. "Of course. I can't stay in bed forever."

"Perhaps you should."

The caustic murmur made her stomach sink. "What do you mean?"

Jennie sighed, though her curt tone offered no sympathy. "I have never witnessed the falling sickness before. I must say, it was quite alarming. And you should have seen Mr. Hill. He was mortified."

Heat tingled through Keziah's body. She longed to recoil from the slice of her cousin's words, but she had no place to retreat.

"Your episode may have chased him away completely. I suppose we shall see if he accepts your mother's invitation to Christmas dinner." Jennie turned to study her own reflection in the vanity mirror as she prattled on, oblivious to the deep barbs she'd flung with her flippant words. "You really should focus your attentions on domestic pursuits, darling. If something like that happened to me, I'd never desire to set foot in public again."

Keziah's breath thinned, her heart throbbing against the dark, cold weight pressing upon her. If only she had some place to hide.

She heard little of what else her cousin had to say. The daggered sentiments lodged deep in her mind as they continued to taunt her. Was she really such an embarrassment that her own cousin preferred not to be seen with her?

Once Jennie had exhausted her thoughtless words, she departed and Keziah fell back into the bed.

Useless.

A humiliation.

Her throat clogged and she pushed herself up from the bed, crossing the room to stare at her reflection in the vanity mirror. Her hair hung in limp waves over her shoulders. Her skin was far too pale. Dark rings framed her eyes. Jerking away, she looked out her window at the gray yard and barren trees.

This last attack had been fierce. Her legs had been uncooperative for hours upon awakening, an occurrence that had never happened before. What if she were someday left paralyzed? A new, more terrifying darkness enveloped her. What if she died? Suffocating as her body thrashed for breath? She fisted the lace curtains and squeezed her eyes shut.

Why had the possibility never occurred to her before?

She pressed her cheek against the cold window glass, lips trembling even as the first warm tear escaped.

Was this what her life would be? Trapped in her own body? Fearful of dying young? A sob scraped for release, her breath fogging the glass. She'd been treated like delicate china on display for half her life, and placed behind glass and tucked out of sight the other half, when the china was too chipped and broken for prying eyes. The only thing of worth she'd done was help the runaways. Even in that, she lived in fear her illness might compromise their flight.

Swiping at the tears running down her jaw, she firmed her lips. She had no control over the breadth of her days. That was in God's hands alone. But if her life was to be short, she must make each day count. A sudden urgency pressed through her spirit. She would do all she could to help others find freedom . . . even as her own was siphoning away.

She sniffled, heartsore, until a cheery thought popped into her mind.

If Mr. Hill was so repulsed by her condition, perhaps he would forgo their courtship. A bubble of laughter pushed through the swirling sadness in her chest.

Happy day.

Christmas dawned cold and sunny. Keziah had prayed Mr. Hill's repugnance with her ill spell would keep him at bay or discourage him altogether.

It was not to be.

He arrived precisely at noon, bearing a saccharine smile for her parents. Her hopes were dashed as Jennie's brows rose into her hair.

They gathered in the festively trimmed dining room, the lace-covered table adorned with silver trays, sparkling crystal, and holly. Despite the lack of their normal Christmas delicacies, the intoxicating scent of cinnamon and oranges permeated the air, a lavish treat in the midst of war. But Keziah's appetite refused to respond to the splendid aromas. She eyed Nathaniel's empty chair, and a lump settled in her throat. For once, she was grateful for Jennie's silly chatter. At least she kept the dinner conversation stimulating.

"So Mama refused to let me join in the party, claiming the occasion was only for adults."

Father smiled and sipped his champagne. "I take it you acquiesced like an obedient child." The twinkle in his eyes betrayed his true thoughts and Jennie giggled.

"You do not know me well at all, dear Uncle, if you think that. No, my thirteen-year-old heart was set on enjoying all the glory of the party. Just when the guests had settled down to dine in our home, I rode my horse, Lady, right into the house and declared, 'If I'm old enough to master this marvelous beast, I do believe I'm quite old enough to attend a simple dinner party.'"

Laughter peppered the table. Keziah felt her own lips tugging upward, though she would never dream of doing anything so outlandish.

Mother dabbed the linen napkin against her mouth. "If I had been your mother, I would have swooned, young lady."

Jennie washed down a delicate bite of ham. "She looked as if she might, but the amusement of the guests kept her from fainting completely. They seemed to think it a rather spectacular joke. Of course, I was allowed to dine after all. How could they turn away the evening's entertainment?"

Mother sighed. "Speaking of entertainment, I wonder what our Nathaniel is doing on this Christmas Day." She sniffled and pressed the napkin to her eyes, murmuring, "His first Christmas away from home."

Father reached out and patted his wife's hand. "Don't fret, Elsie. We should be thankful for such a strong, courageous son. One willing to give his life, if need be, for our great Confederacy."

Keziah's stomach lurched and she placed her fork on the plate, what little appetite she'd had forgotten. Whether it was the thought of her brother in danger or knowing he was fighting for a cause whose ideals she was actively working against, she couldn't say. Perhaps both.

Jennie waved a dismissive hand. "I'm sure Cousin Nathaniel is having a lovely time. No doubt the soldiers find some way to entertain themselves. Cards. Music. Writing letters home."

Mr. Hill grunted, scooping up his creamed peas. "Unless they are engaged in battle."

Jennie gasped. "Surely not on Christmas! Not even the Yankees are that coldhearted."

He chewed and swallowed, his face stormy. "We are engaged in war. Not a garden party."

Father shifted back in his chair. "Quite right."

Her mother's face twisted, and Keziah couldn't refrain from offering comfort, however meager. "Why, just last week I received that long, delightful letter from Nathaniel. He told me that the week before they'd had a bit of recreation time and played an enthusiastic game of horseshoes. I've no doubt they are being rewarded with some kind of pleasure today if at all possible." She judiciously chose to omit the part of his letter where he confessed a favorite pastime was carving dice out of chicken bones. The idea would catapult Mother into sobs.

Sniffing, Mother straightened. "I trust you're right. At least we have the noble Stonewall Jackson at the helm. Our boys are in good hands with such a man. Far better than the Yankees, I daresay."

Father waved his hand. "Praise Providence we have no devils like McClellan or that loathsome General Butler."

Mother's mouth pinched tight. "A more horrid man I've yet to hear of."

Jennie leaned forward, dropping her voice low, though why, Keziah didn't understand. "Have you heard the latest about vile General Butler?" When she was certain she had everyone's rapt attention, she continued. "I was on the square just last week and saw one of our merchants selling chamber pots with dear Butler's face emblazoned on the inside!"

Mother gasped. "Mercy, Jennie! Is there nothing sacred about dinner conversation? And Christmas dinner at that."

Father chuckled. "Polite conversation or no, I had not heard that particular tidbit. Amusing, I must say."

Ignoring Mother's scolding, Jennie sent a pointed glance to Mr. Hill. "And what say you, Mr. Hill? Do you think General Butler has the gumption to take on our brave soldiers?"

Mr. Hill took a sip of his wine, his look dark. "Oh, he has the gumption for certain. But it will be for naught. The Union is caught up in a fool's errand. Providence is on our side." He smirked at Keziah.

She bit the inside of her cheek and stirred the peas on

her plate. How many times would Mr. Hill make the same blanket statement? Would a loving God align himself with slaveholders and tyranny?

Jennie settled back into her seat, eyes astute. "It would be horribly unpatriotic to our glorious Confederacy to disagree with you, sir. I concur. But what is the reason for your certainty?"

Keziah held her breath, trying not to grimace at Lyman Hill's condescending smile from across the table.

"Common sense, Miss Oglethorpe. Aside from states' rights, Lincoln and his demons have angered the Almighty by insisting the Negro is equal to his master." He shook his head. "A preposterous claim."

Images of little Solomon trembling in the dark confines of the stable stabbed at Keziah, followed by face after face of those she'd led on their way to freedom. Men, women, children, infants, not to mention sweet Hiriam and Elizabeth. She'd detected no difference between herself and those poor souls other than the cruel life they'd been forced to endure. She'd found none of them lacking in intelligence or heart. In fact, in some ways, they surpassed the wit of their taskmasters by virtue of breaking free.

Jennie's titter clamped down on Keziah's wayward thoughts. "But of course you're correct." She sipped her wine, her eyes meeting Mr. Hill's over the rim of her goblet. "Who could possibly defeat us?"

Father wiped his mouth and boomed, "I've no doubt we will crush the Yankees into powder and will finally be blessedly free of these absurd conversations." He pushed back his chair and nodded in Mother's direction. "A fine Christmas dinner, Mrs. Montgomery."

Mother blushed and accepted the praise, and Keziah found herself glancing toward Elizabeth, quietly gathering up dishes from the table. Mother had done nothing other than give orders. The house servant had done all the work.

As the others rose, Keziah lingered just long enough to catch Elizabeth's eye. "You prepared a wonderful feast. Thank you."

The servant lifted her face and smiled, her expression filled with surprise. "Thank you, miss. The good Lord gets the praise. Only him what got us our ham when so many other folks are scraping for enough to eat."

"And you managed it marvelously."

"Keziah? Are you coming?" Mother's censure floated into the dining room.

With a final glance toward Elizabeth, she walked out of the room, but her heart felt pricked. She had glimpsed the loveliness inside Elizabeth's heart. How many years had she crafted and served these elaborate meals and never received a simple thanks? It wasn't right. It just wasn't right.

As she entered the parlor, Jennie called out, "Come, Keziah dear. Play us a merry carol on the pianoforte."

Mr. Hill held up a restraining hand. "Ah-ah. First I must have a conversation with Miss Montgomery, if I may. In private."

Heart pounding and mouth dry, Keziah turned to Mother,

desperate for any reason to decline. But Mother's face lit up and she shooed them away. "Go to the library, then."

Mr. Hill left the room without further ado. Keziah remained behind, searching for a way to escape this madness. "I don't mind playing a carol now—"

Father eyed her sternly. "Pishposh. There's plenty of time for merrymaking later. He doesn't care for music anyway, if you remember. Go. You mustn't keep him waiting."

Resignation stifled her like a wet blanket as she complied. Surely no prisoner facing the gallows experienced so much dread.

He awaited her in the musty library, where Keziah shakily inhaled the lingering scent of Father's cigars and old books. When the door clicked shut behind her, it felt like a blacksmith's strike—a hammer delivering the final blow to iron shackles.

Lyman Hill offered a tight smile, the silver in his hair shimmering from the sunshine slicing through the window.

"How are you feeling this evening?"

Swallowing hard, she smoothed her sweaty palms down her skirt. "Some better. Thank you."

He turned away from her and toyed with the cigar box perched on the edge of her father's gleaming mahogany desk. "I confess, I was quite taken aback by your episode. Your parents had not divulged your, uh, condition to me before agreeing to our courtship."

She remained silent, praying he would say he wanted out of the arrangement. *Please, Lord . . .*

"The entire episode was quite disturbing and more than a little embarrassing."

The cold, familiar feeling crept through her again, even as her neck flushed hot. Lowering her head, she stared at the plush blue rug beneath her feet.

"Upon further reflection, I've concluded that some matters are out of personal control. I refuse to believe that your epileptic fit was willful."

Of course it wasn't willful. Resentment burned in her chest. Why did no one seem to understand?

"I thought your condition might be the end of our courtship, but I confess your charms considerably outweigh your faults."

Teeth clenched, she choked out, "How kind."

He opened his mouth to say more, but a harsh pounding vibrated through the air, followed by muffled shouts. Alarm flooded Keziah and she turned to flee the library, Mr. Hill on her heels. She burst into the parlor from the side door as a red-faced man with a wiry beard pushed through the main entrance, past a protesting Elizabeth. Mud clung to the man's clothes, and he had a month's worth of grime glued to his pants and coat.

Father stood quickly, his expression stern. "What is the meaning of this disturbance?"

The stranger's eyes narrowed. "You harboring any fugitives on your property?"

Father's neck mottled red as Mother gasped. "Most assuredly not! Who are you and what are you doing trespassing in my home? And on Christmas Day!"

With an exasperated huff, the filthy fellow yanked his worn hat from his head, revealing mussed brown hair. "Name's Jonah Peterson. I've been tracking an escaped slave for the past week. A young man. Belonged to a feller about fifty miles south." He tipped his head in respectful deference to Mother but never lost the harsh, calculating look, nor the hard press of his whiskered lips. "I've tracked this slave to your home. I believe he's hiding out back."

Keziah's heart hammered wildly. A runaway was hiding out back? She'd forgotten to check the padlock on the stable door, caught up as she was in Christmas festivities. Mother had kept last evening packed full. She'd meant to ensure the lock was clicked into place, allowing no fugitives in on Christmas Eve, but time had escaped her. Her breath thinned.

What had she done?

Father waved a hand. "I know of no such thing."

"You ain't one of them turncoats, are you?" Peterson snarled. "A Union sympathizer?"

Jennie shoved forward, unable to quench her outrage. "Certainly not! Why, my auntie and uncle have a son at war this minute, fighting for the Confederacy!"

Father glared. "I have no love for the Union and am a staunch supporter of slavery. I own some myself. If a slave has snuck onto my property, I have no knowledge of it."

Peterson smiled, his teeth resembling stained and chipped piano keys. Keziah shuddered.

"Then you would not oppose me if I asked to search the property?"

"Not the outbuildings, no. In fact, my driver and I shall accompany you." Father turned and bellowed, "Hiriam! Come immediately!"

"Father!" Keziah ran to his side, desperate for any way to keep the odious bounty hunter from obtaining his prize. "You aren't really going to let this horrid man search through our buildings, are you?" she whispered. "He may be nothing more than a thief! What if he tries to steal Hiriam or Elizabeth with the intention of turning a hefty sum at the auction block?"

He patted her hand. "Don't fret. These are matters you know nothing of. Leave it to the menfolk."

Did he think her a child? Before she could conjure any other plausible reason to detain them, Hiriam appeared, and he, Father, Mr. Hill, and Peterson left the room. At their departure, Mother and Jennie launched into a tirade.

Unable to think of anything other than what was transpiring outside, Keziah rushed to grab her cloak, swinging it over her shoulders, and ran to the servants' door at the back of the house. She watched the men's purposeful strides as they entered the stable. *Please, Lord, let the slave remain undetected. Please, please—*

Shouts erupted from inside, and the bounty hunter crashed through the stable door, wrestling with a lean Negro man. They fought and writhed in the dry grass. Keziah covered her mouth with shaking fingers.

Peterson slammed the butt of his gun into the slave's head, momentarily stunning him. Moaning, the fugitive rolled to his side and held his head. Peterson pushed to his feet and looked down at the man with a sneer before spitting on him. Beyond the scuffle, Father, Mr. Hill, and Hiriam looked on as if they were watching a game of croquet.

Keziah's chest heaved with repressed sobs as she watched from the back door. This was all her fault.

Her heart froze when Peterson yanked the slave to his feet, preparing to clamp his wrists in irons he'd pulled from his coat. Instead, the slave lunged and snatched the gun from his belt. Peterson cursed but froze when the runaway pointed the pistol at his heart. But instead of dropping the paddy roller to the ground as Keziah expected, the slave slowly pointed the gun at his own temple, his tears falling in earnest.

Keziah gasped, understanding his dark intention. She murmured under her breath, "No . . . " and took a halting step forward, but the roar of the pistol shattered her.

Screaming, she pressed her fists to her mouth as the fugitive crumpled into the blood-spattered grass. She tasted tears as her heart ripped in two. Her legs shook so violently, she collapsed into the dirt.

Within moments, she heard the men approaching, even as the sound of her sobs echoed in her own ears. Father exclaimed in frustration, "I had no idea Keziah was out here. Her sensibilities are far too delicate for this kind of gruesome display."

Mr. Hill's clipped tone invaded. "I'm sure once the shock

wears off, she'll be fine. The real tragedy is how much this slave's master has lost. What would you say he was worth? Seven, eight hundred, Benjamin?"

Father grunted. "At least."

She clutched a fistful of dirt as the paddy roller's curses rained down. *Horrible brutes . . . murderers . . .*

Hiriam's gentle hands pressed into hers, and his soft, soothing voice finally penetrated her foggy mind. "You shouldn't have seen that, missy. No one should have. Come with old Hiriam. I'm going to take you inside."

He pulled her to her feet and she dropped her head against his shoulder, hearing his steady heartbeat through the coarse fabric of his shirt as she cried. "Oh, Hiriam . . ."

"Shush, missy. Weren't your fault."

Guilt tormented her. He was wrong. It was all her fault.

# CHAPTER 14

JANUARY 3, 1862

Keziah wrapped the cloak around her shoulders and eased her bedroom door open, wincing at the gentle creak that echoed down the dark hallway.

She'd sobbed within the privacy of her room for a full day after that terrible moment on Christmas. The family all believed her distress was due to seeing the runaway take his own life. That was only a part of her crushing grief.

She had failed him. Unintentionally, but failed him still. She'd berated herself, wallowed in guilt, and sobbed to God, oscillating between believing the call to assist the slaves was certainly from him and wondering if she'd somehow misunderstood.

Grief had given way to anger, and then anger hardened into determination, fanning the flames of her righteous indignation into a raging fire.

She would not fail another slave. Not again.

Word must be sent to Brothers. What if he had heard of the incident and thought her no longer a conductor? She must put such an idea to rights as soon as possible.

Creeping down the stairs, she meticulously avoided the seventh and tenth steps, knowing their squeaks might alert the sleeping house to her movement. She padded along the carpeted hallway on bare feet and tiptoed through the kitchen, grimacing at the cold floor against her toes before she slipped out the servants' door. Pulling on her shoes, she breathed a sigh of relief and crept toward the stable, anxious to see if a passenger awaited her.

*Go back.*

She froze, her breath fogging to whispery ice as she stood silently on the frost-covered lawn.

*Go back.*

The directive impressed her soul with an undeniable urgency. Was it God or her own instincts? She didn't know, but the sensation was far too strong to ignore.

Retracing her steps, she entered the way she'd come, thankful for the kitchen's meager heat that chased away winter's grip. She removed her cloak and shoes, tucked them in her arms, and had just started across the floor when a voice cut through the dark.

"I was wondering where you were."

Keziah nearly yelped. Jennie.

Placing her hand over her heart, she gave a shaky laugh. "Mercy, but you startled me."

The sizzle of a match rent the air just before her cousin coaxed the oil lamp to life, placing the globe over the top with a clink as honeyed light dissipated the darkness.

Jennie smiled as she straightened, though the gesture seemed cold. Alarm skittered down Keziah's spine.

"I couldn't sleep and came down to sneak a mug of milk. Imagine my surprise when I heard you leaving the house in the dead of night, much later than your usual jaunt to visit Magnolia."

Keziah found two cups in the cabinet and placed them upon the counter, forcing a light laugh. "A bad habit of mine, I confess. I couldn't sleep either."

Jennie frowned. "But you walked out into the cold night air."

With an unladylike shrug, she crossed to the icebox and located the pitcher of milk nestled in the back. "I thought perhaps the cold might shock my senses. I can't explain it. It tends to clear my mind and I'm able to rest afterward."

Jennie gave her a long look, and her shoulders relaxed. "I suppose that's true enough. You certainly weren't out there long enough to get into any mischief."

Keziah kept her face neutral, but her insides nearly melted with relief. *Thank you, God, for urging me back.* If Jennie had become curious and followed her, she might have discovered a runaway. And then chaos would have erupted.

Pouring the thick, creamy milk into the cups, she shook her head. "No, I couldn't stay out long. It's far too cold." She carried the full cups to the table and handed one to her nosy cousin. "What steals your sleep this night?"

Jennie played with the rim of her cup and sighed. "I don't know. I feel restless. Unsettled."

Keziah took a sip of milk. "Perhaps it's because you're away from home. You aren't in your normal routine."

"Perhaps." Jennie took a long pull. "Still, I think it might be something more. I feel a bit useless, I suppose. You know, with Nathaniel and so many others off fighting while I sit at home and do needlework. There are few parties, no distractions, and it's driving me mad."

Keziah understood. Were it not for her work with the Railroad, she would likely have felt the same. "In and around Savannah there are all manner of relief and charitable organizations, like the Ladies of Savannah Charity League. Mother is a member. Volunteering might fill that void."

After taking another sip, Jennie licked the corner of her mouth. "That's precisely what I've been considering. In fact, there's one organization I'm particularly interested in joining."

"Do tell."

"An organization I discovered just yesterday. I heard them proclaiming their mission in Liberty Square and was quite moved. The Vigilance Committee to End Abolition."

Keziah nearly choked on her milk but managed to do little more than swallow hard. "I've never heard of it."

Jennie leaned in, warming to her subject. "It's perfect. Not one of those dreadfully dull organizations that rolls bandages or packs lint for the army hospitals. This group focuses its efforts on silencing those zealot abolitionists who have caused so much trouble."

Keziah lifted the cup, using it to hide her grimace. "Interesting."

"Quite. Not only does the Vigilance Committee seek to inform the public of the abolitionists' lies; they work to destroy their very efforts. They have a spy network that serves a great purpose."

Keziah's stomach tightened. "And what is that purpose?"

Quirking her lips upward, Jennie whispered, "Have you ever heard of the Underground Railroad?"

Her mouth went dry. "No. What is that?"

"It's a group of abolitionists and traitors who steal away slaves from their masters and smuggle them into free states. Sometimes even Canada."

Keziah longed to scream at the unjust description but managed to keep calm. "How awful." The lie dripped off stiff lips.

"Oh, they are the worst sort of traitors. Just think of that horrible man who snuck onto the property at Christmas. He couldn't have come all that way alone. Those dreadful abolitionists must have been aiding him. And poor Uncle Benjamin. The authorities have been out twice, still unconvinced he didn't have something to do with aiding that runaway."

"I know, but—"

"If I join this Vigilance Committee, I would be able to help."

Keziah placed her cup on the table. "It sounds so dangerous. What if something happened to you?"

Jennie's brows rose. "But think of the excitement! I would be on the front lines, fighting just as valiantly as any of our brave soldiers. I might even be famous when this is all over. Jennie Oglethorpe . . . patriot and spy for our great and glorious Confederacy!"

"Usually a spy who becomes famous for spying does so because they were caught," Keziah muttered.

Jennie sat back against her chair with a pout. "Fiddlesticks. You're no fun." Her countenance brightened. "I think I've decided. Yes. I'll join. Danger is far better than wasting away in this house day after day." She put aside her cup and stood, brushing Keziah's cheek with a light kiss. "Thank you for listening, Cousin. I promise I shall endeavor to be wise as a serpent and harmless as a dove."

Dread coiled in Keziah's stomach like a serpent itself. "Please be careful."

"Don't fret so. I shall conquer. I always do." Jennie winked and turned to leave. "If you're so worried about it, come with me."

"Oh, I don't think—"

"What harm is there in one meeting?" Her green eyes narrowed. "You're not an abolitionist, are you?"

"I—of course not."

Grinning smugly, Jennie gave a curt nod. "Good. It's

settled. We'll go together." She clapped her hands like an eager child and squealed. "Keziah dear, this will be such fun! I will investigate their next meeting time and we shall attend." She heaved a sigh of satisfaction. "And now I think I'm properly tired enough to sleep. Good night."

Keziah offered a wan smile that evaporated quickly once Jennie had left. The Vigilance Committee to End Abolition. What had she gotten herself into? How would she ever be able to attend such a meeting and not give her true beliefs away?

Micah rubbed bleary eyes with one hand as he clutched his horse's reins with the other. Shadow's normally pert step dragged with fatigue.

He looked up, noticing the position of the half-moon shedding its light over the outskirts of the city. He patted Shadow's neck, his own body aching from the dreariness of riding in a saddle. "Almost there, boy."

Two weeks stationed at the prison camp was far too long. After the first horror-filled days, he'd nearly written the Relief Commission to request a transfer of assignment. The prison's infirmary was hell on earth.

But if he didn't try to alleviate the suffering of wounded prisoners who had received insufficient care, who would? Their haunted, dull eyes beckoned him even in the few precious hours of sleep he'd snatched between amputations and treatments.

Contained within the infirmary walls was agony he could never forget, nor would he ever discuss. It was far too gruesome for the human heart to bear. But every time he feared he could take no more, one sweet face drifted through his mind. He clung to the memory with a fierceness that gave him courage, yet taunted him with bittersweet pangs of remorse.

The war had not even filled a year and he was already weary. Weary of dysentery and gangrene. Weary of sawing limbs and treating lice. He was heavyhearted over the disease, fevers, and malnutrition running rampant through the troops.

He was weary of war . . . of its inevitable suffering and death.

When William Still had summoned him for medical checks along the Railroad line, he'd breathed a sigh of relief. Not that the work would be much different, but at least it meant a change from the stench of disease within the prison walls. It meant he could provide more substantial comfort, praying his efforts would give slaves life instead of numbing broken soldiers from the pain of impending death.

Just ahead he could make out the frame of the African church's simple steeple. Not wanting Shadow to attract unwanted attention from late-night revelers and drunks roaming Savannah's streets, he pulled his horse to a gentle stop, tying him to a small tree where he could graze until Micah's work at the church was finished.

Keeping to the darkness, he stopped at the hidden entrance, his fingers scraping brittle leaves and dirt until they found the latch hidden in the underbrush. The rustle of the breeze covered the squeak of resistant hinges as he pulled the tunnel trapdoor open and plunged himself into the damp blackness of the underground passage.

Familiar as he was with the tunnel, there was no need to light a torch. Instead, he felt his way along the crumbly, sodden wall, breathing a sigh of relief when, long moments later, his eyes detected the faint, gray shaft of light at the end of the tunnel.

He'd only emerged from the darkness for a few seconds, brushing the dirt from his coat, when Rose's familiar matronly form burst into the hidden room under the church, the whites of her eyes large as she held a glowing lantern aloft. The woman was rarely rattled.

"Doc! You're an answer to prayer."

A rush of adrenaline surged through him, chasing away his fatigue. "What's wrong?"

She swallowed as the lantern light danced across the creases of her face. "One of our conductors was dropping off the next passengers at the blacksmith's shop and collapsed."

Discarding his coat, he began to unbutton his shirt cuffs and roll them up, prepared for any possibility. "Do you have any idea what's wrong with the fellow?"

She shook her kerchief-covered head. "Ain't no man, Doc. This here's a woman."

Micah's heart lurched. A woman conductor? His mouth went dry, praying it was not who he suspected.

She motioned toward the dark hallway. "She just kind of stared into space after she fell, Brothers said. Wouldn't respond and eventually passed out, so Brothers and the passengers brought her here."

Micah cringed, ducking under the wooden beams as he followed Rose into a small room. A candle burned next to a lumpy cot, casting dancing patterns across Kizzie's unconscious form. His breath hitched, but he shoved the panic away, scrambling to assess her condition.

He knelt and opened his bag, looking up at Rose. "Where is the blacksmith? And the other men?"

"Brothers done scurried back home, and I've got the menfolk in the other end of the tunnels. They busy feeding their starving stomachs. I told them to get some rest. Didn't know what day you'd be arriving; only knew it would be within a week or so."

He grunted and pulled the stethoscope from his bag, placing the cone against the soft rise and fall of Kizzie's chest. "Providence knew I was needed here now."

Rose nodded. "Just so. Poor lamb. What do you need me to fetch?"

He moved to feel the pulse at her neck, pressing gently against the smooth skin, his eyes trained on her face. "Perhaps a bowl of water and a clean cloth."

"Yes, sir." She scurried away to obtain the items, leaving him alone with Kizzie in the small, dim room. He smoothed her hair away from her face, the silky, reddish-blonde tresses glowing like sunset in the light of the candle.

Her pulse was good. Steady and strong. Stroking her cheek, he softly urged, "Wake up, sweetheart."

No response. He frowned and let his voice rise until it resembled the commanding professional he was and not the doting friend he wanted to be.

"Kizzie Montgomery, you stubborn thing, wake up."

# CHAPTER 15

Keziah heard a voice calling her through the darkness. Everything was murky and thick.

"Kizzie, I'll drop you in the water trough if you don't come around."

The urgency in the masculine voice invaded, but it was the name Kizzie that somehow penetrated the fog. *Micah?*

Shifting aside the heavy veil over her mind, she forced her eyes open only to see Micah studying her with a familiar intensity. His handsome face lifted into a gentle smile.

"I knew a good bossing would wake you."

Where was she? Confusion swirled through her, and her head pounded with a dull, throbbing ache. She tried to rise up on one elbow, but his strong hands gently urged her to relax against the cot.

"What's the last thing you remember?"

She rubbed her temples with trembling fingers and tried to think. "I—I don't know." Her tongue was thick, her throat dry. She sorted through vague images and memories. "Supper with Mother and Jennie. Readying for bed . . ." Sharp as a knife blade, the memory of sneaking through the woods to deliver the frightened slaves to the smithy pierced her. She sucked in a harsh breath and sat up with a speed that made her head swim. "The passengers!"

The warmth of Micah's hands on her shoulders penetrated through her sleeves. "The passengers are safe," he reassured her. "You collapsed just as they were entering the smithy. Thankfully, Brothers was there and brought you here to Rose." He rubbed his thumbs against her shoulders. "Do you remember any of that?"

Her lips quivered and the confession slid past the knot clogging her throat. "No." Sitting upright, she wrapped her arms around her bent knees and turned her eyes away from his compassionate, probing stare, willing the tears to vanish. It was no use.

He drew her into an embrace and rested his head on top of her hair, murmuring comfort as the muscles of his arms held her shaking form. Undone, she finally gave way to a harsh sob and wept as he rocked her gently on the tattered cot.

When she'd expelled the last cleansing sob, she melted into his embrace, both warmed and embarrassed. As she grew calm, he eased her back and wiped the tear tracks from her face with the pads of his thumbs.

"You stubborn, wonderful, brave woman."

He seemed to mean the words as a compliment, but they unsettled her all the same. "No, I'm foolish." She pushed away from his touch, standing on shaky legs and willing the room to stop swaying around her. As she found her footing, a silent fury consumed her. "I could have compromised those frightened men. I almost ruined their flight." She suppressed the rising bile in her throat. "I could have drawn attention to Brothers and brought the authorities or paddy rollers down on his head." Swiping away a stray tear, she covered her face with her hands and whispered with an aching throat, "I couldn't bear it again."

She felt Micah's warm presence step close. "What do you mean *again*?"

Unable to speak, she shook her head as a sure footfall approached. Lifting her face, she observed the approach of a middle-aged woman with a sturdy build and kind face, bearing a bucket of water and a bundle of cloth. "Here you go, Doc."

He offered a smile. "Thank you, Rose."

The woman nodded and, smiling shyly in return, slipped back into the darkness of the tunnel.

Unwilling to share more, Keziah perched on the edge of the cot and desperately tried to shift Micah's focus from her verbal slip. "What happened when I collapsed? Convulsions?"

He lowered himself next to her, shaking his dark head.

Dipping a cloth into the bucket of water, he wrung it out and dabbed it across her brow. The cool liquid was welcome relief to her burning cheeks.

"No, no tremors this time. Rose says the men claimed you merely stared into space, unresponsive to their questions, and then fell unconscious."

Collapsing was mortification enough. If she'd jerked and thrashed around, she could have alerted someone to their presence. Unforgivable.

A muscle ticked in Micah's jaw as he dipped the cloth back into the water. "Has your father relented to let you try some of the remedies I suggested?"

She dropped her gaze. "No. He says I am to be resigned to my condition."

She heard his sigh and braved a glance as the familiar crease appeared between his brows, a sure sign he was frustrated but refrained from further discussion of the matter.

Instead he offered a smile as his fingers grazed the inside of her wrist. She jerked away as if seared by a hot coal.

"Wha—what are you doing?"

An amused smile flitted across the planes of his face. "Only checking your pulse. Nothing malicious, I assure you."

"Oh, of course." He must think her daft. Still, she couldn't repress the skitters of pleasure that traversed up her arm as his fingers pressed tightly against the tender flesh inside her wrist. What was wrong with her?

"Pulse is satisfactory." She resisted the urge to snatch her hand away. She felt . . . odd. Jittery.

"How do you feel?"

"A little shaky but better."

He stood and offered his outstretched hand. She looked up, confusion flooding her.

"Would you like a tour?"

Keziah realized she had no idea of their location. "Where are we?"

He grasped her fingers and gently tugged her to standing. "In the tunnels below the Negro church."

Excitement chased away the confusion nipping her insides. She'd longed to see where the slaves sought their safety. "Please, show me."

Claiming the candle and its tin holder from the floor near the cot, Micah led her down the musty corridor. The loamy scent of earth clung to her as he swatted away a cobweb.

She rested a steadying hand against the tunnel wall. Her fingers brushed across crumbling mortar and slid onto damp stone blocks as she hunched low in the tunnel. Micah swung the candle wide and pointed into the blackness. "Rose has the passengers you conducted in a small room down that way. Thanks to you, they will receive food and rest tonight."

She stayed silent, recognizing his attempt to bolster her spirits. Still, they sagged. What kind of safety could she ultimately offer to escaping slaves if she couldn't even control her own body?

Oblivious to her tumultuous thoughts, he whispered softly in the echo of the narrowing tunnel. "In a minute, you'll see the structure of the walls change. We'll have to sit and scoot, I'm afraid."

"I don't mind."

They rounded a sharp corner and the air changed. It was slightly warmer and smelled altogether different. The faint scent of beeswax and lemon tickled her nose. A large step plunged them deeper into a dank abyss. Micah jumped onto the lower level and offered her a hand. Grasping his hand lightly, she lifted the edge of her skirt and felt her feet drop sharply before thudding against hard-packed dirt. The candle's flicker grew smaller and she couldn't help stepping closer to Micah's comforting presence, hunkering low to avoid whacking her head against the shrunken ceiling.

"Where are we?"

"Under the floorboards of the church sanctuary."

With a soft gasp, she reached up and felt the low ceiling. Splinters of wood met her reverent touch, but she could see little beyond the faint circle of light the candle cast. Setting down the candleholder, Micah dropped to his knees in the near darkness, urging her farther into the odd space. She followed his lead, doing her best to adjust her tangle of skirts as she scooted across the floor.

His low voice near her ear caused pinpricks of awareness to skim down her back. "It's impossible to see at night, but just overhead there are small holes drilled into the sanctuary floor."

"Why?"

"For breathing. When paddy rollers are in the area, neither

the basement nor the tunnels are safe, so the slaves sneak into this space and bar this room with a block. The holes ensure they can breathe for as long as they're here."

For the first time that night, she smiled in wonder. "Brilliant."

Seating himself on the floor, Micah allowed her to relax. She slipped down next to him, enjoying the quiet serenity of the still room and the faint flickering candlelight.

"So what did you mean when you said you couldn't bear it again?"

Her eyes slid shut. Of course he wouldn't forget. He knew her too well. Micah had let her think he'd dropped the subject but was simply biding his time before asking again.

She exhaled a shaky sigh and laced her fingers. "Have you been in Savannah for long?"

"No. The Relief Commission sent me for a spell to a prison camp."

Her brows rose. "For captured soldiers?"

"Yes. Many of them grievously wounded or ill." He leaned his head against the wall and stared straight ahead. "The supplies in the infirmary were limited, the so-called camp surgeons incompetent. I did what I could, but—" he shook his head—"it's a deplorable situation."

"I'm sorry." She spoke no more, feeling as if her own troubles were but a pittance compared to the suffering he must have seen.

A thick silence fell between them for a long moment

before his low voice pierced the heaviness. "So what has caused you such anguish?"

———⟨⚬⟩———

Micah fought the urge to reach for her hand.

Dropping her eyes to her lap, Kizzie took a breath. "I don't suppose you've heard about the incident then. What happened on Christmas Day."

"No."

"It was my fault. I didn't think to go to the stables the night before. I never forget to check the padlock. Ever." She pinched her eyes closed. "Foolish of me."

Unease filled his stomach.

"You know how busy Christmas Eve is, and honestly, Mother kept me so muddled it never crossed my mind." As she stared straight ahead, he watched her lips tremble. "I had recently suffered another epileptic attack as well. The spell knocked the starch from me. It's been . . . difficult."

He ground his jaw. Her attacks would be reduced if her father would listen to reason. Stubborn man.

"Christmas Day, after our midday meal, a filthy man burst into the house, screaming and accusing Father of harboring runaways."

Micah struggled to suppress his groan. "A paddy roller?"

"Yes. Father was understandably outraged but agreed to let the vile man search the outbuildings, I suppose as a way to prove his loyalty to the Confederacy." A sharp inhalation snagged in her chest as her eyes flitted back and forth across the unseen memory in her mind.

"How I prayed the bounty hunter was wrong. Prayed the fugitive had already made his escape despite my neglect. I had to watch as that horrid man pulled him fighting from the stable." A lone tear escaped, tracing a golden streak down her cheek in the candlelight. "Just as he prepared to clap him in irons, the slave managed to extract the paddy roller's gun. He pointed it to his own temple and he—he—"

Kizzie's sudden sob eradicated the need for any more words. With a groan, Micah pulled her close, a hand on her back. If he could only erase the gruesome moment from her memory.

Her muffled voice pressed against his chest. "I'm to blame. Just like tonight."

He cupped her face in his palms, staring hard and trying to impress the truth straight into her hurting soul. "What we do—fighting to obtain freedom for those unable to speak for themselves—it's risky, emotional, and exhausting. But ask yourself if it's worth it."

Her cinnamon eyes met and held his long before she nodded ever so slightly. "Yes, it's worth it."

He stroked her soft cheek with the pad of his thumb. "Bad things will happen. We cannot save everyone, but we keep fighting. We save those we can. We move forward. We run toward the prize."

Kizzie's lips parted, her expression filled with anguish. "How can I possibly be of benefit when I cannot even maintain control of my own body? What if my collapse tonight had cost those men their freedom?"

He drank in the sight of her, the feel of her. "It didn't, though. Yield yourself to God, and he will take care of the rest. The fate of man does not rest in your hands, Kizzie. Be willing, and let God do what he will."

But faith warred with the very real possibility that all she said was true. What if she collapsed at the wrong moment? What if fugitives were captured or she were imprisoned due to one moment out of his control?

Ma Linnie's admonition drifted through his mind. He released the tight breath trapped in his chest. It *was* out of his grasp. He must trust the Almighty or drive himself mad.

She frowned. "I must say, this is a far cry from the speech you gave me mere weeks ago. You thought it too dangerous and were sure I would be caught or ruin the operation."

His heart constricted as the words spilled from his lips. "In truth, I spoke out of fear."

She drew in a shaky breath. "What fear?"

He swallowed, chest burning. "Fear I would lose you."

A wave of longing, of yearning and love, crashed over him, so strong he was helpless to fight its unyielding current. His gaze dropped to her full lips, his heart hammering as one hand reached to cup the back of her head. His other hand slid down to her waist, pulling her body closer to his.

Micah's pulse sped like a galloping horse as her lips melted into his. Desire consumed him. He let his fingers roam through her tumbling, silky curls. His breath grew erratic.

Soaring. Her soft moan sent fire through his veins, and he feared he would crush her in his embrace.

He was losing himself in her. If he'd ever doubted the depths of his feelings, this moment confirmed the love he harbored was no childish infatuation. No, this was real.

He smothered her face with sweet kisses, each caress conveying a thousand different meanings, and she responded with an intensity he'd never dared dream possible.

*You're making her care, toying with her. You know you can't have her.*

A cold fist slammed into him, and he broke away, heart pounding like a drum. She blinked, her lips swollen from his kisses. What had he done?

He'd dishonored her, yielded to his feelings. He was not worthy of her. Indeed, being linked to him would only bring her harm.

Anguish washed over him as he moved farther away, fighting the desire to draw her to him again. Surprise, confusion, hurt . . . all of it painted her shifting expression. He shook his head, his body still on fire, his mind reeling.

"Forgive me." His heart felt as if it were ripping into tattered pieces. "It won't happen again."

Keziah blinked, hurt drowning the heady euphoria she had been swimming in mere moments before. Her lips still burned from his passionate kisses. And her spinning emotions . . .

she'd never known a feeling like it. His touch and his passion had undone her completely.

And now he recoiled, his shoulders slumped, face filled with shame. Was she so repugnant? Or was it something else entirely?

It didn't matter. He'd spurned her, pushed her away. She wanted to collapse in on herself, flee to some place where she could not be hurt, where the deep knife of rejection could not shred her apart.

But it was too late already.

Scrambling away from him, she fumbled through the narrow space to find the way out. His hoarse plea only fueled her desire to flee. "Kizzie, wait—"

Just ahead. She pulled herself up, free of the cramped space, and plunged into the dark tunnel, shivering against the temperature, the dampness of the stone-and-earth passageway. Only blackness surrounded her. Her body trembled as she felt her way along the grimy wall, hurrying as fast as she dared. Away from light. Away from the cold slap of rejection. Away from him.

A soft glow illuminated the tunnel ahead. Her steps scraped against the gritty floor. She lurched forward only to halt suddenly when she turned the corner and nearly collided with Rose.

"Land's sakes, child! You done near scared me outta ten years!" The woman's wide smile belied her scold.

"Forgive me."

"Kizzie?"

Micah's soft call from farther down the tunnel made her stiffen, an action Rose was clearly shrewd enough to note. Her dark eyes became knowing, perhaps even a tad amused. Before Keziah could make her excuses and thank the woman for her care, Micah appeared, his face creased with angst.

A burning hurt rushed through her veins, and she turned away from his gaze. "I must leave soon or risk being found out. Thank you, Rose."

The woman nodded, her face gleaming in the lamplight. "Thankful I am to Providence that he kept you and the others safe. Yes, you best get going. Dawn is just beginning to lighten the sky."

Alarm slammed like a door in her chest. "What?" Her breath thinned. It was far later than she'd supposed. Even later than the night she'd ended up at Ma Linnie's. She would surely be discovered by her parents and accused of some late-night dalliance. Regardless of what they'd suspect, her reputation would be in tatters.

Feeling as if she might cast up her accounts, she barely heard Micah's soft directive. "Don't fret. I'll escort you home."

She shook her head, her mind spinning. "No! That will look far worse!"

He reddened slightly and handed the spent candle to Rose. "I have a plan."

⁃⊷⧟⊶⁃

Micah shifted his weight in the saddle, cringing against the gentle squeak of leather as Shadow trudged down the square.

His breath constricted when Kizzie's back brushed his chest. As if sensing her wilting posture, she straightened in the saddle. Was she avoiding all contact with him? Or perhaps she was desperate to maintain a sense of propriety. A propriety he'd all but taken from her in his passion.

He could kick himself for the ardent kisses he'd unleashed, yet he did not wish them back. Not when he could still taste her sweetness, feel her wildly beating heart, and relish the knowledge that she had responded to him fully and completely.

He was a fool.

She'd said not a word to him since leaving the church in the chill morning air. The sun peeked over the gray horizon, lightening the sky, yet it brought no warmth from the January fog. If Kizzie was cold, she uttered no complaint.

His own breath clouded as he exhaled. He prayed all was quiet in the Montgomery household so she could slip in undetected. If not . . .

He swallowed. The uproar would be intense.

He murmured softly near her ear. "If it's apparent you've been missed when we arrive, let me do the speaking. You need only play along."

He felt rather than saw her frown as she gave him a view of her profile. "Play along with what?"

Clamping his jaw, he explained, "I'm going to tell them that I found you wandering the road past the house, deep in the throes of an epileptic spell."

She sucked in a breath. "Do you think such a plan could possibly salvage my honor?"

Guilt gnawed him for the liberties he'd taken, yet he knew she was thinking of far greater concerns. "Possibly. If they believe your wandering is from their own inability to care for you properly, your parents will be likely to blame themselves, rather than you."

"It will make any future escapades far more difficult."

He smiled to himself, trying to ignore the sweet scent of her hair tickling his nose. "Perhaps. But knowing you as I do, you'll find a way."

Indeed, such a turn of events would make her clandestine activities nearly impossible under Benjamin Montgomery's austere eye. Guilt stabbed him for the relief flooding him at such a thought. Yet what would happen to the fugitive slaves seeking refuge without Kizzie there to guide them?

She emitted a dry laugh. "You give me far too much credit."

He tightened his grip on the reins. "Not at all. You're a treasure, Kizzie Montgomery. Don't ever believe otherwise."

She lapsed into silence again as he directed Shadow toward the sprawling Montgomery home. Kizzie suddenly trembled, and his heart tugged in sympathy. He spotted Hiriam and her father conferring together inside the gate, their movements hurried, tense.

Any hopes he had for sneaking her quietly inside evaporated.

He whispered, "Act dazed. I'll explain."

He called a soft "Whoa" to Shadow and stopped just outside the iron barrier separating the brick home from the street.

At his approach, both the servant and Mr. Montgomery stepped forward. When her father witnessed her atop Micah's steed, his face mottled scarlet.

"What is the meaning of this affront?" Montgomery yanked the gate open, his eyes bugging out in a grotesque fashion.

Micah remained outwardly unaffected, holding Shadow in place as the horse shifted his weight, his unease with the furious man palpable. "I was going to ask you the same, sir."

Glaring at him with nothing short of hatred, Montgomery shifted his gaze to Kizzie. "Daughter, explain yourself."

With an air of confusion that would put the best actresses of the stage to shame, she blinked, her voice cracking. "Father?"

"Come here at once!"

Micah interjected, "Begging your pardon, sir, I fear the young miss is a bit befuddled. I found her walking past the square, dazed and incoherent."

Montgomery's scowl deepened. "Then what is she doing with you?"

Micah met his venomous expression directly. "I feared for the poor girl's safety. She was mumbling and seemed not to know where she was when I questioned her." Feigning indignation, he shook his head. "Really, sir, with your daughter's falling sickness, it's a wonder this hasn't happened long ago."

Montgomery huffed. "I did not ask—nor do I care—for your opinion, Greyson. Hiriam!" He turned to his servant.

"Assist Keziah from that man's horse immediately and take her into the house posthaste. Elizabeth will see to her."

With a nod of quiet submission, Hiriam approached Shadow and lifted his aged hands up to grasp Kizzie's slim waist. "Come on, missy. Old Hiriam is gonna take you inside. Elizabeth got a hot toddy for you and a bed warmer for your feet."

Kizzie let her arms hang limp as the slave tugged her free from the saddle. Micah assisted, even as Montgomery's stare burned a hole through his middle.

"Hiriam?"

"I's here, missy."

Micah watched them go, his heart already missing her yet proud of her ability to keep her wits about her. He shifted his focus back to her irate father.

"And just what were you doing out so early, Greyson?" Suspicion dripped from his pinched lips.

Micah smiled tightly and patted his medical bag, securely tied to Shadow's saddle. "I was summoned early to assist in a birth." He shrugged. "Babies know no schedules, sir."

Montgomery chewed the inside of his cheek, no doubt oscillating between whether to believe the claim or not.

Undaunted, Micah forged ahead. "I remember upon our last meeting my medical advice was not well received, but I beg you to consider altering your daughter's regimen. Clearly her current treatments are not working. Have you tried the peony root or mugwort I recommended?"

Fury flashed across Benjamin Montgomery's countenance.

"Indeed I have not, and I will not consult nor take advice from the son of abolitionist trash. If I ever see you lurking around my home again, I'll shoot you on sight."

Stubborn man, held hostage by hate and ignorance. There was nothing Micah could say or do to sway his opinion. The thought saddened him greatly. If Benjamin Montgomery knew even half of Micah's family history . . .

Choosing the high road, Micah gave him a curt nod, tipped his hat, and turned Shadow away from the house, but not before he witnessed the flash of a pink gown and a strange woman studying him from a second-floor window. When he glanced up at her, she disappeared behind the curtains.

# CHAPTER 16

FEBRUARY 10, 1862

The stark grayness of winter crept by at a sluggish pace. Ever since Micah had returned her home in January, she'd been watched like an explosive oddity. If she thought her existence before was stifling, life inside the Montgomery home now was torturous.

Many nights she had to keep the stable locked, the lantern extinguished. With every day that passed, a dark cloud of foreboding grew. Their home, situated as it was in the city, was key to transporting slaves to the blacksmith shop, where they would be one step closer to escape from Savannah. Every night she was unable to conduct, the fugitives' chance of capture multiplied. She would lie in her darkened room, tucked between warm blankets, and pray. *Father God, keep them safe. Guide them safely to freedom.*

They had received no letters from Nathaniel of late. With every passing week, the silence screamed louder. Mother paced incessantly, murmuring that of course Nathaniel was fine since his commander had sent them no letter indicating otherwise. Still, the quiet was unnerving.

It didn't help that the papers carried news only of war, casualties, and the dead. The strains of Handel's "Dead March" had become so regular a refrain for passing funeral processions, Keziah no longer reacted or noticed its mournful cadence.

Still, she would rather be locked in the house, listening to the drone of dirges, than be where she was at present: sitting in a hall with Jennie, surrounded by feverish radicals. Her first Vigilance Committee meeting. Lord willing, it would be her last.

She'd only come to silence her cousin's insistent pleas. Perhaps this would be beneficial for appearance's sake. No one would ever suspect her of transporting runaways if she were recognized at an antiabolition meeting.

Jennie clutched her arm and leaned in, whispering, her eyes aglow. "Isn't this exciting? And look at the turnout. Nearly all the seats are full."

The very idea of so many wanting to see their fellow humans locked in chains—and to hunt down those who would try to free them—made Keziah nauseous.

The meeting hall was bright with sunlight streaming in through the windows. Men and women of all ages filled the space, most chattering in rapid staccato. The sharp scent of floor soap permeated the air. A lectern, polished to a gleam, stood ready at the front of the room. Such a contrast between this gathering and the antislavery meeting she'd attended with Micah. There was no need to hide or cower in fear here, yet Keziah's shame had rarely been so strong. Absurd what society deemed acceptable and what they then spurned as vile.

Jennie released a light squeal and pinched Keziah's elbow. "Ooh, it's starting!"

A large man with a barrel chest stuffed inside a black suit and a too-tight vest ambled to the front. His bushy gray side-whiskers did little to mask the scowl on his face. As he took his place behind the lectern, the chattering in the room quieted until only a faint cough could be heard.

"Ladies and gentlemen, I thank you for attending this afternoon's meeting. I am Edgar Glass, president of the Vigilance Committee to End Abolition, and we thank you for your interest in this most important cause." His voice boomed and echoed through the cavernous space.

"Our glorious Confederacy is currently engaged in a war—a war to determine whether a people can really and truly be free. The treacherous Union told us we were free to live as we pleased, but from the travesties of Bleeding Kansas to Harper's Ferry to the election of the devil Lincoln, we have been spurned, our liberties stolen and trampled, our economic systems threatened, and our very way of life insulted."

Several male voices lifted: "Hear, hear!"

Keziah wrung her fingers in her lap. What of the *slaves'* liberties? Their lives were the ones being threatened, insulted, even stolen at the tempestuous whims of their overseers.

Mr. Glass gripped the edges of the podium in a dramatic fashion, as if the weight of the world hung on his next statement. "Much of this disgrace lies solely at the feet of a band of renegades. Zealots intent on their own misguided ideals, ripping apart the very fabric the old Union was founded upon. These same betrayers have infiltrated themselves among our beloved Confederacy, spreading their poison, their lies— indeed, stealing our very property!"

Cries of outrage peppered the room. Jennie leaned forward, enthralled. Keziah swallowed and tried not to wince. Surely he wasn't referring to—

"You may know these horrid radicals by another name: abolitionists."

The outrage escalated. She dropped her gaze to the floor, fighting the heat within.

"Yes, my friends. You know their ilk well enough. Murderers like John Brown."

Hisses followed the name, but Edgar Glass wasn't finished.

"Or hystericals like William Lloyd Garrison, or traitorous authors like Harriet Beecher Stowe who publish garbage for the masses." His gray brows dipped low. "I praise Providence her libelous trash is banned in this most righteous land of Georgia."

"Hurrah!" Cheers erupted, causing Keziah to jump. Jennie clapped and waved her lace-trimmed handkerchief.

Mr. Glass gestured for silence. "But our enemies are not content with the severance of the old Union. No, now they have set their sights to fracture this new nation. Our Confederacy. Do not be deceived, my brothers and sisters. These wolves in sheep's clothing do not flaunt their beliefs in the marketplace with trumpets and banners. No, they prowl about, sly as foxes. They may be merchants or bankers, teachers or carpenters. The devout Quaker who masquerades as pious but is, in fact, a bloodthirsty thief."

A woman gasped behind Keziah, and she resisted the urge to roll her eyes.

His melodramatic plea boomed over the electrified crowd. "Did not our Savior himself declare he would turn father against son and mother against daughter? Beware, for some of these villains may be among our own families."

She felt Jennie stiffen beside her. If Edgar Glass was trying to stir the crowd into a riot, he was doing an admirable job.

"Lest we forget, the apostle Paul himself declared a slave should be subject to his master." He pointed to a man in the front row. "You, sir. Would you ever think of breaking God's sacred law?"

The man shook his head. "Never."

Mr. Glass pointed to another fellow sitting on the opposite side of the aisle. "And you, sir? What about you?"

The elderly man harrumphed. "I should never think to do so!"

He then pointed straight at Keziah. Her heartbeat thudded dully in her ears as the light narrowed down to a small point. "And you, miss? Would you dream of breaking God's holy law?"

Hundreds of eyes watched her. Breath grew faint. She

scraped for a semblance of thought. "I—that is, the Scriptures say all men and women have broken God's law. Thus the need for a Savior."

Mr. Glass reddened. She must not be seen as unsympathetic. Before he could respond, she continued. "But would I purposely choose to disobey him? May it never be so."

He nodded in satisfaction and moved on in his speech. Keziah heaved a sigh and fell back against her chair. Jennie patted her hand and whispered, "Well done. Isn't this too thrilling?"

Managing a weak smile, she pressed her hand to her trembling stomach, relieved when Jennie turned her attention back to the orator once more.

"These, these . . . apostates—" he sneered as if tasting something bitter—"think themselves to have the moral high ground. They believe they have the right to steal men's property by any means necessary, often resulting in bloodshed and enormous loss of capital. Such horror is unfathomable."

A chair creaked in the back as someone stood. A masculine voice sounded. "I would like to hear more details. By what methods do the abolitionists seek to steal our property?"

Mr. Glass straightened his shoulders. "An excellent question. We have recently learned more of their system. A system by which abolitionists and Union sympathizers aid runaway slaves to freedom, conveying them from house to house until they are in free territory."

Ripples of shock burst across the room.

"Why, I've even heard these abolitionists steal slaves from

their very beds, against their will, and carry them across state lines!"

"I've heard of this. It's true!" a man shouted from the back.

The buzzing conversation grew into a roar. Keziah bit her tongue until she tasted blood. She wanted to scream at the unfairness of it. Preposterous!

Jennie shook her head, russet curls bouncing. "Can you imagine?"

She clenched her teeth. "No, I cannot."

Glass held up his hands. "Calm yourselves, my friends. All is not lost. This is precisely the reason we are meeting today."

A woman called out, "What can be done?"

He cleared his throat. "Much. With your help, we can stop these devils in their very tracks. Restore order. Return stolen property. Maintain freedom and our way of life." He steepled his fingers and pointed them toward the crowd. "In short, we need you to be our eyes and ears."

A ribbon of unease unfurled through Keziah.

"Savannah is teeming with these vile traitors. We must ferret them out, but it will take all of us working together. Their system employs codes. Lights in windows at odd hours of the day and night. Secret messages passed between homes and people. It will take listening ears and sharp eyes. You must suspect everyone. Many of us—" he placed a hand over his chest—"are too old to enlist. Gentlemen, this is how you may serve in the glorious cause. Ladies, do not bemoan the fact that you cannot pick up arms and fight. Indeed, this may be your shining moment to make your mark on the world. History books will write about you one day. You were born for such a time as this. This is your call to engage the enemy."

Jennie sat straighter, her chin lifted high, even as Keziah's spirits plunged low.

Glass scanned the crowd. "Anything you hear, see, suspect—anything at all, even if you think it unimportant—must be shared with the Vigilance Committee. We will work with the authorities to bring lawbreakers to justice."

A man spoke up. "And what if the authorities turn a blind eye to our suspicions?"

Glass's jaw hardened. "Then we take matters into our own hands. Either way, justice will be served."

The next day, Keziah sat in the parlor, still edgy from all she'd heard and witnessed at the meeting. Her beloved Savannah had become a place of menace and spies, sinister figures and wolves lurking around corners.

Across the room, Mother laughed lightly at something her friend Mrs. Ward had said and sipped her weak tea. The two matrons had spent the past hour draining each other of gossip—most of it related to the war and where Nathaniel might be, although their conversation drifted from scandal to courtships and back again.

Neither the tea nor the conversation held appeal for Keziah, though her mother had required her presence. No, her heart remained decidedly fixed on a church several squares away, along with weary slaves and one particular doctor whose memory refused to leave her be.

She'd only been able to transport one passenger since that disastrous night beneath the church. With rising temperatures, the Railroad's work would greatly increase, and she would need to find a way around her father's scrutiny. Instinct, however, screamed that her house had been compromised as a safe station. Once a bounty hunter discovered a runaway on the premises, word would spread.

At any rate, the extra rest had been good for her. She'd not had a falling spell since that night last month. Even when Father was away, Jennie's sudden clinginess and curiosity over her every movement left her desperate for any measure of time alone. She was doing well if she could even get to the stable to check the lock, much less light a signal lantern.

This afternoon, at least, gave her a reprieve from her probing cousin. Jennie had bonded quickly with the insatiable extremists on the Vigilance Committee and was meeting with them yet again. For the first time in weeks, Keziah found herself able to relax.

"Darling, play us a song. I'm so desperate for any kind of music."

Mother's plea scattered her pensive thoughts. Keziah left her chair and moved to the rosewood pianoforte in the corner of the parlor.

Mrs. Ward exclaimed, "Oh, how lovely! I was just telling Polly the other day how I've longed for a bit of merriment. There's been none since Christmas."

"Small wonder." Mother took another sip of her tea. "It seems since news broke of our defeat at Fort Henry, the starch has been washed from everyone's sails."

Seating herself on the bench, Keziah ran her fingers lightly over the polished keys. The hammers struck the strings inside the instrument, but a twinge accompanied the sound. She wrinkled her nose. The piano had not been played enough of late. It sounded as if it had been soaked in brine. Tinny. Was there anything the war had not tainted?

Instead of listening, the two women launched into another round of gossip, leaving her free to consider a piece of her own choosing. Nothing seemed to suit. Beethoven sonatas were too grim. Bach minuets too jaunty. The only tunes that filled her heart these days were a scant few hymns offered in church worship and simple melodies spun by the slaves from neighboring homes as they hung wash outside or tended their gardens. Many days Keziah would sit on the porch and listen to the gentle rise and fall of the mournful tunes. One she remembered for its rolling melody that reminded her of swelling waves against the ocean shore.

With a steadying breath, she gave herself to the music, her fingers dancing across the instrument and coaxing out the gentle strains of "Swing Low, Sweet Chariot."

Falling in love with the song once more, she closed her eyes as she played . . . until she heard a soft intake of breath.

Her eyes popped open to see Polly, Mrs. Ward's slave, staring at her from the corner, bewilderment on her face. With a start, Keziah realized her mistake. She'd played a song used by the Railroad. The subtle code, she had learned, alerted slaves to an engineer's approach. Would Polly report the slip to her mistress?

She grew still and met Polly's stare as the two matrons chattered on, oblivious to what had just transpired under their very noses as they held their dainty china and fussed about the price of lace. Keziah shook her head ever so slightly and watched Polly's eyes widen a fraction before the slave responded with a measured nod. She lowered her gaze back to the floor.

Keziah sought a deep breath, but her stays prevented it. What would Polly do?

The front door banged open, and the women hushed as Father stood in the parlor doorway, his face ashen. A telegram was clutched between his stout fingers. Cold dread snaked through her.

"Father, what is it?"

The lines of his face deepened as he spoke through lifeless lips. "We've a telegram from Nathaniel's captain. He was killed in the line of duty on February 6, defending Fort Henry from General Grant's assault."

The last of the color leached from his face as Mother cried out. He seemed not to hear her heartbroken sobs.

"My son is dead."

Then her strong, stoic father collapsed to the ground.

# CHAPTER 17

A COOL BREEZE TUGGED a wayward tendril of Keziah's hair free from her snood as she eyed the black crepe hung over the doors and windows, a sign to all who passed that the Montgomery family was in deep mourning. Life had been snuffed out of their home in one crushing blow.

Since Father's collapse, he'd not left his bed. His pallor refused to budge from its sickly gray. Dr. Kelsie had been sought and had come several times over the past two days but only shook his head, countenance stern.

His voice was grave as he stood at the end of the ornately carved bed. "I'm so sorry, but there is little to be done. It's his heart. To be honest, it's only by Providence's hand that he's still here. The damage is no doubt extensive."

Mother did little but stare blankly at Father's sleeping form or weep hysterically into her clutched handkerchief, its substance no more than a fluff of lace. Ineffective and helpless against her cries.

Helpless. That's exactly how Keziah felt.

Nathaniel. Her heart stung just at the thought of his name. Her vibrant, joyful brother struck down in the bloom of youth. He was so clever. Had so much life yet to live. A lump settled deep in her throat. Well-meaning friends only made the wound worse, saying time would heal the gaping hole he had left behind. That she would eventually forget this horrid pain.

She didn't want to forget. Such a thing would make light of his sacrifice. Of him. No, losing Nathaniel was an ache that would never heal.

Hiriam descended the rickety ladder over the door, startling her from her wayward thoughts, the small iron hammer clutched in his hands.

"There, missy. That should hold the mourning crepe in place unless a storm rolls in."

Offering a sad smile, Keziah reached for the hammer so his hands would be free to move the ladder. "Thank you, Hiriam. March winds will soon be upon us. How thoughtful you are to secure the crepe over the door."

He squeezed her shoulder in a grandfatherly fashion. "Ain't no trouble. Seems like a pitiful amount to do considering the sorrow you're bearing up under, but I'll aid you any way I can."

Tears swam in her vision, blurring his face. "How would I manage without you?"

He chuckled softly in the gentle way he had. "Probably dance a jig. These old bones of mine ain't useful for much."

She reached up on tiptoe and kissed his gray-whiskered cheek. "Old or no, I couldn't function in your absence. Besides, it's not your physical strength I usually seek. It's your wisdom and kind heart."

His face lit with a kind of sadness, though his mouth smiled. "Most wisdom comes through trial."

"And you've had your fair share of that, have you not?"

His expression shuttered. "That's true enough, and I wrestled with the Almighty through most of it, but there's great peace in surrender."

Lines crinkled the corners of his eyes as he patted her shoulder once more and hefted the ladder toward the corner of their brick home. Another gust toyed with her hair. She looked up, glancing at the darkening sky.

At the squeak of an iron hinge, she turned and saw Polly tentatively walking up their stone walkway, a basket clutched in her hands.

Keziah swallowed, suddenly uneasy. Why was Polly here alone?

The slave woman kept her head down, her face almost completely obscured within her large bonnet. She stopped before Keziah and timidly lifted her eyes. "Miss Keziah?"

"Polly, how lovely to see you."

Reaching into her basket, Polly pulled out a square tin

and held it toward Keziah. "This here is a gift from Mistress Ward. She heard about Mr. Montgomery's continuing poor health."

Keziah gently took the tin from Polly's fingers, noting the way the slave's hands trembled. She studied the label and smiled in appreciation. "Ceylon black tea?"

"Mistress Ward said it ain't much, but with the blockade still hemming the city in, she thought this tea might be a small comfort."

Keziah hugged it to her bodice in gratitude. "I know this comes dear. Especially now. Please convey our deepest thanks to Mrs. Ward."

Polly nodded and dropped her head once more but did not move. A cool wind swirled around them, ruffling their skirts, but still she stood mute. Was she afraid of something?

Clearing her throat, Keziah shivered against the cool and braved a word. "Was there something else you needed?"

The woman's chin trembled as her lips parted. "A friend of a friend sent me."

Keziah's heart slammed. There would be no reason to use the cryptic phrase unless Polly was seeking escape with the Railroad. She glanced side to side to make sure no one was about, then stepped close, collapsing the wide space between them. "Why do you seek me?"

Polly held herself erect as if she'd decided to spill her thoughts and suffer the repercussions whether they were favorable or not. "I knew you was to be trusted since I heard you play that song in the parlor. Take me. I'm seeking Canaan."

Was this a trap of some kind? Keziah struggled to form a coherent reply. She did not want to incriminate herself if the request was some kind of ploy, but neither could she ignore the plea if it was sincerely petitioned.

"But why? Is Mrs. Ward not good to you?"

Polly's expression hardened, her shoulders stiff. "Mistress is right kind to me. It's Mr. Ward that has me wanting to leave. He comes into my room at night, and . . ." She fumbled, struggling to say the words.

Keziah's eyes slid shut. "Say no more, please."

The slave woman gripped her basket so tightly, Keziah feared the handle would snap.

"Is there no one else you trust?"

Polly took her measure with a direct gaze that bored into Keziah's soul. She met her focus evenly, refusing to look away.

"I have no one. I came because . . ." She swallowed. "If I'm mistaken to come to you, correct me."

Keziah's breath hitched as she whispered, "Await my reply. Within a month, if the Lord wills. Instructions will be forthcoming."

The faintest trace of moisture pooled in Polly's eyes, her shoulders slumping with relief. "God bless you, miss." Something caught Polly's notice from the side of the house, and she quickly dropped her gaze into meek submission before turning to leave.

Keziah called to her retreating form, "Please thank your mistress for the thoughtful gift."

With only a momentary pause, Polly nodded and let

herself through the iron gate, disappearing down the lane in a swish of skirts.

Keziah turned to see Hiriam watching her, his face a mask. Had he overheard?

Heat enveloped her and she offered a thin smile before making hasty steps toward the door and shutting it behind her with a relieved click.

The steady ticking of the grandfather clock in the parlor reminded her time was not on her side. It slipped away, second by agonizing second, as she scrambled for the best way to smuggle Polly into the Railroad.

Setting her feet on the path of freedom would be easy. Evading capture in the process would be difficult.

The thought of her cousin's inquisitive stares rushed to her with sickening dread.

A difficult task indeed.

FEBRUARY 17, 1862

Micah plunged his hands into the tepid water of the washbowl and watched it turn a murky pink. The man lying on a threadbare cot in the church basement heaved a sigh, his face dotted with sweat.

"Don't know how I can thank you, Doc. That bullet was paining me something awful."

Micah wiped his hands on a fresh cloth and gathered up his instruments to clean them before they were needed again. "A bullet wound is nothing to ignore. Could have infected your blood if it were in much longer. I think your shoulder will mend fine now, though." He eyed the fugitive's cotton-swathed shoulder with satisfaction. The spot of blood soaking through the fabric was minimal.

The man's bass timbre floated through the quiet. He was the only passenger at the moment. "I'm mighty beholden to you."

Micah shook his head. "The Almighty is the one who deserves the gratitude."

"Yes, sir." He broke into a smile, revealing crooked teeth, and shifted against the cot, wincing with the strain.

"Here. I don't know when you'll be moving, so I'll give these to you now. Three rolls of fresh bandages, lint to pack the wound each time you change the dressing, and a small vial of whiskey for cleaning it out." Micah gave a look to intimidate but knew the threat was thin, especially considering the man's thick-corded muscles. "The whiskey is for cleaning, not for drinking."

Crooked teeth flashed again, accompanied by a low chuckle. "And here I was all excited." The man suddenly sobered and stilled, his dark eyes moving to the doorway of the inner room. Fear flickered across his face.

Micah whirled around to see a slight woman, her mousy-brown hair pulled into a tight bun, standing on the threshold. Despite the poor cut of her worn dress and her lean frame, she was attractive with her large eyes and high cheekbones.

"Dr. Greyson?"

Straightening slowly, he moved to block the woman's view of the hurt slave. "I am."

Relief sagged the tight lines in her forehead. "Forgive me. I know I gave you a start. I'm Mr. Brothers's wife."

The band of iron around his gut slowly unclenched. "Why didn't he come for me himself?"

"He's been asking me to help him of late. It allows him to be at the bellows and iron more often, reducing the risk of suspicion. Here." She reached into the pocket of her soiled apron and pulled out an envelope. "This was delivered to us by a young lad I have never seen before, but the contents bear your name. We figured it must be from another conductor, since only one of them would know to get you a message through us."

His brows knit as he took the missive. "Thank you kindly, ma'am."

With a quick nod, she fled from the room.

Micah moved toward the closest oil lamp, broke the seal, and pulled a single sheet of paper from its depths, noting the elegant, feminine script.

*Dear Dr. Greyson,*

*I trust this letter finds you in good health. I know you bear a terrible strain aiding our brave soldiers as they heal from the devastation of war. May Providence bless you as you have blessed others.*

*I write to beg your wisdom and expertise in a certain medical matter. A dear friend of mine is suffering from a horrid malady, an illness which has virtually imprisoned her in her own home much of the time, with no seeming hope for relief. All current treatments for improvement have led to naught. My dear friend has become so vexed in her current circumstances, she laments she wants nothing more than to leave this earth and seek her reward in the Promised Land.*

*I humbly seek your wise counsel. If you desire to consider her case and would like further details, please write posthaste.*

*With kindest regards,*
*KM*

Micah's mind reeled. Kizzie trusted him, yet to have penned such a desperate request, even in a seemingly normal manner, meant smuggling out the slave seeking escape would be an unusually difficult task. How high were the stakes that she had to solicit his aid through a letter?

He shook away the thought. The stakes were always high. It was human life, after all.

His brain spun with possibilities. To conduct this person through the Confederate-infested land between Savannah and the Ohio state line would be foolhardy at best. Since Grant's Union victory in Tennessee, Confederate forces had been trying to hold their ground. How many troops lay between Savannah and the Ohio River? Far too many to think the normal routes would meet with success.

The best option was to travel by ship, a feasible possibility since the Confederate Navy had abandoned Tybee Island altogether.

He studied Keziah's curving letters, and the desire to help rose thick in his chest. *Father, help me not to fail her.*

He would move heaven and earth to rescue this woman or die trying.

# CHAPTER 18

FEBRUARY 22, 1862

Keziah pushed the front door open, clutching the laden basket to her middle. Raised feminine voices floated from the parlor and met her ears.

"Jennie Oglethorpe, your behavior is nothing short of scandalous!"

Keziah frowned and removed her shawl, thankful that the chill had left the house of late, due to milder temperatures. Yet judging by her mother's harsh tone, a cold wind still blew.

Approaching the two women squared off in the middle of the blue- and gold-trimmed parlor, she noted Mother's face was flushed, but Jennie didn't look even slightly perturbed at the outburst. Instead, she grinned like a fox in a henhouse.

Upon seeing Keziah enter, Jennie quickly turned to her, ignoring Mother's ire. "Oh, Keziah dear, please tell Auntie Elsie that I am not an immoral reprobate."

Keziah looked between the two of them, their expressions as opposite as sunshine and storm clouds. "Why the fuss?"

Mother shifted toward her, her black bombazine dress releasing a gentle swoosh. "Your cousin is making a spectacle of our entire family with her outlandish behavior. Do you know what she's done now? A regiment marched by and Jennie opened our second-story window and leaned out of it, giggling and waving at the soldiers. Waving!" Keziah had rarely seen her gentle mother so undone as she twisted her fingers together. "No proper young woman ever waves at a man, much less a whole group of men . . . and in a house of mourning, at that!"

Jennie puckered her lips into a pout. "Honestly, Auntie, societal rules are becoming so antiquated." She moved to slip her arm through Keziah's in a show of camaraderie. "I've no doubt Nathaniel would want us to continue our lives much as before. He never was one to stand on ceremony. Don't you think so, Keziah?"

Truth be told, her cousin's behavior was scandalous indeed and becoming more daring with every passing day, yet was Keziah any better, with her clandestine activities? The irony was not lost on her. Instead of fueling either of the women's fires, she tried to change the subject.

"Since I did not see the incident, I will refrain from giving an opinion. I'd rather get these goods to Elizabeth."

Jennie's brows rose at the sight of the bulging basket. "Please tell me you were able to acquire a sweet cake or ginger pop. How I crave them!"

"I'm sorry. There were none to be had. I suppose with prices soaring, merchants are concerned with keeping only staples on hand. But here—" she reached in and pulled out a narrow box—"I did manage to find you a package of Necco wafers."

Her cousin reluctantly took them, her face puckered into a petulant scowl. "It's not a ginger pop, but it will do."

Mother sidled close and peeked into the basket's contents. "Sugar? Flour?"

"I found only a small package of sugar but procured enough flour and cornmeal to last for a good spell and even snagged the last rasher of salt pork."

"Combined with what we already have on hand in the larder, that will do." She sighed and Keziah noticed the dark circles beneath her eyes, a sure sign of her recent emotional strain. "Times are growing leaner."

Keziah patted her slim hand. "Praise Providence we have plenty to eat. Many do not."

Nodding, Mother eyed the basket. "Did you acquire anything else?"

Keziah had no intention of announcing the messenger boy who had greeted her outside the house just before she'd left for the market, nor would she mention the letter he had delivered. It was safely nested in her reticule, awaiting a stolen moment when she could read it. When she'd witnessed Micah's distinctive scrawl on the envelope, her heart had beat wildly within her chest. Waiting for privacy to soak in its contents was growing more torturous by the second.

"No, nothing else." What a smooth liar she was becoming. Her conscience pricked. Not an admirable trait.

Mother took the basket from her with a small smile. "I'll take these to Elizabeth. It was kind of you to run her errands for her."

"I could do nothing less considering she's down with the quinsy." Keziah grimaced. "Miserable malady."

"Indeed. I shall have to summon a doctor if she does not improve soon. You go on and see your father. He's been asking for you."

"Yes, ma'am."

Mother shot a warning glance to Jennie. "I shall refrain from telling your uncle of your brazen behavior. In truth, I fear his heart could not take the shock."

Upon her departure, Jennie sighed. "Mercy, but Auntie is in a snit today."

"Perhaps, considering her recent strain, you could temper your impulses a tad."

Jennie's lips twitched into a smile. "But, dear Cousin, how boring that would be!"

Keziah made a quick path to her room before going to see Father. The unread letter from Micah burned her mind with possibilities. Had he understood her plea? Did he think her forward or addled? In truth, she could not accomplish such a feat, to sneak away a well-known and much-relied-upon slave, without the aid of a partner. After the way they had parted, would he agree?

The memory of Micah's ardent kisses assaulted her once more as she stepped into her room. As quickly as the snatched memories of pleasure came, she snuffed them out, pushing them away with effort. It would do no good to dwell on such a mistake. Micah did not once say he loved her.

Allowing the hurt to wipe away the blush of sweet memories, she pulled the letter from her reticule and opened the stiff paper with trembling fingers.

*Dear Miss Montgomery,*

*Thank you for your kind regards. I am well and doing what I can to help our brave men, although war weighs heavy on my heart, as I know it does on yours.*

*In regard to your friend who has been dealt such a vicious blow of ill health, I would need to know more of your friend's symptoms to advise the best course of treatment, but hereby pledge my willingness to aid her in whatever manner possible. Barring a lung malady, I might suggest that breathing in ocean air is a wonderful way to combat a wide array of troublesome ailments, particularly in the area of melancholy.*

*I shall be passing your way soon and will make every attempt to visit your friend, if she is willing. Look for me on the third at the place where memories were made, and I shall endeavor to do whatever I can.*

*Kindest regards,*
*MJG*

She exhaled a shaky sigh, her heart bursting. He was going to help Polly escape. She scanned the contents again, wondering why he'd mentioned ocean air. Ocean air? Salt water, the stench of decaying fish and sea life . . .

She sucked in a breath. He was planning to smuggle Polly out by ship.

Such a move would hold its own risks but, once executed, would be far less risky than traversing the many miles of Confederate fortifications between Savannah and any free states.

The third of March where memories were made. He had to mean the schoolhouse. That's where their collective memories and friendship had bloomed and grown.

Stuffing the letter into her desk drawer, she straightened, her thoughts spinning like carriage wheels as she shoved the walnut drawer shut with a decisive click. There was little she could do before their arranged meeting but still, trying to calm her scattered wits and taut nerves would prove difficult.

She walked down the hallway and noted the way her boots connected sharply with the polished floors, echoes trailing in her wake. The house seemed so desolate. Nathaniel's death and Father's subsequent illness had laid a bleak pall over the home like a damp blanket. No wonder Jennie sought adventure. Even the traces of sweet tobacco from Father's pipe that had always lingered in a welcoming embrace had evaporated.

Grasping the knob, she pushed her father's bedroom door open with a light squeak. Benjamin Montgomery looked pale and listless beneath the dark-green duvet, his color far too gray, his eyes far too glassy and bright.

"Father? How are you feeling today?"

With a light cough, he beckoned her in, ignoring her question. "Come closer."

As she entered the room and moved to his side, a familiar, unwelcome voice intruded.

"Miss Montgomery."

She gasped and whirled around to see Lyman Hill standing somberly in the dark corner, illuminated by the faint light filtering through the curtained windows.

"Mr. Hill." She itched to ask him to leave but knew such a demand would be unseemly. He'd done nothing wrong, yet why hadn't Mother mentioned he would be present?

Turning away from him, she focused on her father and perched uneasily on the corner of a chair next to his bed.

Ever the businessman, Father addressed her, his gravelly voice sharp. "I'm going to speak plainly."

Keziah couldn't suppress the curving of her lips. "You always have."

"True enough." He coughed again and winced but waved her off when she tried to reach for his glass of water. "No water. Not until I'm done. I'm not long for this world. Soon I'll be joining . . . Nathaniel." His eyes fogged with pain as he fumbled over her brother's name. An aching sadness pierced her chest. She suspected her father was not just suffering from a physical heart ailment, but was grieving himself to death.

She longed to reach for his hand but feared the gesture would not be welcome. He was an unemotional man, prone to turn up his nose at sentimentality. Still, a person ought to feel their impending passage into glory would be a sorrowful parting for their family.

"You are well into marriageable age, and since Providence has seen fit to take me soon, I request you marry Mr. Hill immediately."

Venomous dread coiled through her. "Father, please, I—"

He held up a silencing hand. "I cannot rest in peace until I know that you and your mother will be taken care of. Mr. Hill has graciously agreed to house your mother for as long as she has breath. My only fear has been leaving her in duress, without a strong man to care for her needs. Your marriage to Mr. Hill would allay my fears."

What of her own feelings in the matter? She longed to scream, to make him see reason. With a sudden flash, she imagined life with Lyman Hill, his cold manner, stiff disdain . . . the thought nearly made her retch.

Mr. Hill stepped out from the shadows. "I know this comes as a bit of a shock. I'd hoped we would have more time for affections to grow, but your father is quite right. Practicality trumps emotional matters, especially during the uncertainty of war."

Keziah's mouth was dry as cotton. "There's no rush, Father. Mayhap you'll recover. I certainly have no intention of burying you anytime soon." She forced a laugh but grimaced when it sounded more like a choked gasp.

Even in his frail condition, the stubborn set of his jaw told her she would not persuade him. "Would you begrudge your dying father his only wish?"

Heart sinking, she swallowed the bile rising in her throat. She had prayed that courting Lyman Hill would allow her family to see how ill-suited they were for each other, but to no avail. She was trapped.

"If you're agreeable, my dear, we can set the wedding date for three weeks from today."

The room spun as she slowly stood. She nodded even as her mind screamed for release. How could she possibly pledge her troth to love, honor, and obey a man she barely knew when Micah's kiss still burned her lips and the memory of his touch haunted her each night?

The future loomed ahead of her, bleak and cold as a January night.

---

MARCH 3, 1862

Micah watched from the grove of trees behind the schoolhouse, thankful for the warmer temperatures of early spring, as Kizzie walked with a rapid step toward their arranged meeting spot.

How many years since he'd seen her walking to school on a day almost exactly like this one, her braids resting against her shoulders, lunch pail swinging from her fingertips, books hugged to her chest? He remembered thinking her so pretty as she strolled toward the schoolhouse.

And out of nowhere, Charlie had crept up behind her, knocked her books from her hands, and run away.

Micah had burned with anger as she'd stooped to gather

her scattered primers, a dozen emotions flitting across her face. She looked so forlorn. So . . . alone.

If only she realized Charlie teased her because he could think of no other way to capture her attention. All the boys knew Charlie was smitten with her. But the troublemaker was none too bright about showing his affection.

Unable to watch Kizzie struggle anymore, Micah had rushed to her side, kneeling in the dirt, picking up the dust-smudged books. She kept her head bowed, no doubt to hide her flaming cheeks from his perusal.

She tried to juggle the stack of primers and rise, but he gently tugged them away. "Here. Let me carry them for you."

Her bleak whisper pained him. "Why does he torture me so?"

He'd swallowed and shrugged. "Charlie just wants attention. How about I walk with you from now on?" At her stare, he felt a strange heat crawl up the back of his neck. "You know, as protection."

A soft smile broke across her face. "I'd like that. I'd like that a lot."

He didn't understand the odd way his heart pounded or why he suddenly felt taller when she smiled.

Micah blinked. She was no longer a girl but a woman, yet his chest thundered now just as it had that day so long ago. Her strawberry-blonde curls were tucked loosely into a fashionable snood. Soft blossoms of pink dusted her cheeks. But why was she wearing a black bombazine mourning dress?

She hadn't seen him yet, hidden as he was, and he enjoyed

the rare pleasure of drinking in his fill of her. She slowed, sauntering past the mournful cemetery to the east of the schoolhouse, her face downcast. Something was troubling her deeply.

Stuffing his hands in his pockets, he emerged from his hidden spot among the trees and strode in a lazy fashion toward the cemetery, trying to look nonchalant should anybody see them upon passing. At his hushed footfalls in the greening grass, she turned, her eyes lighting with happiness just before a dark veil shuttered them.

He stopped several feet away. "Miss Montgomery."

Offering a smile that seemed forced, she nodded but avoided his gaze. "Dr. Greyson."

"Would you be so kind as to walk with an old school chum and relieve my boredom?"

"Of course." Her voice was soft as ever yet her manner seemed distant as she fell into step beside him. When they'd walked to the far side of the cemetery, away from any listening ears that might be frequenting the uneven road, he could contain his curiosity no longer.

"What has happened? Why the mourning?"

She stopped but looked straight ahead, intent on a mossy tombstone with fading letters.

"Nathaniel is dead, shot down during the battle of Fort Henry."

He groaned, wishing he could take her in his arms, loathing the fact that he must keep his distance. "I'm so sorry. Nathaniel was one of the finest men I've ever known. Never met a stranger." He sighed. "I can't imagine the world without him."

She shook her head slightly, dropping her eyes to the grass. "We knew the risk he took, but—" she faltered, her profile somehow expressing her stark grief—"Mother and Father have not fared well with the news. Father collapsed upon receiving word and has not regained his strength. Our family physician says his heart is barely functioning."

Micah winced, knowing words would be inadequate comfort in the face of such loss. "I'm sorry."

She sighed and finally lifted her eyes to meet his, resignation flickering in their depths. "I know."

"And yet in the midst of your own sorrow, you're attempting to aid a passenger to freedom."

With a dry twist of a smile, she looked back over the quiet cemetery. "She requested my help. How could I do anything less? Of course, it all depends on your wisdom. Without you, I fear I'd be lost." As if realizing how her words might be construed, she lowered her gaze to her feet and blushed prettily.

He lowered his voice. "There is little I can do to alleviate your family's suffering, but thankfully I can do something about the latter. If you're agreeable, here's the plan. . . ."

# CHAPTER 19

KEZIAH SAT INSIDE the family carriage, willing the moths to cease their fluttering torrent in her belly. Hiriam flicked the reins, urged the mares to keep pace as they pranced past the square to the Wards' lofty home.

As she gripped the worn handles of the large bag in her lap with one hand, she pressed the fingers of the other to its lumpy insides and reassured herself the needed gown had not been left behind.

She was more likely to lose her courage than misplace the gown.

She peered anxiously for Micah as the carriage approached the street corner they had agreed upon two days prior. Sure enough, he stood ready in his black suit, far too handsome for his own good. His dark hair shone in the sunlight, and an easy smile lit his face as he recognized their hack.

This was the moment.

"Hiriam?" She raised her voice to be heard over the rumble and clatter of wheels. "Stop for a moment, please. I see an acquaintance up ahead I wish to greet."

With a nod, Hiriam pulled back on the reins, stopping the glossy mares. Upon seeing her, Micah feigned surprise and lifted his hand in greeting. "Miss Montgomery? What a pleasure to see you today."

"And you, Dr. Greyson. Do you fare well?"

"Well compared to our suffering soldiers. After months of treating their wounds, I have no right to complain about any personal discomforts."

Was Hiriam listening, or had he tuned out their silly formalities? Talking in such a manner to Micah felt as phony as pretending tea was cream. "Well, I don't wish to take up any of your time. I know as a physician you stay extremely busy."

He smiled, his white teeth flashing and blue eyes twinkling in the tanned lines of his face. Her knees suddenly felt weak. Thank Providence she was sitting, so they could not betray her.

"I'm never too busy to say hello to a schoolmate. I'm on a matter of business, heading to the Ward home. I need to inform several of the families on the square about an illness affecting many Negroes throughout Savannah. The Ward family is next on my list of contacts."

She could plainly see the humor longing to peek through his gentlemanly demeanor. "How fortunate! I am heading there myself. I have a matter of business to discuss with Mrs. Ward. I would be happy for you to accompany me. No sense walking when our destination is the same. Hiriam?" He turned his head to the side to catch her request. "Would you be agreeable to conveying the good doctor to the Ward home as well?"

Hiriam tipped his hat to Micah, giving him a moment to lift himself into the open-air carriage. The bench seat beneath her tilted and bounced as Micah settled his weight beside her. Once Hiriam's back was to them once more, Micah's subtle wink caused her cheeks to warm. The carriage rolled gently along the road, and with his strong presence, she felt her nerves calm . . . that was, until his knee jostled hers.

Then the fluttering moths in her stomach nearly took flight.

They traveled in silence for long minutes. With every block the horses clopped past, her unease grew. She had not yet informed him of her betrothal to Mr. Hill. He deserved to hear the news from her first.

*Tell him.*

"Dr. Greyson, there is something I must tell you."

His brows rose. "Oh?"

Words abandoned her. Why was this so difficult? She'd opened her mouth to speak when the carriage slowed to a stop.

"Here we are." Hiriam turned toward them, oblivious to her inner turmoil.

She offered a smile. "Thank you, Hiriam."

Micah studied her. "You were preparing to share something with me?"

"I—that is, it can wait." *Coward.*

As Micah descended and offered his hand to assist her, a sob lodged in her chest. Nathaniel was dead. She was engaged to Lyman Hill, and Micah was all but lost to her. As a little girl, she had sketched her dreams in journals, imprinting them upon her mind and building them into castles of hope. How different her life had turned out to be.

There was little she could do for her own future, but perhaps there was something yet to be done for Polly's. She must focus on the task at hand.

All other dreams had been cut to ribbons.

Micah perched on the stiff, horsehair sofa in the stuffy green parlor of the Ward house, praying he didn't look as uncomfortable as he felt.

Mrs. Ward had welcomed them warmly, inquiring about Mr. Montgomery's health. When both Micah and Kizzie relayed how they'd come to arrive together, the matron said two visitors were better than one.

The hospitality of the robust woman sipping her tea across the parlor was meant to set him at ease, but the woman who sat primly on the opposite end of the sofa from him caused him some disquiet. The yawning expanse between them on the couch was nothing in comparison to the odd distance she maintained. Ever since meeting at the cemetery, Kizzie had seemed . . . different. Aloof and skittish as a newborn colt.

At first, it appeared she was merely committed to her role as an old schoolmate running into him on the street. But even when Hiriam had turned his back to them, sending the carriage into its lurching sway, her demeanor had not changed. He'd continually felt her eyes on him, but when he braved a look, she reddened and averted her gaze.

Had his foolish kiss ruined their friendship completely? He hated this stiff tension pulsing between them. Yet she'd come to him for help in spiriting Polly away. That counted for something, didn't it?

The wayward thoughts cluttered his mind and he shook them off. He had a job to do. Woolgathering over his failures with Kizzie would not help matters.

"I agree, dear. The price of yard goods is utterly ridiculous in my opinion." Mrs. Ward's strident tone speared his attention as Kizzie leaned forward, gently cradling her delicate saucer and flower-patterned teacup.

"Actually, that is why I'm here. I pray you won't think me too forward, but your kind gift after the passing of Nathaniel was much appreciated. I know this isn't much, but our house slave Elizabeth has an abundance of dresses—more than she could ever need. And your servant Polly looks to be about the same size required to fit Elizabeth's gowns. I noticed her cuffs were just a bit frayed when she dropped off your lovely gift and wondered if you'd be opposed to letting me give her several of Elizabeth's dresses, times being what they are."

Mrs. Ward's round face softened. "Very thoughtful of you and your dear mother. I confess, with yard goods so costly now, I've fretted over how we are to afford clothes for the staff in light of the coming social season."

Micah suppressed a frown. Social season? In the middle of a war? Didn't the societal elite understand the gravity of the battles raging around them? Images of bloodied stumps and disease-ridden men flooded his mind. What good were dance cards when men lay sprawled over barren, pockmarked fields, their bloated, bloody bodies piled three feet deep?

Oblivious to his irritation, the matron prattled on. "If you're sure your servant will have no further need of them, I'd be grateful to receive them."

Kizzie nodded. "Of course. I brought several of them with me. Would you like her to try one on now?"

Placing her empty cup back on the silver tray with a clink, Mrs. Ward dabbed her lips daintily with a crisp linen napkin. "Indeed. That would be the best course of action. Polly?"

Mrs. Ward had barely raised her voice, keeping it cultured, as proper women tended to do, yet the meek maid appeared at the doorway all the same. "Yes, ma'am?"

"Go upstairs and try on these gowns. The Montgomery family said you're welcome to them."

Micah noted the hint of a smile around her mouth but she hid her pleasure well, instead dropping her gaze to the floor with a meek bob of her head. "Yes'm."

Kizzie stood, grabbing the bulging carpetbag. "I'll make sure they fit."

Mrs. Ward waved a dismissive hand. "If you wish, but don't let her keep you. She moves as slowly as molasses."

Kizzie ignored the barb and followed Polly from the room, leaving Micah alone with Mrs. Ward. Smoothing an invisible wrinkle from her skirt, the buxom woman straightened and arranged her hands primly on her lap. "Now, Dr. Greyson, you said you have some medical information to relay to me."

With a final sip of the watery tea, he set the cup on the tea service. "Yes, ma'am. Thank you for the refreshment." He cleared his throat, launching into his pretense. "I'm attempting to alert everyone in my circle of acquaintance to the danger spreading among the Negro population."

Her brown eyes reflected concern. "Oh? Do tell."

He paused and twiddled his thumbs, wondering how long he should stall. Surely Kizzie would need only a few minutes to lay out the escape plan to Polly before she tried on the gowns.

"There seems to be a peculiar ailment making its way through the area, and Negroes appear to be especially vulnerable to this malady."

"Nothing life-threatening, I hope."

"No, in most cases, the illness will resolve itself in due time without loss of life. But I wanted to make your family aware of the possible implications."

Intrigued, Mrs. Ward leaned forward. "What are the symptoms?"

"Sore throat, headache, and fatigue, primarily. Sometimes fever and stomach ailments might accompany this particular malady, making work nearly impossible."

She wrinkled her pug nose in disdain, clearly ill at ease with the delicate topic. "How . . . dreadful."

He forced his mouth into a grim line and muttered, "Quite."

"What can be done?"

Leaning his elbows on his knees, he tried his best to look impassioned. "Rest. Much rest. Sleep is the single best treatment for this illness. Rest and creature comforts. Since exhaustion is the most vexing and weighty symptom, it's the most integral one to treat. Oftentimes, the sick will need inordinate amounts of rest, even up to one month after contracting this horrid disease."

Her eyebrows puckered as she frowned. "One month of sleep and rest? Forgive me, Doctor, but that seems excessive. Especially for a slave. Why, who would see to the work?"

How he longed to laugh at her consternated expression, but he schooled his features just in time. "Indeed. It seems you understand the gravity of the situation. And an intelligent woman such as yourself knows how crucial rest will be, since failure to treat these aggressive symptoms could lead a slave to total collapse. In extreme cases, even death."

"But I—"

Micah shook his head, forging on. "You wouldn't believe how many people I've spoken to who have yet to realize the full consequences of disregarding this advice. Failure to do so would mean unnecessary loss of life and, consequently, the financial loss of a dead slave." He clucked his tongue. "Many don't have your foresight, Mrs. Ward, if I may be so bold as to say so."

The ignorant woman blushed pink and took to the flattery like a fish to a worm and nodded in agreement. "If any of our slaves contract this terrible illness, I will certainly insist on a month of rest. We will make do or hire someone else in the interim. Slaves can do no work if they expire."

"Quite right."

Mrs. Ward visibly relaxed, her shoulders losing their tight appearance. "I shall warn Polly of this new malady when she returns downstairs."

He stood, indicating his intention to leave. She rose with him. "Well then, with your blessing, I'll take my leave."

"Of course, Doctor. I would ask you to stay a bit longer, but I have no idea how long Polly will be with Miss Montgomery. Kind of her to give you a ride today."

He smiled, a genuine one this time. "Miss Montgomery is very kind. My feet appreciate her willingness."

The matron laughed lightly and gestured toward the door to show him out, chattering idly all the way down the carpeted hallway. "A sweeter person the Almighty never made. I'm so glad Miss Montgomery will finally have her chance for happiness."

Something about the woman's tone set his nerves on edge. He slowed his steps. "Oh? What happiness has befallen Miss Montgomery?"

Mrs. Ward raised a brow. "Why, her engagement to Lyman Hill. Surely you've heard."

His blood froze, his pulse roaring in his brain. His lungs were tight, bereft of air.

His Kizzie? Engaged? A cold numbness robbed his body of sensation as he choked out a reply, "No, I hadn't heard."

"It was rather a sudden announcement, but I believe it's a good match. Mr. Hill is quite a bit older—past fighting age. And with his financial success, he'll well be able to take over her father's holdings. I hear it was Mr. Montgomery's wish."

Her babbling buzzed in his ears like pesky flies as his heart slowly shredded. What was Benjamin Montgomery thinking? Promising his vibrant, beautiful daughter to a man twice her age? A man known for his biting tongue and cold business practices? Life with him would shrivel lovely Kizzie into a limp, empty flower.

"When is the wedding to take place?"

Mrs. Ward resumed her brisk pace to the door. "Less than a fortnight."

Now Kizzie's odd behavior made sense. The sadness and resignation. The distance. His chest pinched with a pain that nearly took his breath away.

Yet he'd always known this moment would come. Life with him was far too dangerous. He'd known she would eventually marry someone else . . . hadn't he?

The thought of her married to sour Lyman Hill, her slim waist swollen with his babies, the dreariness of the Hill house . . . the dark imaginings consumed him, filling him with anger, mingled with a misery there was no remedy for, no medicine. No cure.

*Kizzie, what have you agreed to?*

---

Within the small, dreary confines of Polly's windowless room, Keziah yanked the blue dress with its front row of white buttons and gentle tucks from the carpetbag, looking over her shoulder to ensure no one had followed them.

Polly lit the oil lamp next to her bed, the light casting eerie silhouettes against her face. "Oh, Miss Montgomery, you sure about this? If you are caught because of me—"

"Nonsense." Keziah forced a bravery she didn't feel. "I have no worries. God's will be done, either way. Look here." She flipped up the fabric, showing Polly the underside of the gown's wide hem. "In two days' time, I will send a message, asking your mistress if I can borrow your talents for the day in helping Elizabeth prepare for my wedding." The very word stuck in her throat. But now was not the time to lament her future. "Wear this dress. I've sewn a bit of money into the hem."

The poor woman gasped, mortified. "Miss Montgomery, I couldn't!"

Keziah grasped Polly's fluttering hands, calming her frantic movements with a gentle touch. "Don't fret. It isn't much, but it will help. The important thing is that you have a way to start a new life when you are free. You will be given what you need along the way. Bring nothing else with you."

With a dense breath, Polly nodded.

"I will arrange to have a driver come for you by coach. I'll be inside the carriage, but do not acknowledge me. When we arrive at my house, I will leave the coach, but you will remain inside." She leaned forward and whispered, "We will be wearing matching blue dresses."

Understanding dawned. "So it will appear that I am entering the house."

"Correct. You'll be taken to a safe place where you will change coaches, and my friend Dr. Greyson will escort you to the port."

Her dark eyes widened. "I am to go by sea?"

"Yes." Keziah sensed her fear. "It is the safest route."

"But what about Mistress Ward? Won't she find it suspicious that I disappeared while at your home?"

"Once I know you're safe, I'll send a message to your mistress, telling her I sent you on an errand and you never returned. No doubt they will begin searching immediately, but I think by taking the initiative to contact them, suspicion will be deflected from me."

Polly exhaled a shaky sigh, her eyes brimming with unshed tears. "How can I ever thank you?"

Grasping the woman's thin shoulder, Keziah gave a gentle squeeze. "Live well. Be happy. I pray wherever you go, God Almighty will direct your steps."

# CHAPTER 20

PEBBLES CRUNCHED under Keziah's boots as she shifted her weight uneasily from foot to foot. She held her breath, praying, hoping Hiriam would agree to the plan she proposed to Polly yesterday.

A gentle breeze rife with the perfume of irises and jonquils brushed tendrils of hair across her face as she stood outside the stable. Hiriam ran his calloused thumb up and down the wooden handle of the shovel propped steadily in the gravel between them. He pursed his lips, contemplated the ground. She'd never seen him so serious.

Finally he lifted his eyes to hers, concern snuffing out any hope of affirmation. "I don't know, missy. What you're asking . . ."

Mouth dry, she swallowed. "I know. And I wouldn't ask unless there were no other alternative."

Sighing heavily, he leaned his weight against the thick wall of the stable and gave her a long look that made her squirm. "You remember that little boy what we spirited to the Negro church months ago?"

The odd question snagged her curiosity. "Of course. Why?"

"That wasn't the only time you helped an escaped slave, was it?"

Her heart skidded. She would not confess to such a thing, but neither would she lie to Hiriam. Instead, she met his gaze boldly, studying its depths. The aged lines in his face softened.

"Missy," he murmured, "you got the sweetest and kindest heart I know. But this thing you're doing . . ." He shook his head. "It's dangerous. Not just for you but your family as well."

The words were gently spoken but stung nonetheless. Hiriam had never disagreed with her on any other subject, and she felt like a wayward child. Hurt lumped in her throat.

"I thought you, of all people, would understand."

Groaning, the elderly man rubbed the back of his neck. "I do, missy. I do. But your choices affect your family. And you got to know that not every slaveholder is cruel."

She recalled Amos's mutilated back. "Not every slaveholder is kind either."

"True enough."

Agitated, she began to pace. "Am I so wrong to want all those in chains to taste freedom? Why must people remain enslaved at all? Why should pale skin be the distinction between bond and free?"

Hiriam spoke slowly, his deep voice soothing as a goose-grease compress on burned skin. "You're right, missy. Shouldn't be no difference, but there is. At least for this scrap of time. All I'm saying is, weigh the consequences."

"I have."

He firmed his lips and jutted out his chin but said nothing.

"I don't understand you, Hiriam. Why do you refuse me?"

He absently ground the point of the shovel into the gravel. "Did you ever stop and think that maybe the Almighty has a greater purpose in mind for folks than physical freedom?"

She frowned. "I don't follow."

He studied her for a long moment, expression thoughtful. "I never did tell you about my past, even when you asked." A sudden sadness covered his aging features. "Reckon it's time. Leastwise, maybe you'll understand why I'm hesitant."

Her ears pricked. Finally. She stepped close as his face took on a faraway look.

"I was born on a plantation down in Mississippi. Don't remember much about my early years. I was sold to a master on the other side of the state when I was a young fellow. Separated from my mother and siblings when I was just on the cusp of manhood."

He clenched his jaw tightly. His knuckles grew taut around the shovel's smooth handle.

"Master Dean was the meanest man I ever did know. He'd whip a slave just for the sport of making him scream and bleed."

Her eyes slid shut at the thought.

"When I was a strapping young fellow, Master Dean gave me permission to jump the broom with my sweetheart." His eyes misted. "That was a happy day. One of the few happy days I remember from that time."

"What was her name?"

"Anna. Prettiest little thing I ever laid eyes on. When Providence seen fit to give us a baby girl, I near burst my buttons with pride."

Keziah sensed a coming doom and tried to brace herself. "I had no idea."

He dropped his head and brushed under his nose to hide the telltale signs of emotion. "One day, Master comes down to slave row, screaming and hollering, saying one of the slaves been stealing eggs from his chicken coops. For some reason, he seemed to think it was me or two other field hands. None of us confessed, even after he'd whipped us to a bloody pulp, so for vengeance, he sold off our wives and children."

She gasped, pressing her hands to her mouth. "Oh, Hiriam, no."

With a balled fist, he swiped away the moisture running down his cheek. "Never did see my Anna or my little girl after that."

Her eyes stung and her throat ached. "A fate more cruel I cannot imagine."

Gathering himself, he lifted his face. "Master Dean died not long after, and his overseer had to sell off some of the slaves to pay Master's debts. Took me all the way to the Lumpkin's Alley auction block in Richmond. I thank God Almighty Master Montgomery bought me that day."

He took a faltering step closer, gazing at her with tenderness. "Your father—he's shown me kindness. Decency. Even though I'm his slave, he treats me like a human, not an animal. He never once laid a hand on me or even threatened to. He's a good man. And what's more—" Hiriam smiled—"he has a special daughter who makes me feel like my own isn't so far away."

Her chin trembled. Tears left warm trails down her skin.

"Those days after my Anna and daughter was taken from me, they was hard. Hardest I ever seen, but the Almighty walked me through. Some of them abolitionist folks say I'm trapped in a system of property and ownership. I guess to their way of thinking I am, but the way I figure it is this: where man sees limitation, the Almighty gave me a kind family to serve and a sweet girl to watch grow up. You have a way about you that makes folks feel special. Seeking me out and asking so many questions when you was but a wee thing—" he chuckled—"made me feel like your grandpappy. You brought love into my life again."

Hiriam patted Keziah's head like he used to when she was little, his calloused hand smoothing her hair. "What you're doing is a good thing. A brave and noble thing. I just don't want to see you or your family hurt. I'll do whatever you tell me to do, but I want no part of the scheming or the knowing."

Her heart leapt. A slow smile spread across her lips. "Thank you, Hiriam. May Providence bless you."

He laughed softly through his crooked teeth. "He already has. You tell me whenever you want a ride and I'll be at your service."

He started to turn away to put up the shovel when her gentle question brought him back around. "Do you think you'll ever see Anna or your daughter again?"

His shoulders drooped, though the smile never faded. "No, I reckon not. Not on this side of eternity, leastwise. Someday, though. In glory."

Nodding slowly, Keziah left him to his work, her heart thrumming with heavy sadness at all he'd endured. Before she could take ten steps, she spun back. "What was your daughter's name?"

With a long look over his shoulder, he murmured, "Her name was Ruby."

Ruby. A jewel. Keziah's eyes smarted as she walked away.

Perhaps, if God blessed her with a daughter someday, she would name her Ruby.

Keziah eyed the market vendors clogging the roadway and grimaced.

Winter's chill had dissolved into sticky Southern humidity. Although not overly warm in the open, the press of people crowding around the peddled goods was stifling. The normal boxes of thread and ribbon, soaps and creams were present and proudly displayed on peddlers' stands, but the lack of foodstuffs like coffee, sugar, cornmeal, and smoked meats was noticeable. Worse yet, where barrels of sorghum and flour once stood, a display case filled with odd jewelry beckoned curious onlookers. Pushing through the chattering shoppers, Keziah pressed close to inspect the unusual trinkets. Upon identifying the goods, she shuddered.

There on the table were necklaces made of teeth and goblets made of skulls. The hawker behind the stand contorted his whiskered face into a gruesome grin. "Miss, might you be interested in my secesh goods?"

Tasting bile, she hazarded a question. "What are secesh goods?"

He fingered his suspenders with a lazy air and raised bushy brows. "Jewelry, bowls, and trinkets made from Yankee traitors and soldiers. Would you like to look at any item in particular?"

She shook her head and turned away from the morbid display before she became ill. The man's strident voice called out, begging her to return. "If you have no currency, many merchants are accepting sewing pins in lieu of coinage."

Sewing pins as currency, indeed. Money was scarce and food was growing scarcer still.

Already she'd witnessed signs of the crushing press of Northern blockades. Ready-made boots were disappearing, replaced with the makeshift fashion of palmetto and raccoon-skin shoes. The newspaper carried reports of Atlanta jewelers setting breast pins with coffee beans instead of diamonds.

The unsavory aroma of dry goods, unwashed bodies, and cheap chicory made her yearn to flee the market, but determination kept her in place. She couldn't leave, not until she checked for Micah's message.

The hastily scrawled note she'd received at the post office gave few details, only to meet at the market road near Liberty Square and await his arrival. *I will find you and relay instructions.*

She twisted the strings of her beaded reticule and squelched a sigh of irritation as a hawker bellowed nearby.

As she searched the crowds for Micah, she startled when his low voice murmured near her ear.

"Good afternoon."

Jumping, she turned to him with a soft gasp. His faint laugh lines creased ever so slightly, and she felt her pulse leap in response.

*You're betrothed to another.*

She masked her pleasure at seeing him, stiffening as he cupped her elbow and maneuvered her to a quieter corner.

"We do not have long. Everything is set for tomorrow."

She sucked in a breath. "Tomorrow."

With a curt nod, he shoved his hands in his pockets and looked over the crowd in a disinterested manner, but he did not fool her. He was alert to every sign, every sound, every face.

"When?"

"Early afternoon. Whenever you send Hiriam, I'll be ready." His eyes narrowed, making her feel undone somehow. Exposed. "Are you sure you're ready for this?"

"I'm ready."

After a long, inscrutable look, his gaze flickered back to the teeming street. "And does your intended know of your . . . shall we say, nocturnal pursuits?"

Her breath froze. Staring at him, she felt robbed of speech when his eyes aligned with hers. For a moment, she witnessed a spark of something in his expression. Something stark. Pain? Yearning? In a flash it was gone, replaced with a cold shutter that seemed utterly incompatible with the man she knew him to be.

"You know, then?"

She watched a muscle twitch in his jaw. "I know." His voice was clipped. "Let me be the first to congratulate you and Mr. Hill on your upcoming nuptials."

"Let me explain."

"No need. I'm sure your father had his reasons." He looked away and muttered, "Don't forget. Early afternoon. Tomorrow."

And then he was gone, stepping quickly into the crowd that obscured him from her view.

Cold water could not have doused her spirits more than his brisk, formal demeanor. Her breath was shaky as she turned away from the market and set her face toward home.

He was angry and rightfully so. She should have told him. Unless he was upset for an altogether different reason.

Perhaps he cared for her more deeply than she'd thought possible.

Forcing back burning tears, she walked as quickly as she dared toward home. It made no difference. Father had laid Mother's well-being and his dying wishes at her feet, daring her to refuse him. Her own feelings and dreams did not figure into the equation.

And they never had.

Micah arrived at his childhood home, his mood dark. He knew he'd hurt Kizzie with his curt, clipped words, but he saw no way around it. He must sever any sweetness or affection now. She was betrothed to Lyman Hill and would be his wife in less than a fortnight.

His wife.

Bitterness coated his tongue as he trudged up the steps of the two-story brick home. Mother kept it so well-maintained and welcoming. Ivy climbed along the trellis framing the gate. Happy spring flowers lined the stone walkway. Though in a more modest part of Savannah than the Montgomery property, he'd always been proud of his family's home.

He'd neglected his mother since returning to Savannah most recently, but she rarely complained, greeting him with open arms whenever he dropped in. He must see her before he transported Polly around the military lines to the next safe stop north. If something went amiss, he'd regret not saying he loved her one last time.

He knocked and waited, pinching the bridge of his nose with his fingers. She deserved better. A son who looked after her, not one traveling all over the country, leaving her to fend for herself in her widowhood.

The door swung open to reveal Hattie's familiar face. He'd known the elderly servant since he was a boy, only this time, her mouth drooped down instead of the wide smile he was accustomed to.

"Master Micah, praise the Lord! I been praying we would find a way to get ahold of you. Lo and behold, here you are on this very doorstep." She pressed her veined hands to her lips. A sob escaped. "Thank you, Lord."

He placed a comforting hand on her shoulder. "Hattie, what's wrong?"

"It's your mother. She collapsed yesterday. Ain't risen from her bed. Only sleeping. The doctor . . . he don't know what to think. I've been so worried, and with me not knowing how to find you . . ."

He tugged the distraught servant close and let her cry on his shoulder, his own heart sinking like lead.

"May I see her?"

Hattie stepped away and wiped her eyes. "Of course. Come."

He followed her through the foyer, past the parlor, and up the stairs to Mother's bedroom. After all these years, his father's presence still loomed large. Close, yet absent. Missed. Always missed.

Hattie pushed the door open with a soft creak and went

to the far side of the bed, giving him room to approach his mother as she lay so still in the too-large mound of blankets and pillows. Her dark hair, with its threads of silver, flowed loose over her shoulders. Her skin was as pale as the white nightdress she wore. Were it not for the gentle rise and fall of her chest, he would have thought her departed.

Throat clamping shut, he moved to her side and grasped her slender, limp hand. "Mother, it's me. Micah. I've come to see you."

No movement. No flutter of the eyelids. Only breath. In. Out.

He blinked back the moisture collecting in his eyes. "Hattie, were you with her when she collapsed?"

"No, sir. I was downstairs, preparing the midday meal. I had just come in here to tell her it was ready only to find her lying on the floor." She sniffed, her chin quivering. "Poor lamb."

He slid open one of her eyelids, then the other, watching for her pupils to contract. "What did the physician say?"

"He thinks it could be anything from apoplexy to bleeding in the brain." She clucked her tongue and smoothed the blankets around Mother's shoulders. "I maybe wonder if it had something to do with that journal she was holding."

He turned to her with a start. "What journal?"

Hattie's eyes widened and she retrieved a small leather book from the bedside table. "When I found her, the bottom bureau drawer was pulled out and this was clutched in her hand. I don't know what it says, but . . ."

She held it out and he grasped it, his hands clammy. Unease crawled through him. "Thank you, Hattie."

She nodded. "I'll leave you alone with her for a few minutes. If you need anything, just call."

He barely noticed her soft steps or the rustle of her skirt as she slipped from the room. Without delay, he opened the journal and drew a quick breath. Father's bold penmanship greeted him. Had she been reading it when she succumbed to some horrid malady?

He ought not intrude on Father's privacy. His most personal thoughts were etched on the pages. Still, a strange foreboding pressed in on him, like a hot iron burning its mark.

Scanning the contents, he felt the disquiet in his soul rise into a tumult. The book fell from his fingers. He lifted his eyes to watch Mother's lifeless form on the bed. Numb. Empty. Was that what discovering the truth about her husband—and her son—had done to her? Struck her with such vehement force she was rendered incapable of function?

With a moan, he dropped his head in his hands. Why hadn't Father told her before? Why write her a note, praying she might find it upon his demise, leaving Micah to watch the flotsam and wreckage the truth left behind?

And if a mother's love was not strong enough to embrace him and his shattered existence, what hope was there for him?

# CHAPTER 21

FROM HER CROUCHED POSITION in the confines of the enclosed carriage, Keziah's pulse thrummed heavily in her ears. This was it. The start of Polly's journey to freedom, provided all went as it should.

The floor of the carriage bounced beneath her, pounding her poor knees until she feared they were bruised. The vehicle hit a rather sharp dip, and she winced when the back of her head banged against the underside of the carriage seat. Her breaths came in shallow pants from behind the thick curtain covering her hiding place beneath the seat.

She heard Hiriam's low "Whoa" just before the carriage tilted to a gentle stop. In moments, a woman's light footsteps approached the carriage. The door opened and the conveyance dipped, settling the woman's weight inside.

The door creaked shut. Hiriam shifted in the driver's seat, making the carriage sway, before the soft snap of the reins set them back in motion.

Peeking from between the cracks of the curtain, Keziah looked up to see Polly's face pinched in distress, her lips bloodless.

Keziah couldn't repress a gentle groan as she pushed aside the cover and unfolded herself from the cramped space. Polly's eyes widened but as promised, she uttered not a word. Keziah winced at the pain shooting down her limbs, but she laid aside her discomfort as she slipped into her seat and offered a smile.

She mouthed, "Are you ready?"

Polly nodded, though the furrow between her brows only deepened as she twisted her fingers so tightly they resembled wet sheets pulled from a washtub. Her apprehension was palpable.

With a calming hand over the woman's cold fingers, Keziah looked into her eyes and willed her all the courage she could muster. Polly stilled.

Despite the danger of speaking, Keziah lowered her head while clasping Polly's trembling fingers and murmured a prayer. "Father, I ask you to guide Polly to safety, health, and peace. Be the light to her path. Give safety to those who will be aiding her. Amen."

The clip-clop of horse hooves slowed as the carriage

pulled to a stop. Time to switch places. Giving the slave one last smile, Keziah took a deep breath and eased the carriage door open, her face down, nestled in the shade of her wide-brimmed bonnet. With a hasty step, she scurried to the back entrance of her home and managed to slip into her room undetected.

She shed the replica of Polly's bonnet and pressed a hand to her quivering stomach. Soon she would need to compose a note to Mrs. Ward, inquiring of Polly's whereabouts. The first step of the plan was complete. The greatest danger still awaited.

*Please, Lord, keep Polly, Hiriam, and Micah safe.*

⁓❧⁓

Mother paced in front of the lacy-curtained windows, her brows knit. Keziah took another sip of her lavender-infused tea, praying the dwindling luxury would calm her tattered nerves.

Upon receiving the concerned message from Keziah, Mrs. Ward had flown into a frenzy, demanding Hiriam, as well as her own staff, scour the town for the wayward slave.

The search had turned up nothing, and twilight was quickly approaching.

Mother pressed fingers to her temple and rubbed her head. "And she said nothing to you, dear?"

Shaking her head, Keziah replaced the cup in its saucer and set it aside. "No, nothing. She told me she would go to Landry's to purchase the thread needed to alter my wedding gown. With Elizabeth seeing to both Father's needs and all the other household tasks, Polly seemed more than willing to lend her assistance." She blinked, trying her best to look stunned. "I never imagined she wouldn't return."

Across the parlor, her cousin sipped the tea. "You had no idea the slave would run away?"

Keziah frowned. "How do we know she's run away? What if she's fallen ill or has been mistreated or taken by someone?"

Jennie harrumphed. "Don't be naive, Keziah dear. In my opinion, these slaves are all alike. The Yankees have put any number of ideas in their heads about equality." Arching a brow, she muttered, "You best watch your own slaves or they'll be running too."

Mother waved a hand. "Elizabeth and Hiriam would never dream of doing such."

"I hear Mrs. Ward thought the same of Polly."

Mother eased down into the upholstered chair of pink-and-cream brocade. "True. Poor Nannette." Sniffing, she pressed a dainty handkerchief to her nose. "The distraught woman is beside herself with grief."

Keziah picked up her tea once more, if for nothing else but to give her hands something to do. She doubted Mrs. Ward was mourning Polly's disappearance so much as bemoaning the loss of her worker. And Mr. Ward . . . Keziah shuddered to think of the man's vile treatment of the slave.

With a deep sigh, Mother stood, her black bombazine swishing lightly. "I will not tell your father of this development. It would only distress him. Say nothing to him about this travesty, Keziah. Besides, we have enough to concern him, with your wedding a week away."

"Yes, ma'am."

Mother took the tray filled with his dinner from Elizabeth's waiting hands. "I'll carry this to Mr. Montgomery, Elizabeth. He'll suspect something is amiss if I dally any longer."

Mere moments after Mother swept from the room and up the stairs, the solemn ticking of the grandfather clock in the hallway was interrupted by her faint cry of alarm, followed by the shattering of dishes.

Keziah discarded her refreshment and lifted the hem of her skirt as she fled the parlor and rushed into her parents' bedchamber. Broken dishes and spilled soup lay strewn across the floor. Mother was doubled over, weeping into her hands.

Breath snagging, Keziah flicked her gaze to Father. His vacant expression told her all she needed to know.

Benjamin Montgomery was dead.

MARCH 9, 1862

"'For this corruptible must put on incorruption, and this mortal must put on immortality. So when this corruptible shall have put on incorruption, and this mortal shall have put on immortality, then shall be brought to pass the saying that is written, Death is swallowed up in victory.'"

Reverend Moseley's voice buzzed in Keziah's ears, but she scarcely took in what he said from the grassy knoll of the cemetery. Within the wrought-iron fence surrounding the burial ground, mourners clogged the old site, standing precariously between worn headstones jutting from the ground and fresh mounds of dirt spaced throughout the area. Pink wisteria tangled through the limbs of large willows overhead, its sweet scent carrying through the spring air.

The faces blurred. Keziah saw little, save the image of Father's ashen face staring at her blankly just after he'd passed. Mother's sniffle into her tatted lace jerked Keziah back to the present.

"'O death, where is thy sting? O grave, where is thy victory? The sting of death is sin; and the strength of sin is the law. But thanks be to God, which giveth us the victory through our Lord Jesus Christ.'"

Thumping his Bible shut, Reverend Moseley nodded toward the crowd of mourners, his pinched face dour. "May God Almighty bless the memory of Benjamin Charles Montgomery."

At Mother's whimper, Keziah slid an arm around her waist and gave a gentle squeeze. Poor Mother. The stoic, proper lady had been through much in only a matter of weeks. First the loss of her son and now her husband.

Lyman Hill's low grunt to her left caught her off guard. She had forgotten he stood at her side. In truth, she didn't even want him there. His stiff countenance and stern expression were a stark reminder of the future that awaited her.

As the black-clad mourners moved to Mother to offer their sympathies, Mr. Hill took her elbow, steering her away from the crowd.

Looking up into his steely eyes, she murmured, "Yes?"

He released his grip and shoved his hands behind his back. "I'm sorry again for your loss, my dear. Your father was a wise, discerning man."

She dropped her gaze to the ground, emotions swirling like a whirling dervish. Her relationship with Father had been complicated. She was in awe of the authority he wielded and his sharp business mind but had always cowered under his domineering ways. She knew he had cared for her in his own way, yet she had never felt his affection. That fact, perhaps, was what she was truly mourning with his abrupt passing.

Instead of voicing her turbulent thoughts, she whispered, "Thank you."

"I trust you've reiterated to Mrs. Montgomery that I will be caring for her needs upon our union."

The odd question rankled, combined with the impropriety of his businesslike approach at such a moment. Frowning, she searched the hard lines of his face. "I'm sure she knows. After all, our nuptials were Father's dying wish." Uttering the words out loud left a sour taste in her mouth.

"I pray this unfortunate turn of events does not delay our marriage."

She blinked. In the shock of Father's passing, she'd failed to consider the changes it might bring. *He's concerned about mourning rituals.*

Feeling as if she'd been granted a stay of execution, she fought the rush of relief that bubbled inside her chest. For once, society's ironclad rules of decorum would grant her a measure of freedom.

With feigned innocence, she offered a tight smile. "The marriage shall take place as Father wished. Although, of course, we must delay it until after the mourning period has passed."

A flicker of annoyance sparked in his eyes. "I would rather not. The country is at war. Half the nation is in mourning and will be for quite some time."

"All the more reason to wait. To marry before a full year has passed would be disrespectful to Father's memory. We had only laid aside the mourning time for Nathaniel because of Father's desire to see us married, but with his passing, the need to rush is gone. I'm sure Mother would agree we mustn't marry in haste and bring dishonor to him."

Frown lines deepened around his mouth, and his displeasure was palpable. Instead of cowering, she straightened and pressed her lips together. A reprieve, however temporary, had been granted, and she would not relinquish it.

Just as he opened his mouth to respond, Jennie's quiet call allowed her to turn away from his dark glare.

"Keziah, Auntie Elsie is longing to sit and gather her bearings. She is requesting you act on her behalf to greet those who want to pay their respects and offer condolences."

Another reprieve. "Of course. Thank you for seeing to her needs."

She watched her normally vivacious cousin move with subdued quiet as she lent Mother a steadying arm. The sight of Mother's black-draped form bent over with grief pricked Keziah's heart.

If she refused to marry Lyman Hill, what would become of Mother? She would be as lost as a piece of flotsam on an ocean current. Elsie Montgomery had never lived without a man's guidance. For all of Father's blustery ways, Keziah had never realized how deeply Mother relied on his decisive nature. He was her security, and now she had no mooring. The past two days had been especially trying. The smallest decisions had sent Mother into hysterics.

The noose of responsibility tightened around Keziah's throat. No matter the reprieve provided by mourning, she would eventually have to face her duty.

Heavyhearted, she trudged her way through the cemetery to where a handful of men and women waited to offer their sympathies. Despite his aggressive personality, Benjamin Montgomery had been considered an astute businessman and a pillar of the community.

After thanking an older couple for their kind words, she glanced up and startled to see Micah standing not ten feet away, his blue eyes staring oceans into hers.

He studied her so intently, she began to feel a telltale flush staining her cheeks. What was he thinking? He'd seemed so different upon their last encounter. Unbidden, the memory of his kisses, his touch, surged through her, choking out her breath. Heat bloomed up the back of her neck as she dropped her gaze from his stare.

In three strides, he stood before her, fingering the brim of his hat as if uncertain what to say. He swallowed and spoke, his voice tender. "Kizzie, I'm so sorry to hear of your father's passing."

An undefined emotion stung the backs of her eyes, and she could do little more than nod and murmur, "Thank you."

"Is there anything I can do?"

A thousand things skipped through her mind, but she gave none of them voice. "I—no. Thank you, though."

He scanned the cemetery as a gentle breeze ruffled the long, feathery limbs of the willows overhead before he searched her face once more. "I wanted you to know that the medical aid you requested for your friend was met with success."

Relief unfurled through her. "Praise Providence." One bright burst of joy against a canvas of gloom. She studied the planes of his face, the handsome features, eyes bright as the summer sky . . . even the dark stubble covering his jaw. She longed to etch the lines and hues of his face into her memory.

He dropped his gaze to the ground, mouth moving, searching for words. "I wasn't sure if you'd heard, what with your own sorrow, but my mother passed yesterday."

Gasping, she lifted her hand to her lips, heart aching for him. Unable to resist, she placed her fingers upon his sleeve. "I had not heard. I'm so terribly sorry. I liked your mother very much. Such a kind woman."

He looked up then, skimming her face, a soft smile playing around his lips. "She liked you as well. I believe when we were younger, she called you 'that sweet little Montgomery beauty.'"

"I take it her death was sudden?"

He hesitated a moment. "Yes, mostly. She grew ill just before I left, and although I hired a nurse to care for her during my absence, she passed away not long after."

"I wish there were something I could do."

Warmth spilled through her as he placed his hand over hers. "Kizzie, I—" he dropped his voice to a hoarse whisper—"I'm leaving Savannah. For good."

Micah? Her dear friend and confidant, abandoning the town? Their work? Her?

He stiffened. "New opportunities await, just as they do for you. You'll be married soon, after all."

She longed to protest. Yet what could she possibly say? She was trapped, a pawn in the hands of Lyman Hill and her father's legacy.

"Micah, I—" Her tongue stalled, a thick sadness expelling the air from her chest. "Thank you . . . for everything."

He made as if to say something else, but after a long moment he pressed his lips shut and gave a small smile instead. His low whisper teased her senses. "You are a treasure, Kizzie Montgomery. Never let anyone tell you differently."

Before she could breathe, he grasped her fingers between his and lifted her hand to his lips. Her pulse skittered as his warm breath caressed her skin. Pressing a gentle kiss to her hand, he released her. "God go with you."

Her heart hammered as she watched him walk swiftly away, his form growing smaller moment by moment. She longed to call his name again, to see his roguish smile, to study the humor and intelligence that often danced in his expression.

Instead she stayed silent, knowing that prolonging their farewell would only prolong the pain. He was lost to her.

Sensing the weight of eyes upon her, Keziah turned to see Jennie studying her with barely veiled suspicion. The cold emotion reached across the space between them, wrapping its tentacles around her heart. Though she pulled her gaze away from her cousin's, she couldn't shake a quiver of unrest more intrusive than a heavy cloak settling over her shoulders.

Even after she returned home, the odd sensation refused to leave her be.

---

MARCH 22, 1862

Micah scanned the bold script of the telegram as he walked from the telegraph office, his thoughts jumbled.

The Relief Commission had found him a new assignment—traveling alongside the Union army to treat their wounded and ill. If he thought military prison was bad, it would no doubt seem pristine compared to treating those maimed and dying in the heat of battle. He had only a few days to settle his mother's affairs, and then he would leave to report to headquarters in Washington, DC, with no plans to return to Savannah.

Shoving the telegram into his pocket, he frowned and skirted the crowded street. Though the task would be difficult, he would welcome the change. Perhaps the hectic schedule of war, the exhaustion, would blot out the maddening memories of Kizzie—the taste of her lips, her gentle laughter, her strength and compassion.

He growled under his breath, then exhaled sharply. Perhaps the gruesome horrors of war would make him stop wondering how she fared. Perhaps he could stop tormenting himself with thoughts of her pledging her life to Lyman Hill. Perhaps he could forget the memories they'd shared. The dreams and comfort that tied them together.

Perhaps. But he feared even the nightmares sure to follow him would not erase Kizzie from his mind. Or his heart.

What of Ma Linnie or the fugitives he treated? What would become of them when he left?

Pushing away the bleak thought, he slowed and sniffed. The distinct scent of briny salt water wafted around him, tainting the air. He frowned as he glanced around the bustling thoroughfare. The scents of the bay usually could not be found this far inside the city. The wind was not up. Odd.

He crossed the square, continuing on his way, and moved with steady steps toward Mother's home. The closer he came, the more the crowds thinned. The perfume of daffodils hung heavy in the spring air . . . until the sharp odor of dead fish assaulted him again.

As he rounded the corner, the hair on the back of his neck stood on end. He stopped abruptly. Something was wrong. The thick croak of an Irish brogue sounded from behind him.

"That's him."

Spinning, Micah came face-to-face with a straggly

fisherman staring him down with a jaundiced eye. From the shadows of a hotel, three more burly men crept out of their hiding places, each of them approaching with venomous intent.

Micah's heart thudded as he turned slowly, meeting each one of their hostile glares with a steely one of his own. "Gentlemen, may I assist you?"

One of the largest men, with graying-blond hair and a slight paunch, narrowed his eyes. "Dr. Greyson?"

"I am he."

"You're under arrest for aiding a fugitive slave."

Before he could utter a word, a meaty fist slammed into his mouth. The metallic taste of blood coated his teeth as his head snapped to the side. The world spun.

Hissing through the throbbing ache, he sucked in a deep breath and tried to straighten. But pain exploded in the back of his skull just before the light was snuffed out.

# CHAPTER 22

Elizabeth sighed as she stirred the bubbling black water
with a wooden paddle, churning up billows of steam from
the large cauldron outside. A fire blazed underneath the wash
pot as Hiriam approached with an armful of wood weighting
his stooped shoulders.

"Can't believe there's not a merchant dyer what can do
this," she groused.

Keziah shook out another of Mother's day dresses, preparing them for the sharp thrust of Elizabeth's dye paddle. The
servant was being forced to dye all of Mother's dresses for her
period of deep mourning, as well as the rest of the clothes in
the house.

Keziah tried to keep her voice chipper. "At least Mother's will be done soon. There are only two more of her dresses to dye. And you know how busy the merchant dyers are. Half the country is steeped in mourning."

Pushing back a damp tendril of hair, the house servant frowned. "Humph! That's why we need more dyers in Savannah . . . to save the rest of us folks from the foul stench."

Keziah couldn't disagree on that point. The pungent steam rising from the bubbling pot of inky fabrics was not pleasant—almost offensive in the sticky oppression of humidity. Their only consolation was that with the shortage of available merchant dyers, most of Savannah smelled of dye pots. Their neighbors likely never noticed. Still, her eyes and nose stung from the sickly stench.

Hiriam dropped the remaining wood at Elizabeth's feet with a clunk. "You need some more, or will this finish the job?"

Not even sparing him a glance, Elizabeth wiped the beads of moisture from her forehead with the back of her hand and stirred the dye water again. "This should finish it. I don't plan on dillydallying with this job. Uh-uh. I'm ready for those last two dresses, Miss Keziah."

Dropping the remaining garments into the steaming tub, Keziah dabbed the sweat collecting above her lip. "At least we've been spared the task of dyeing Mother's fans, gloves, and handkerchiefs black as well. Dooley's had plenty of mourning accessories ready-made. Even a plenteous amount of black-banded writing stationery."

"As they should. With the war raging, no end in sight, the two things every family seems to need is food and mourning clothes." Elizabeth shook her head, the lines around her mouth drooping. "More's the pity. Death is everywhere, seems like."

A wave of sadness crashed over Keziah again, and she could do nothing more than nod. Nathaniel, Father, Micah's mother, friends, cousins, schoolmates, neighbors . . . every family she knew had been dramatically stung by the war's bloody reach.

"Miss Montgomery, I request a moment of your time."

Lyman Hill's hard, commanding voice caused her to whirl in fright. Pressing a hand to her bodice, she released a shaking breath with a light laugh. "You startled me. I wasn't aware you'd come to call."

His perpetual glare only deepened. Dread curdled within her.

"I'm currently in the middle of helping Elizabeth prepare Mother's clothes for mourning. Can our discussion take place here?"

A muscle twitched near his eye. "It cannot."

Her stomach clenched.

Elizabeth muttered under her breath, "Best go on, Miss Keziah. I can finish."

Keziah swallowed at the servant's look of fear and wiped her hands on her apron before unknotting it and casting it off with trembling fingers. Before she could say anything further, Mr. Hill turned on his heel and marched toward the house.

She followed his terse steps, her mind racing. Had he discovered her work with the fugitives? She mentally retraced every nuance of her last excursion, desperate to know how he'd uncovered her deepest secret. Surely he must know. There could be no other explanation for his ire.

As she trailed after him into Father's library, she smoothed her palms down the folds of her black balzarine skirt, unsure what to do or say. What words could she possibly utter in her own defense? She took in Mr. Hill's cold glare from across the musty room and decided to remain silent. Let him say what he would.

The silver hair at his temples caught the light streaming through the window and winked. If only his disposition were as comely.

"You have not been honest with me, Miss Montgomery."

Her heart squeezed but she held her peace, her heartbeat thready.

"Here we are, betrothed to one another, and I discover you are not who I believed you to be."

Warmth crawled up her collar, braising her cheeks until they felt aflame. He came close and she instinctively took a halting step back.

"How long has this been going on? How long have you harbored feelings for him?"

Uncertainty buzzed through her mind, and she could do little more than blink. What was he rambling about? "Pardon?"

His gray eyes narrowed. "I saw you. All the mourners for your departed father witnessed the scandal as well."

He didn't suspect her of aiding runaways? Her thoughts felt foggy and dull. "I have no idea of what you speak."

Straightening, he assessed her with a suspicious eye. "Surely you know. The shame you thrust upon me seemed obvious to everyone else."

She was becoming weary of his obscure accusations. "I'm sorry, but I have no inkling what has perturbed you so."

"Really?" He tilted his head to the side, studied her as if she were a pesky puppy. "It never once struck you as inappropriate when that man kissed your hand at the cemetery?"

Awareness dawned. Mr. Hill truly had no knowledge of her abolition work. He'd seen Micah's tender good-bye in the cemetery and had assumed the worst. She breathed a sigh of relief as her galloping pulse slowed.

"You mean M—Dr. Greyson? I remember a gentlemanly kiss on the hand but nothing more."

He barked a dry laugh, face darkening. "There was more than sympathy in his touch, I'd wager."

"No, that isn't true."

Mr. Hill gave her a condescending look and dropped his voice low. "I witnessed the expression on his face when he touched your hand. I saw the unspoken language in his body when he released you. He's in love with you."

She nearly staggered backward, her heart a tumbling riot. Micah was in love with her?

"My only question is whether you return his affections."

Her breath thinned. "This accusation, it—it comes as quite a shock. Dr. Greyson has been a dear friend since my youth." She shook her head. "You must be mistaken. Why, he even told me he was preparing to leave Savannah permanently."

He scowled. "And go where?"

She lifted her hands. "I have no idea."

"So you and this 'old friend' of yours—" he spoke through gritted teeth—"have no romantic overtures toward each other?"

Memories of Micah's hungry kiss filled her mind, but she forced out a lie. "None." With a start, she realized it indeed *was* a lie. Her feelings for Micah ran deep, far deeper than she'd dare admit.

But to delve into such vain wishes would only make reality harder to bear. Sweet dreams of a life with him would merely serve to make her future seem more bitter and empty than it already promised to be. Besides, he'd never confessed his love for her. The kiss was nothing more than a mistake—Micah had said as much. Mr. Hill must be confused.

At her answer, Mr. Hill's shoulders visibly relaxed. "I admit relief. It's just as well anyway. I asked your cousin about the fellow. She said he comes from a traitorous family. His father was a close companion of John Brown's. Abolitionist trash."

The urge to defend Micah flashed hot and strong, but Keziah clamped her lips shut. She would only worsen matters. And why was Mr. Hill plying Jennie for information? The sickly feeling of dread crept over her once more.

"Nevertheless—" he clasped his hands behind his back, looking like the captain of a seafaring vessel instead of a stubborn man of means—"I want your assurances that you harbor no feelings toward this fellow, and I expect you to behave with better decorum from here forward. Otherwise I shall be forced to reconsider my generous offer of marriage."

His patronizing tone rankled, and she longed to bite back with a caustic remark. What would that feel like, to finally stand up and speak her mind? Would it be a rush of blessed relief or a regrettable moment of shame?

The old fear clawed at her throat. *Keep silent. Mother is counting on you. You can't fail her.*

The bonds of duty choked her, their grip tighter and more suffocating than before.

Hating every word slipping past her lips, she murmured, "I shall endeavor not to shame you. Forgive me."

Micah's head throbbed as rough hands shoved him into the small jail cell, throwing his battered body against the unforgiving wall. Groaning, he managed to see through puffy eyes as his sneering attackers slammed the bars of his cell door shut with their dirt-encrusted fingers.

A large man with jagged yellow teeth and greasy hair grinned, leering at Micah. "Rest up, Doc. Traitors like you need to be at their best when they face trial. Not that it'll matter too much when you're swinging from the end of a rope."

With a slew of profanities, the odious man laughed and walked away, his gravelly mirth fading, leaving Micah alone in the cold cell.

He scanned his surroundings, fighting to stay upright against the searing misery in his ribs and the dull pounding in his skull. The cell couldn't have been more than ten by twelve feet. A single window high on the wall let in precious little light, covered as it was by thick bars and streaks of grime. The room boasted a lumpy iron cot and a broken chair that sagged next to a splintered table in the corner. A chamber pot was shoved under the cot.

Injured in body and spirit, Micah sank into the putrid mattress and dropped his head in his hands. He winced as his fingers roved through his hair, brushing against swollen knots of misery and crusted blobs of blood dotting his scalp. Sucking in a deep breath, he cringed when the pain in his side slashed like fire. Broken ribs most likely.

The ruffians, with the sheriff's snide approval, had beaten and kicked him to a pulp. At some point, Micah had passed out, waking only when they half dragged him into the jail carriage, their murderous insults stabbing his clouded senses back to life.

He must be inside the jail on Wright Square. Pain blurred his thoughts, but one thing he knew: just beyond the jail was the infamous hanging square.

His hopes for escaping the dreaded fate evaporated, his heart crushing with fear for those he worked with and loved. Had his failings compromised them?

*Father, please keep all those you've entrusted to me safe. Especially protect Kizzie and Ma Linnie. Don't let them suffer because of me. Please . . .*

———◦⊛◦———

APRIL 4, 1862

Keziah stared at the clock over the fireplace in her parents' bedchamber, its spindly hands frozen in time.

Upon Father's death, Elizabeth, ever superstitious, had stopped the clock to ensure the family would not be cursed with bad luck. Weeks had passed, and yet the clock remained fixed in place.

Picking up the ornate piece of machinery, she turned the hands to the correct time and began the tedious process of winding it into motion again. The gentle clicks and whirring grated her nerves.

If only time would stop and freeze the horrors of war. Stop long enough to let them grieve their losses without marching on, scrambling to catch their breath. Stop its dreaded ticking that counted down her year of mourning until she would be wed.

She replaced the now-functioning clock with a gentle thud and turned. Mother was finally emerging from the recesses of her gloom, spending less time in solitary weeping. Even now she was in the parlor taking tea. Perhaps she could coax Mother out into the spring sunshine later. It would do Keziah good as well. With her middle-of-the-night conducting excursions becoming more frequent of late, the ominous signs of fatigue signaled that another spell of illness might befall her soon.

She could not afford any more convulsions while transporting passengers through the streets of Savannah. It had already happened once. Once was one time too many when lives hung in the balance.

Her stomach ached as she descended the stairs, her cousin's animated chatter drifting from the parlor.

"It seems like traitors are all around us, Auntie. Only last week one of Savannah's most elite newspaper editors was arrested for passing military information to Union troops."

Wincing, Keziah prayed Jennie would not plunge Mother's fragile spirits into further melancholy with her talk of war.

She entered the parlor, and Mother's eyes latched on to hers with a grateful wisp of a smile. "There she is, Jennie. Now our tea is complete."

Jennie sipped daintily from her delicate rose-trimmed cup. "I was just catching Auntie up on all the latest gossip."

Keziah seated herself on the settee and reached for the last cup, avoiding Jennie's gaze. Her cousin's brash ways and glib tongue were beginning to wear her thin. "Nothing too dismal, I pray."

Jennie tittered. "In the middle of war? Nothing but, I'm afraid." Nibbling on the edge of a tea biscuit, she shook her glossy red head as if ashamed of the state of the world, but Keziah knew she thrilled to every dramatic detail. "Thanks to the Vigilance Committee, traitors to our Confederacy are being turned over faster than Stonewall Jackson can cut down a blue wool coat."

"I suppose I've not heard all the fracas then, but I would prefer Mother not be bombarded with discouraging news."

Mother sighed, her face more drawn and weary than Keziah had ever seen it. "You don't need to protect me, darling. In such a time as this, there is little else consuming minds and hearts."

"Quite right." Jennie leaned forward. "It really is scandalous what is going on in our city. Widow Simmons was here only two days ago. She lives near Wright Square, you know. She was telling me how, a couple weeks ago, she watched the sheriff and a passel of men drag an abolitionist into the jail. Poor fellow had been beaten black-and-blue."

"Do tell. Did she know his identity?" Mother asked.

Jennie grunted softly. "She wasn't sure but thought he looked like someone named Greyson. Kept prattling on about how he had gone to Philadelphia for his education."

Keziah almost dropped her cup. Warm tea splashed over the edge. She caught it before it careened to the rug-covered floor.

*Please, God, no . . .*

Mother turned to Keziah, eyes gentle. "You remember him, don't you, dear? He was at the Ballinger house the night you were ill, and then—" she coughed lightly, cheeks blushing—"arrived several days later and argued with your father."

Her heart constricted so hard, it nearly choked her of breath. "I—yes, Mother. I remember."

Jennie sniffed. "Of course, Mrs. Simmons wasn't sure it was him. In the condition that fellow was in, it was likely hard to tell."

Mother frowned. "What are his charges? Did Mrs. Simmons know?"

"No, but if it's Greyson, his father was an abolitionist—so any number of things would make him a suspect of wrongdoing. Especially during this war."

The stays of Keziah's corset felt as if they were shrinking, robbing her of precious air. *Not Micah. Please, God, not Micah.*

With a smirk, Jennie took another sip of tea. "If he's an abolitionist, good riddance, I say. The last thing our city needs, with all the trouble on our doorstep, is Yankee sympathizers roaming the streets and stirring up hornets' nests of havoc."

Mother placed her cup gently in its saucer with a soft clink. "Still, I hate to judge the man unfairly. Just because his father made poor choices does not necessarily speak ill of the son." Her face lined with regret. "I pray he's not guilty of treason. Despite our family's differences, I always found him to be a kind fellow."

Warmth curled around Keziah's heart at Mother's praise of Micah. She had certainly never voiced any in Father's presence.

Jennie frowned. "There's nothing more dangerous than a traitor with a deceptive tongue and a handsome face."

"True, but I still choose to think the best of the man. After all, if found guilty, he'll likely be hanged, and that's a fate I take no delight in, no matter the offense."

Hands trembling, Keziah set her untouched tea back on the silver service platter.

"Darling, are you quite all right?" Mother fretted. "You

look frightful. Pale as rice powder. Are you about to have another of your spells?"

Panic clawed her throat, but she managed to stand on shaking legs. "I—I fear I'm not feeling well. Pardon my leave." She grasped the excuse of her illness like a lifeline. "I'd like to retire to my room, if it's all right. If I do succumb to my illness, I'd prefer to be in the comfort of my own bed."

"Of course, darling. I'll call Hiriam to escort you up the stairs. We want no accidents."

Nodding dumbly, she waited for Mother to find Hiriam and willed the black spots dancing before her eyes to dissipate. She felt Jennie's gaze fix on her as she fled the suffocating parlor and waited for Hiriam in the blessed quiet of the hallway.

She must go to Micah without delay.

# CHAPTER 23

"I DON'T LIKE THIS, MISSY. Not one bit."

Keziah grimaced at the stubborn set of Hiriam's whiskered jaw as he stared at the imposing Chatham County Jail. It had taken two full days of begging before he'd finally relented to drive her, though his acquiescence did not stop him from muttering under his breath the entire carriage ride over.

Now, as she stared up at the imposing towers and fortress-like structure, her courage nearly fled. They had timed their visit for when the rest of the household was occupied. Mother was locked in the library, penning letters to family, and Jennie was abed with a spring cold. Still, Keziah wore an oversize brimmed bonnet to hide her features from curious eyes.

"I wish they would let me accompany you inside."

Though she'd never admit it, she wished Hiriam could escort her as well. She shot a glance toward the stern-faced guard standing watch at the outer door.

The man narrowed his eyes at their conversation. "No Negroes."

She offered Hiriam a reassuring smile, trying to ignore her nerves, and patted him on the arm. "I'll be fine. Wait here. I shan't be long."

Mustering her grit, she walked into the prison. Her insides quivered like jelly.

The surly-faced guard muttered under his breath. "You sure you want to see this traitor?"

She did her utmost to ignore the leers of the prisoners as she walked behind the barrel of a guard, her footfalls echoing loudly in the grimy hallway. The clanging sounds and scraping of chairs against stone floors tangled her nerves in knots. Splotchy black dots of mold clung to the stone walls and coated the rows of bars she passed. And the stench—the acrid odor of urine and unwashed bodies nearly robbed her of breath.

They walked so long, she was dizzy from exertion when the guard paused before a cell near the end of a long hallway. His bark nearly caused her to shriek in alarm.

"Doc! You got company!"

A rustling sounded from the far corner of the cell. The giant of a man nodded curtly. "You got ten minutes. I'll be at the other end of the hallway if you think better of talking to this trash."

As he slunk away, she turned to see Micah staring at her, his mouth slack with wonder. At the sight of his bruised face, she could not repress the cry of horror that escaped her lips.

"Kizzie?" He stared at her as if she were an apparition. "Am I dreaming?"

She rushed to the bars and curled her fingers around their cold grittiness. "No, you're not dreaming. I'm here."

He moved slowly toward her and wrapped his fingers around hers despite the unrelenting iron keeping them apart. She noted his evident exhaustion, the stubble darkening his strong jaw. One of his eyes was circled by fading bruises. Cuts marred his hairline. The telltale signs of a split lip snagged her attention. What had he endured?

"What are you doing here? You can't be seen coming to visit me. It's too dangerous."

She ignored his soft protests. "What happened? Why are you here?"

He dropped his gaze, and a lock of dark hair fell over his brow. She longed to push it back but remained still.

"I don't know. When Sheriff Cole and his posse arrested me, a fisherman was with them. Said something about the Vigilance Committee contacting him. He thinks he saw me ushering Polly onto the boat."

With a groan, she slid her eyes shut. The soft touch of his fingers against her cheek popped her lids open once more. His gentle smile was a tonic to her aching heart.

"Kizzie . . ." His whisper undid her completely, and she leaned into the roving graze of his fingertips. "You must leave. There is nothing I want more than to see you, but you mustn't come again. It's far too dangerous. You cannot taint your name by mingling it with mine."

"Hush." Plucking her courage, she fought the tears that burned as she reached out and cupped his jaw in her hands. She heard his sharp inhale of breath as he relished her willing touch. "Don't deny me this, Micah."

He traced the lines of her face with his eyes. Some kind of invisible thread bound them together, despite the bars separating them. "I mean it. You can't come again."

She smiled wryly. "I'd think you would know me better than that by now."

"I'll not have you hurt because of me. You already play with fire as it is."

She frowned. "Is there not a cause?"

"Of course there is, but I know too well how hot emotions run right now. The memory of my father's convictions has not been forgotten by this town. For years my mother lived in fear, afraid that the vigilantes who opposed John Brown would come after those who believed in his ideals. Father had his share of death threats. That's the reason she sent me away to medical school after his death. Father's reputation is likely what drew the Vigilance Committee's attention in my direction. I'll not see you sacrificed too."

"Stop saying that."

He pushed away from the bars with a huff and ran his fingers through his thick, wavy hair. "You need to forget about me."

"I will not!"

Dropping his head, he muttered, "If you only knew . . ." He rubbed the back of his neck. "If you knew everything about me, you'd understand why things must be the way they are."

"Don't you think I should be the judge of that?" She wanted to shake him, knock some sense into his head. Couldn't he see she loved him?

Her breath froze, her pulse tripping. She loved Micah. She'd never admitted it to herself until now, but she did all the same.

He glowered. "You don't know who I really am."

"I know you're brave and compassionate. You're kind and intelligent. You love God and always think of others before you do yourself."

He stared at her, his body still. She couldn't restrain the current of her feelings as they rushed from her lips.

"You are a man of ideals and conviction. You saw the lonely little girl in school who desperately needed a friend. When all the other children saw a wallflower who was too scared to speak, you saw my need. You see beyond my weaknesses to the heart beating inside."

A warm tear escaped and trailed down her cheek. "I know you, Micah. I know you well. You would rather sacrifice yourself than see an imprisoned slave languish one more day in misery." Her chin trembled. "You give of yourself over and over and over and ask nothing in return. You taught me what it means to live and to love."

He leaned his head against the bars and reached for her, weaving his fingers through her hair and tracing her features with his thumbs. She rested her forehead as close as she could to his. His warm breath fanned her cheek. Their lips were mere inches apart. If either of them were to move . . .

"You don't know my secret, Kizzie. If you did, it would change everything."

She shook her head, tasting the saltiness of tears on her lips. "No, it wouldn't."

He smiled sadly. "Yes, darling, it would." He swallowed, eyes flickering with pain.

"Tell me."

He hesitated only a moment. "I—can't."

"Say it!"

"I'm part Negro."

The revelation hit her like a runaway horse. She gasped and could do little more than blink. "Wh-what?"

His breath hitched. "My grandmother was a slave in Alabama, the product of a hardworking slave woman and—" he frowned—"her lustful owner."

Mind racing, Keziah's gaze flickered over his features, his sky-blue eyes. "You don't look part Negro."

His mouth twisted into a wry smile. "Neither did my father. My grandmother escaped, thanks to the benevolence of conductors, and was able to pass herself off as white. She married a white man and had my father."

"And your mother?"

He shook his head. "Father never told her. Despite her abolitionist sympathies, he feared her Southern heritage was far too ingrained. The knowledge would have scandalized her. He didn't reveal it to me until mere months before his demise." His expression hardened. "I suppose I should say Mother learned of it eventually, but . . ." His stare fixed on some place she could not see.

"What?"

Stark pain clouded his face. "The day she collapsed, she had found one of Father's journals. It contained the truth of his heritage. Of mine. The book was still in her hand when Hattie found her crumpled on the floor."

Her throat cramped.

Micah gripped the bars with white knuckles, his jaw tightening. "My own mother was so horrified by the truth, she suffered an apoplexy and died. What hope could there possibly be that I could ever be accepted by this society . . . or anyone, for that matter?"

Sorrow for the burden he carried overwhelmed her. "No wonder your father was so devoted to the cause."

"Yes. And now you know why I am so passionate about the same." Staring at her as if she were a glossy piece of porcelain he could not touch, he offered a small smile. "Now you know why you must stay away. Society would never accept our union if the truth were to come to light. I couldn't put you through such an ordeal. I won't."

She studied this man, her friend for as long as she could remember. Negro or white, imprisoned or free, it made no difference. Every piece of his history, his life, his struggles made him the man he was.

Clutching his hands through the bars, she started to form a plan.

She whispered, "Hear me well: your heritage and past make no difference to me." A righteous fire began to burn in her middle, fanning out to consume her entire body. "I will fight for you and by your side with all I am, Micah Greyson. And I'll find a way to get you out of this prison or die trying."

# CHAPTER 24

OVER THE NEXT DAY Keziah's mind spun with plans to aid Micah's escape. If she could conduct half-starved fugitives to freedom, conducting a physician from a prison should be no more difficult. And a trip to the First African Baptist Church would set things in motion.

"Rose, I need your help."

The woman looked over her shoulder to ensure she and Keziah were alone inside the church. She motioned quickly. "Come."

Rose led Keziah down the musty stairs and turned to her when they were secure inside the depths of the church's secret tunnel. "You feeling well, miss? What do you need?"

"I'm fine. Listen, next time Smithy Brothers brings a load of passengers, I need you to give him this message."

Thrusting an envelope into her hands, Keziah searched her dark eyes. "Please. It's vitally important."

"Yes'm." Rose tucked the letter into her apron pocket with a frown. "Is it true what I hear? Was Dr. Greyson arrested?"

"Yes, it's true—but not for long. Not if I have anything to say about it."

"Please let me know if there is something I can do to help."

"If you can deliver that message, you'll be doing the most important thing imaginable to help Dr. Greyson."

"I see." The woman's lips curved into a faint smile. "He's done a mighty lot of good. His papa, too. Why, it was his father that got Smithy Brothers working in the Railroad, and because of that work, Brothers heard about my plight, bought me, and then gave me my freedom."

Keziah blinked. "I had no idea."

Rose smiled, her expression tender. "Some days when I'm worn down and tempted to think my meager efforts are too small to make much difference, I remember Dr. Greyson and all the good that came from him igniting a spark in a single man. One person's life can touch so many, can't it?"

Keziah's eyes stung as she squeezed Rose's hands. "Indeed it can. Thank you for the reminder, my friend."

"The tea and sugar are all gone, ma'am."

Keziah watched her mother's face fall. "We have none left? Not even in the cellar?"

Elizabeth shook her head, her lips pressed into a firm line. "No'm. Ain't any to be had anywhere in Savannah, neither."

"How about the cornmeal and flour? Coffee?"

"Coffee's nearly gone. We still have plenty of flour and cornmeal, but it won't last forever."

The three women stood staring at the nearly empty larder. Keziah winced, trying not to let worry consume her. "Hiriam tells me the root cellar still has a few potatoes and onions, though they're small. And there's still a bit of salt pork in the smokehouse."

Elizabeth nodded firmly. "True enough. And we still have some canned fruits and vegetables tucked away in the pantry. As long as the Yankees don't invade, we've got our cow for milk and butter."

Mother heaved a thick sigh. "We've been blessed more than most, that's for certain. Still, we must endeavor to make our supplies last as long as possible. Smaller portions for all of us."

"Yes'm. I hear tell that President Davis is thinking of instituting fast days."

Mother frowned. "I hadn't heard of such a thing."

Keziah interjected. "I just read that in the newspaper this morning. He and his cabinet are considering setting aside days devoted to prayer and abstaining from food."

Mother's mouth pinched in an uncharacteristic way. The woman had never said anything against Jefferson Davis, never offering anything less than glowing praise for the Confederacy's president. But Keziah knew she was thinking that instituting fast days had less to do with prayer and more to do with helping his disgruntled countrymen stay distracted from their gnawing stomachs and empty coffers.

Mother rubbed her temple with delicate fingers. "Be that as it may, we must all endeavor to do our part. Smaller portions and simpler meals."

A heavy knock sounded on the front door. "I'll get it, Elizabeth, since you two are planning meals." Keziah was grateful for the distraction. Her mind never seemed to stop whirring, and she knew it would not desist until she heard word from the blacksmith.

She grasped the cool knob and pulled the door open to reveal a battle-worn soldier staring at her, his bearded face unreadable.

His gray coat was frayed around the collar and wrists. Several buttons were missing. Glancing down, she sucked in a breath when she saw an empty trouser leg had been pinned and tucked behind his knee. The soldier leaned on a worn crutch.

"Yes? May I help you, sir?"

His blonde brows rose. "Keziah?"

That voice. The inflection that had always lurked, though the tinge of humor was absent . . .

She stared into his shuttered eyes and knew. Clasping her throat with shaking fingers, she whispered, "Dear me . . ."

The soldier breathed heavily. "It's me. Nathaniel. I'm alive."

Behind her, a shout of shock rang in her ears. She whirled

in time to see Mother crumpling to the ground in a pouf of black bombazine.

Her brother was home.

Keziah sat in the parlor, unwilling to look away from her battle-hardened brother, fearing that doing so would make him vanish as the spirit she'd thought him to be. Mother fared no better, constantly reaching for his hands or stroking his cheek as if afraid the body of warm flesh and blood would scatter like dandelion fluff.

But he was here, nonetheless. Hearty and healthy. Well, nearly so.

She took in his lean frame, wondering if his whittled shape was due to decreased rations or recovering from the removal of his leg. Perhaps both.

But it was his mind that concerned her the most.

Her lighthearted brother had morphed into a moody, brooding man. Glimmers of his old self would push to the surface until a loud noise of some sort would frighten him; then he would retreat into a seething shadow once more.

He seemed more relaxed here in the parlor, however. Keziah noted all three of them spoke softly, though no one seemed to know exactly why.

"Son, how did such a mix-up occur? Once we heard from your captain—"

Nathaniel patted Mother's hand. "I know, and I'm sorry you suffered needlessly. Apparently, when they were sweeping the battlefield for the dead and injured, the ambulance runner who found us mixed us up. My fellow soldier Charlie was reported to have taken a blow to the leg requiring amputation, and I was reported dead."

Mother's voice thickened. "I've never been more grateful for a mistake. But this friend of yours—Charlie. Was he . . . ?"

Nathaniel stared hard out the window, his face blanching. "Dead."

A heavy tension blanketed the small room. Keziah squirmed in her chair, afraid of saying or doing anything that would cause him more pain.

The boyish looks from when he'd left home had been replaced by hard lines and grooves of unspoken misery. She had no idea how to relieve his burden or even if she could. How could one who had suffered so greatly ever regain his innocence once it was lost?

The front door flew open with a bang and Nathaniel shot up from his chair with a cry, his eyes wild.

Mother stood swiftly, murmuring comfort. "Shh, darling, it's all right."

Laughter bounced through the air and Keziah winced, knowing Jennie had come home from her Vigilance Committee meeting, and judging by her animated chatter, she had brought a visitor with her.

Her flamboyant cousin stopped suddenly when she set foot in the parlor, Lyman Hill just behind her. "Oh! Pardon me, Auntie. I'd no idea we had company."

Mother's smile wobbled. "This isn't company, Jennie dear. Your cousin Nathaniel is alive."

Jennie gasped and moved to embrace him. Keziah glanced toward Mr. Hill. His face was sullen as if he was displeased by the news.

Her heart thumped. If Nathaniel was home to carry the burden of caring for Mother's needs, he would inherit the lion's share of Father's holdings, finances, and business.

And if that were the case, her arranged marriage with Lyman Hill would no longer be necessary.

# CHAPTER 25

APRIL 8, 1862

The clatter of wagon wheels just beyond the prison walls
snagged Micah's attention. Rising on sore, aching muscles, he
grimaced and scooted the chair underneath the window. He
climbed slowly, balanced on the battered piece of wood, and
peered out. A large man pulled the wagon's brake lever and
jumped from his perch behind the matching sorrels.

Something about the giant's stride was familiar, but at this
distance, Micah could not place him. Yanking a crate from
the back of the wagon, the stranger strolled inside the prison
and disappeared from view.

Micah let his head drop against the moist wall as he slowly

slid down onto the unforgiving floor. How many days had he been in this tomb? Two weeks? More? Hour after hour slowly ticked by, each one as dreary and hopeless as the last. He'd heard nothing from his captors since being thrown into the stinking cell. Well, nothing other than the tidbit that a judge had been wired to come for his trial, but the arrival date was uncertain.

Some days he relished the reprieve from judgment. But on others, it was torturous. If God called him to give his life for the cause of freedom, he would give it gladly. But there was little comfort when the process was a drawn-out, agonizing affair.

And when he'd looked up to see Keziah's beautiful face outside his cell, he feared God was doing nothing more than taunting him, forcing him to yearn for things out of his grasp.

He scratched his itchy scalp and grimaced. The only thing more abundant in this dreary jail than hopelessness was lice, no doubt contracted from the foul cot sagging against the wall.

He still marveled that after he'd shed his secret, Keziah had not seemed distressed. Only thoughtful.

He was ashamed he'd thought she would react any other way. Then again, he'd not seen her since his confession, either. Perhaps she'd taken his warning to heart. In any case, he was doomed, but there was no reason for her to throw away happiness too. One of them needed to live if for no other reason than conducting the broken to freedom. She would carry on where he had failed.

And to think Ma Linnie had once told him he was like Moses, fighting to lead captives out of slavery. What a poor leader he'd turned out to be.

From down the corridor, a low voice echoed, bouncing off the mildewed walls. Heavy footfalls scraped closer. His senses snapped to life. Crossing to the door, he squinted, trying to focus on the massive figure ambling toward him. The stranger stopped at his cell, the guard a few steps behind. Micah's breath caught.

The blacksmith?

Brothers shook his dark head slightly as if warning Micah not to speak. He reached inside the crate, and his beefy hand pulled out a small loaf of bread and thrust it through the bars. "Looks like you could use a bite. Am I right?"

Micah nodded dumbly, unable to piece together Brothers's presence. It had been several days since the guards had given the prisoners any food, and his mind felt muddled.

"This should help. Cheerfully donated by the Sisters of Mercy to the poor souls and bodies of the Chatham County Jail." Brothers leaned in and gave him a penetrating stare, his voice hushed. "Perhaps this bit of bread will provide what you've been needing."

Before Micah could thank him, the blacksmith moved away, handing out more loaves of bread to those prisoners in an adjacent corridor.

Scooting away from the bars, Micah knelt and, with shaking hands, tore apart the yeasty softness of the bread. His stomach cramped in response and he tried to chew slowly, despite the impulse to cram the sustenance into his mouth. Plucking off another piece, he paused when he realized some sort of stiff paper was nestled inside.

He gingerly tugged at the paper, and his heart flipped when the bread baked around it fell away. Scooping the morsels onto his lap, he carefully unfolded the missive. The inky script was smudged but readable.

*Genesis 40–41. Sometimes a soul must die to live.*

Micah read and reread the message, attempting to wrap his foggy mind around its meaning. He knew that passage of Genesis. Chapters 40 and 41 dealt with the unfairness of Joseph's imprisonment and how he was elevated out of the prison and into the service of Pharaoh.

But the second half of the note was a puzzle. *Sometimes a soul must die to live.* Was this message baked into all the prisoners' bread? Since it was the smithy who had hand-delivered it, he doubted it. Surely it wasn't a jab at the possibility of hanging.

He rubbed his jaw, noting the scruff of facial hair was growing longer, softer. He felt as if he were circling around something incredibly important yet failing to grasp it.

*Sometimes a soul must die to live. . . .*

Keziah winced as Lyman Hill's normally cultured voice rose in fury, disturbing the peace of Father's library.

"Absolutely not! I refuse to bless such a foolish endeavor."

She spread her hands wide. "But this would be a charity mission! Surely you see what a comfort it would be to those hurting souls within."

"Out of the question." He clenched his teeth, and she felt his ire like hot coals. "The very idea! Traipsing through the jail, offering precious food and reading materials to traitors and criminals . . . No wife of mine would dare do something so scandalous."

Stung by his callousness, she grew still, flooded with a measure of peace she'd not felt in many months. "But I am not your wife."

His dark eyes gleamed. "You will be soon enough. No. I forbid you to waste precious resources on delinquents and trash."

The thought of Micah's handsome face, bruised and battered from cruel fists, flashed in her mind, bolstering her with a courage that unhinged her often-shy tongue. "I have no intention of cowering before a man, any man, when God has clearly directed me to move with compassion and Christlike love."

Sucking in a hot breath, Mr. Hill narrowed his eyes and hissed, "What did you say to me?"

She straightened her shoulders. "In other words, I hereby dissolve our engagement. Now if you would be so kind as to leave."

Flabbergasted, the older man grabbed her by the upper arms and squeezed. "I forbid this! Have you no regard for your father or his dying wish?"

She tried to pull away, but his fingers dug into the soft flesh of her arms. "My father's wish was that Mother be well cared and provided for. Nathaniel is home now and will take over his holdings. You are released from this commitment."

He barked a dry laugh. "Nathaniel, indeed. Are you blind? Your brother is suffering from soldier's heart. Do you really think he can manage your father's business? Why, he'll drain your coffers faster than you can blink when he can no longer withstand the lure of alcohol and morphine."

"Leave me."

With a growl, Mr. Hill released her and paced like a caged animal as she rubbed her throbbing arms. "You would be so cold as to break my heart?"

She gave a thin smile. "Come now, is it my heart that you long for or my father's money?"

Neck mottling red, Mr. Hill came close and she took a hasty step back, bumping into the sharp edge of the desk.

"No one discards me like a worn garment, Miss Montgomery. I have plans for that money and I won't let a silly snippet of a girl keep me from it."

Before she could utter a reply, he stomped out of the library. A muffled *oomph* sounded from the hall. Outside the door, she could see Jennie smoothing her rumpled skirts, a copy of *Godey's* clutched to her chest as she stared at Mr. Hill.

Yanking his coat sleeves down with precise movements, he clipped, "Pardon me, Miss Oglethorpe. I did not see you approaching. I fear I am not myself at the moment."

Jennie darted a glance at Keziah, still inside the library,

then shifted to stare at Lyman Hill once more. "Quite all right. Is there anything I can do?"

"Yes." He seethed. "You can talk some sense into your cousin."

With that, he turned on his heel and left. Keziah released the breath she wasn't aware she'd been holding.

Jennie entered the library, all amazement. "Whatever has happened?"

"I ended our engagement."

The copy of *Godey's* went limp in Jennie's hands. "Surely you jest."

"I assure you I do not."

She dropped the magazine on the desk and frowned. "Why would you do such a foolhardy thing?"

Keziah lifted her chin. "I do not love him."

Rolling her eyes, Jennie huffed. "Don't be so simplistic. Marriage has little to do with love. Unless . . ." Her gaze sharpened. She studied Keziah with an intensity that made her long to squirm. "Unless one is in love with someone else."

Keziah looked away. Jennie's fingers clamped around her wrist, and Keziah lifted her eyes slowly to her cousin's.

"It's him, isn't it?" Jennie's lips were stiff.

"Who?"

Jennie released her wrist, her expression hardening. "That doctor. The abolitionist sitting in the Chatham County Jail."

The air grew thin. "I don't know what you're talking about."

Her green eyes glittered like shards of glass. "Auntie mentioned how chummy the two of you were. And I saw how you reacted upon hearing the news of his arrest. Is it not enough to have one beau while I have none? Instead you have two." Jennie stepped close and hissed, "Tell me I'm wrong."

"You know nothing." Keziah made to step past, but Jennie barred her path.

"Family or no, anyone who dallies with an abolitionist is a traitor to the Confederacy. I would hate to see you mixed up with a turncoat."

Stomach tightening, Keziah fought for calm and met her cousin's stare directly. "I am not your enemy. You have nothing to fear from me."

After a long moment, Jennie's stiff posture relaxed. "That's good. Things like this are so vexing on the system, aren't they? I worry about you, dear Cousin. With your poor health, I would hate to see misdirected affections cause your condition to worsen. Why, some think the best place to treat the falling sickness is in an asylum." A single eyebrow rose high. "I would loathe to see you institutionalized in such a place." Cold warning dripped from her tone, even as a guileless expression blanketed her features.

"A more unjust fate I cannot imagine, especially for someone guilty of doing nothing more than living the life she was born to live." With that, Keziah fled to her room, shut the door behind her, and turned the lock with a resounding click. Pressing a hand to her churning stomach, she exhaled slowly. Jennie had no proof. Only suspicion.

Despite the terror that should be plaguing her, she found

little room for anything but relief. Lyman Hill no longer had his claws in her.

*I'm free of him. Free, free, free.*

As she glanced out the darkened window, she caught the outline of her own reflection but imagined Micah's smile instead.

*You would be proud of me, Micah. So proud.*

Mother stared at her, clearly flabbergasted.

Keziah sighed. "Surely you know I have no affection for Mr. Hill."

Mother pursed her lips, toying with the black pendant winking against her coal-colored bodice. "Nor should you! Love comes with time. You and your generation—" she shook her head—"have become infatuated with emotional fiddle-faddle. To break off your engagement, well, it is something I never thought you capable of."

"I never should have agreed to such a scheme from the beginning."

Mother wrung her hands. "It was your father's dying wish!"

"To ensure your comfort, Mother. Now that Nathaniel is alive and well, the conditions have changed."

Dropping into a stiff-backed tapestry chair, she beseeched Keziah. "You should not have been so hasty to dismiss Mr. Hill. In a time of war, the lack of ready men to marry is disconcerting. And he was willing to overlook your faults."

The remark stung. Keziah spoke slowly. "Indeed, I have many, it seems."

"Don't be saucy. You know what I mean. I'm referring to your—your—"

"Falling sickness?" She studied Mother's flushed cheeks. "Why can't you bring yourself to say it out loud?"

Mother averted her eyes and turned to stare out the lace-curtained windows, studiously avoiding the question. Keziah bit back tears. She shouldn't be surprised. Her illness had always embarrassed her family. *She* had always embarrassed them.

Unwilling to speak further, she stood and swept of out the solemn room. Her heart smarted. She had no control over her condition. Yet why did her family's shame hurt so?

Keziah stepped into the musty library and pushed the door shut with a loud click. Instead of ruminating over the strain of her family's disappointment, she should concentrate all her efforts on helping Micah.

She studied the neat rows of tomes, running her fingers over the hard spines. She would need a relatively new book with stiff, thick pages. And she would need to work quickly.

While Mother stewed about the courting rituals of polite society, Micah was running out of time.

# CHAPTER 26

THE PRISON WARDEN, clutching a pencil and a scrap of paper, caught Micah's concerned glance as he stood beside him.

Micah studied the sickly prisoner, watching the slight rise and fall of his chest in sleep. Too shallow.

"Iodide of potassium every six to eight hours. And prayer."

The warden scribbled softly in the crammed sick bay of the filthy prison. Half-starved men moaned on lice-ridden cots. The stench of sickness thickened the stale air. Upon hearing the prison housed a physician, the warden had quickly put Micah to work treating the ill. Despite the putrid odor, at least the work gave his mind a reprieve and allowed him to escape his cell for several hours. Even this early in the morning, he was grateful.

Moving to another fellow's side, Micah considered the man's sallow appearance. Slight yellowish cast to the skin. Deep shadows under the eyes and thin as a rail. But then again, who hadn't grown thin in this place of misery?

Micah knelt beside him, but the man flinched and reared back, his face hostile when Micah reached for his wrist.

Smiling gently, Micah forced himself to speak calmly. "Don't worry, friend. I'm a physician. I'm merely checking your pulse."

The spindly man glared. "Don't need no physician to tell me I'm sick. I'm here, ain't I?"

He chuckled and rocked on his heels. "I suppose so."

The warden leveled the ill man a glare. "You best watch your attitude, O'Keefe, or you'll be hurting more than you do now." He turned to Micah. "I especially need this one kept alive, Doc. He's the key witness in a murder trial and a coconspirator with the murderer himself. After the trial, you're most welcome to pour strychnine in his tea."

Micah shook his head, playing along. "What a pity. And here I am, all out of my poisons."

O'Keefe shot him a venomous look. "Don't want no addle-brained doctor poking me."

Micah lifted his brows. "Why? You have some other matter to attend to?"

Pressing his thin lips together, the man huffed.

"Can you describe what is causing you discomfort?"

The man reddened and looked away.

"As bad as all that, eh?"

The man's knobby throat dipped as he swallowed.

"Tell me, have you visited any, uh, shall we say, less than desirable places in the past year? Perhaps spent time in female company there?"

He muttered, "It's possible."

Micah rose with a sigh. "His condition, if I presume to guess correctly, isn't fatal. However, if you want him in optimal health for trial, he needs a compound of balsam of copaiba, powdered cubebs, and magnesia." The warden scribbled furiously. "If those can't be obtained, applications of black wash can be administered."

"Black wash?"

"A mixture of calomel and lime water."

The prisoner blanched. Micah patted his bony shoulder and moved away. The beefy warden tucked the paper in his shirt pocket and led Micah from the sick bay.

"I appreciate your help."

Micah shrugged. "I have nothing else to occupy my time."

The warden regarded him thoughtfully, rubbing his whiskered chin. "Sometimes the reverend of St. John's comes by, asking if he can hand out Bibles to the inmates. I don't let him give them out to everyone. Some of them don't get such luxuries when they've been raising a ruckus, but perhaps I'll let him hand one to you. A good turn deserves a mercy every now and then."

Having something to read, especially a Bible to look up the chapters from yesterday's note, would prove to be a great comfort. But as the warden returned him to his bleak cell and slammed the iron door behind him, he thought the greatest mercy would be something he'd risked his life to give to others.

Freedom.

"Where is Auntie Elsie?"

Keziah looked up from the breakfast table. Her cousin's tone this morning was curt.

"She said she wasn't feeling well and planned to rest in her room."

"And Nathaniel?"

"Visiting with Dr. Kelsie."

Jennie sipped her tea. "Anything of import in today's paper?"

Smoothing the *Daily Morning News* flat on the table, Keziah glanced at Jennie with curiosity. Her cousin had recently stopped referring to her as "Keziah dear," a nickname she'd used since childhood. Additionally, Keziah now felt Jennie's stares on her at all times, so much so that she'd had to suspend her conducting activities altogether. The lantern had been cold and the padlock secure for nearly a week.

Keziah took a bite of her steaming grits, scanning the headlines. "The same. Fortifications. Battles. Soldiers either dead, wounded, or missing. Desperate letters from loved ones trying to find their lost. And, oh—" her lips curved into a smile—"it appears General Jackson is in a quandary on whether to move his contingent of troops closer to the battle lines or withdraw and enforce his holdings."

Jennie sniffed and wrinkled her nose as she spooned in another mouthful of the bland fare. "I assume he prayed about this. He's the finest Christian man the South has ever produced."

"If he prayed, he must have felt Providence would deem it wise for him to retreat to higher ground, which was what he was planning all along." Under her breath, she murmured, "It seems General Jackson often finds that the Almighty's will lines up with his own. How convenient."

Jennie stared hard. "Treasonous talk, if you ask me."

Keziah felt heat creep up her neck. She'd said too much. Sighing, she lifted her spoon. "Forgive me if it sounded that way. It's really not. It does, however, still seem perplexing to me that both sides claim Providence is fighting for them."

"Let those cowardly Yankees think whatever they like. We know the truth."

Keziah skimmed the back page, refusing to be baited further, and startled when her focus landed on Micah's name. Amid the list of thieves, traitors, and murderers being held at Chatham County Jail, the paper seemed to shout *Micah Joel Greyson*.

She studied the report, hoping against hope for good news.

It is rumored the renowned Judge Harrison Wilbanks
will be arriving in less than a fortnight to commence
hearings on the latest prisoners incarcerated in
Chatham County. Among the mass of usual reprobates

and vile sinners, the esteemed Sheriff Cole has arrested several dozen men on grounds of crimes related to aiding and abetting the Union, spying, and abolition, some of which involve physically transporting escaped property past the lines of our beloved Confederacy.

Judge Wilbanks, a loyal and renowned supporter of Jefferson Davis, is a harsh taskmaster and has been reported to brook no nonsense when it comes to trying traitors. His judgments are swift and severe. We can only pray for his speedy arrival in relieving our fair city of these heinous criminals.

Keziah swallowed the dry lump in her throat and lowered the paper.

"Anything else?" Jennie asked.

Shaking her head, she folded the bad tidings and tried to force normalcy. Her thoughts spun like a cyclone.

The urgency to free Micah had risen considerably. They must move and move quickly.

"Bread!"

Hungry voices called out for sustenance, their thin hands reaching through the bars.

Just like the last time he'd come, Brothers showed no sign he recognized Micah, only handed him the soft bread. But this time, Brothers also plunged his hand into his knapsack and pulled out a volume with stiff binding.

"A gift from the Sisters of Mercy."

Grasping both offerings, Micah murmured, "Thank you."

The blacksmith moved away, leaving Micah alone with his bread, though the book was what intrigued him most.

The tome crackled as he opened it. When he witnessed the ink-dotted inscription inside, his chest warmed.

*Look toward the Light.*

*Ever prayerful,*
*KM*

He ran his fingers over her curving script and allowed himself the luxury of thinking of Kizzie—her smile, the way her eyes sparkled whenever he challenged her to do something new, her soft laughter . . . all of it a tonic to his parched soul.

*Look toward the Light.* Interesting inscription. Did she mean to continue to hold fast to Christ or something altogether different?

With a frown, he thumbed through the almost-new edition of *Gulliver's Travels*. As he flipped the pages, he noticed in the middle of the book there were odd bumps on several pages, nearly imperceptible by sight. But brushing his fingers over the pages revealed something was indeed different.

He went back to the inside cover, letting the inscription soak deep. *Look toward the Light.*

A gut instinct had him turn to the middle of the book and examine it carefully. Tiny holes dotted the page. A message? Excitement tripped through his veins as he ripped the first marked page from the book and held it up to the lone window overhead, allowing the light to illuminate the paper.

He gasped when the pinprick holes took the shape of words. *Two days.*

Sucking in another breath, he ripped the next page out and held it up. *Freedom.*

His hands shook as he removed the next two pages and held them up as well. *Be in the dead house. Midnight.*

Suddenly the bread-baked message of the week before made sense. *Sometimes a soul must die to live.*

Kizzie and Mr. Brothers had found a way to free him . . . if only he could get himself to the prison's dead house.

# CHAPTER 27

"It's him!"

Mrs. Ward burst into the Montgomery parlor in a state of flummox. The matron flapped her ample arms like a chicken preparing to fly the coop.

Startled, Mother looked up from her needlepoint and stood. "Nannette! Whatever is the matter?"

"Haven't you read the day's paper?"

"Honestly, no. It seems to upset Nathaniel so."

"Here." Mrs. Ward thrust the paper into Mother's hands.

Keziah winced, fearing what was coming. Moving to the women's sides, she interjected, "Perhaps we shouldn't upset Mother with dire news."

"Nonsense." Mother scanned the paper and gasped.

Mrs. Ward smirked triumphantly. "Exactly. Widow Simmons was quite correct. The man she saw being dragged into the jail was that physician. The very physician who came to the house to give me some prattle about illness among the Negroes."

Mother frowned. "Yes, he appears to be one and the same. But why the hysterics?"

Easing her girth into a chair, the older woman scowled. "Don't you see? Just after he visited, Polly disappeared."

Keziah's gaze flickered between the two women as she held her breath, needlepoint suspended above her lap.

"So you think this Dr. Greyson had something to do with her disappearance?"

Keziah spoke up. "Were they even alone together? If I remember correctly, they weren't in the same room except in passing."

Mrs. Ward sniffed. "The timing is highly suspicious." She jabbed her pudgy finger into the middle of the paper. "It says right here that some of the new inmates have been accused of crimes against the Confederacy, spying and aiding runaway property to Union states." With a sound of disgust, she began fanning her flushed face.

Keziah lowered herself to the settee and forced back the hysteria threatening to bubble up. "Still, we have no idea what actual crime the man has committed."

"Time will tell. Mark my words: that man bears watching."

Mother's lips tipped into a dry smile. "Likely the very reason he's in prison."

Keziah breathed a sigh of relief. Mrs. Ward had nothing more concrete than suspicion.

The sound of Nathaniel's uneven step, followed by the soft scrape of his crutch, echoed from down the hall. At his appearance, Mother stood and escorted him into the parlor. "I was so hoping you would be feeling better this afternoon."

With a wan smile, he smoothed a wayward lock of his blond hair away from his forehead. His hands shook. "I can't seem to rest any longer." Hobbling toward an overstuffed chair, he sank into its cushions and laid the crutch on the floor. "And what are you conversing about today?"

Mrs. Ward leaned forward, her blue eyes wide. "Didn't you hear? Not long ago my house slave ran away, and I just found out today that the very man who visited our home before she left has been imprisoned. Possibly for property theft and transportation of slaves."

Nathaniel ground his teeth. "Abolitionist dog."

Keziah tried not to wince at his dark snarl.

The matron leaned back, tut-tutting. "Well, we all know what the Good Book says. Man's heart will wax colder and more wicked as the Day of the Lord approaches. These base, criminal sorts are only proof the Almighty's Word remains true."

Heat flushed Keziah's cheeks and she lowered her head toward her needlepoint. She longed to flee, to run from the self-righteous talk, but she knew she must endure it if for nothing more than appearance's sake.

Nathaniel glowered. "If I ever see Yankee traitors lurking

around this house, I vow they'll never come back again. After what I saw them do . . ." His mouth trembled and he swiped it with the back of his fist. "They captured one of our scouts and then bayoneted him to death. Do you know what they did to the town when they discovered the people there had given him shelter? They burned the whole thing to the ground. Innocent women and children . . ." He choked.

Mother shot Keziah an anxious look but kept silent. Nathaniel seemed so volatile since his return. Dark. Consumed with bitterness.

Mrs. Ward cleared her throat. "Isn't Miss Jennie involved with an antiabolition committee of some sort? I hear they are turning Savannah inside out, unearthing a slew of spies and vermin, all loyal to that devil Lincoln."

A muscle twitched near Nathaniel's eye. "If I were ever to discover one of my friends—or, God forbid, a family member—was a turncoat or one of those dreadful abolitionists, I would toss them out on their ear." He clenched his jaw. "Unless I had the privilege of killing them first."

Mother rebuked him softly. "You shouldn't say such things."

His eyes snapped fire. "Anyone who aligns himself with those cursed devils is dead to me. A Yankee bullet took my leg. A person who consorts with them might as well have ripped off my leg with their own two hands."

With a growl, he stood quickly and slunk from the room, his crutch thumping softly as it trailed away.

Shaken, Keziah watched his departure. Thick cords of

sorrow twisted her heart. Poor Nathaniel teetered on sanity's perch.

He was not well. Not well at all.

<hr />

APRIL 10, 1862

Elizabeth slid a steaming plate of fried potatoes in front of Keziah with a sigh. Mother grimaced at the scant breakfast fare. Jennie, as she often did, turned up her nose at the food she deemed "fit sustenance for the poor."

With a thin smile, Mother picked up her fork. "I take it shopping at the market yielded no results?"

Elizabeth shook her head. "Not a crumb to be had in the whole town. The Yankee blockade has made food scarce."

Jennie groaned. "I feel faint with hunger."

Keziah's patience with her cousin's pampered complaints was lessening by the day. "You are blessed, then, since God provided you food."

Jennie pushed away from the table with a sneer. "I'm not hungry enough to eat what those pitiful Irish immigrants on the bay front consume. They might find it sufficient, but my tastes are much too refined for such measly fare." With a huff, she flounced from the room.

Keziah smiled timidly, anxious to relieve the tense moment. "Personally, I'm thankful for it and have found myself looking forward to these simpler meals. I find them quite enjoyable."

Elizabeth dipped her head and excused herself.

"That was kind of you to say, dear."

"I meant it. I have found this simple food is much easier on my stomach. I don't feel deprived or missing our old fare overly much."

Mother arched a brow. "Not even lemon tarts? Or chocolate cake?"

She giggled. "Well, perhaps on occasion."

They ate quietly. The gentle ticking of the grandfather clock in the hall seemed to beat an insistent drum. Keziah felt antsy, though she was loath to consider why.

A distant boom of thunder sounded and Mother glanced out the window. "Odd. It doesn't look like rain."

Another boom. And another.

Jennie threw open the door, her chest heaving. Both women jumped as she managed to choke out her message.

"The word is spreading like wildfire through the streets. The Yankees are firing from Tybee Island. We're under attack."

Keziah walked the length of the prison hallway, the guard on her heels, his stiff movements betraying his annoyance at her presence. She didn't care. Time was running out.

As she approached Micah's cell, she stalled and wove unsteadily on her feet, rubbing her fingers against her temple.

"Miss, are you well?"

"I'm fine. Just a little light-headed."

The lanky guard grunted. "Small wonder. This place isn't

fit for a lady. Why you insisted on doing your charity work now, when the city is on the verge of attack, is beyond me. The smell alone is enough to turn most men away."

Keziah gathered her courage and took another step forward. "Doing the Lord's work is not always pleasant, but obedience is always rewarded." She glanced down the grim row of cells to see Micah's bearded face peering out from behind the bars. She nearly sucked in a breath. He looked so pale, so filthy and thin.

*Forgive me for scaring you so, Micah.*

Letting her eyes slide shut, she fell limply to the moist, grimy floor.

# CHAPTER 28

WHEN MICAH SAW KIZZIE FALL to the floor, his heart lurched. No more so than the guard's, whose eyes flooded with wild terror. When Micah had shouted he was a physician and had been given permission by the warden to treat the ill, the guard wasted no time fetching him. He scooped Kizzie's limp weight into his arms and raced on wooden legs down the stairs and into the sick bay.

Lowering her onto the table, he cupped her cheek and grimaced at the sharp contrast between his filth-crusted fingers and her creamy skin. Nonetheless he reached for her wrist, searching for the reassuring thrum of life.

"What do you need?"

Micah had all but forgotten the terrified guard. "Clean water, please. And smelling salts. I'll let you know if I need anything further when you return."

The skittish man nodded and raced from the room, locking the door behind him.

Micah stroked her brow and murmured, "What are you doing here?"

Her eyes popped open, shocking him speechless. "Saving your life, that's what."

He blinked as she sat up. "Wha—why—?"

She smiled with such mischievous intent, he longed to take her in his arms and kiss her until he'd driven sense into her head.

"Illness is not always such a terrible thing." Her eyes twinkled. "I faked my falling spell."

Micah felt a slow grin spread across his face. "I always knew you were a vixen behind that beautiful face."

She blushed and leaned close. "We haven't much time. Fort Pulaski is under attack, and the Union may very well invade the city. Not to mention a judge is heading this way in a matter of days to sentence the lot of you to the hangman's noose."

"What are you saying?"

"I'm saying your escape must be tonight."

Before he could offer an argument, she began yanking pins from her hair. The pert snood holding her curls fell away as her hair tumbled free. He inhaled sharply at the sight of the silky tresses. Her loose golden waves were tinged with hints of fire. She was exquisite.

And dangerous. Very, very dangerous. He looked away, fearing he would forget himself if given half a chance.

Oblivious to his thoughts, she ran her hands through the waves and snatched a slip of paper and a thin bundle of currency free. "Here." She handed him the treasures and hastily gathered up her hair, trying to tuck it back into submission.

He glanced at the paper and laughed. "You snuck money and identification papers in your snood? Are you mad?"

Giving him a saucy smile, she secured her snood. "Necessity is the mother of invention."

"Where did you get funds?"

"I sold a piece of jewelry."

"Kizzie—"

"Do you not think your freedom is worth much more to me?"

He frowned, fearing for her. "You take on too much. If caught, you could be arrested, your fate no different than mine."

Smoothing her hair back into place, she lifted a brow. "How lovely to be of enough consequence to be arrested." She eased back on the examination table and whispered, "You must find a way into the dead house. Stay there until Mr. Brothers comes for you." She opened her mouth to say more but snapped into a look of dazed exhaustion when the key scraped against the lock and the guard appeared.

"Is she awake?"

Micah swallowed and took the basin of water and salts from his hands. "Yes, though she took a nasty fall. Dehydration and malnourishment, I'd say."

She blinked as if disoriented. "What happened?"

Micah smiled to himself. She really was quite a performer.

The guard cleared his throat. "You lost consciousness, miss. I think it best that you leave as soon as you're able."

"Of course." She rubbed her head. "I'm just so dreadfully hungry. The blockade, you know."

The nervous guard held out a hand to assist her down from the table. "Do you have a ride?"

Blinking harder, Kizzie leaned against the guard's arm. Crimson crept up his neck. "Yes, of course. My driver is waiting just outside."

The guard shot a harried look at Micah. "I'm locking you in here for the time being. Stay put until I return and I'll walk you back to your cell."

He slammed the sick bay door with a sharp clank and Micah released the breath he'd been holding. Stroking his beard, he puzzled.

How could he ever manage to sneak himself into the dead house when he couldn't even figure out how to escape his cell?

Despite Hiriam's grousing, he did agree to drive from the jail to the blacksmith shop so Keziah could pass along a hastily scrawled coded message, pressing Mr. Brothers to extract Micah from the jail's dead house this very night, earlier than planned. If Mr. Brothers was as faithful as he'd been in the past, she knew he would do anything within his power to free Micah, despite the dangerous circumstances.

Still, the urgency of his need pulled her nerves taut. *Father, protect them.*

They arrived home to find Jennie fuming, whispering oaths under her breath as she paced the parlor, her sage dress swirling around her each time she spun to traipse the length of the thick rug protecting the floor from her wrath.

Keziah frowned as she stepped inside and hung up her wrap. "What's wrong?"

Jennie stopped, her eyes flashing with irritation. "Cursed Yankees! Why must they choose this time to attack? I was supposed to have tea with an esteemed brigadier general at the Ballinger home in mere hours, but the tea has been canceled." Steam nearly rose from her russet pompadour.

"I'm sure there will be other times. Other officers to meet over tea."

"But none of them a single, unattached war hero." With a sigh, Jennie flounced into a chair. "And where have you been?"

"Running errands."

Her cousin smirked. "I'm sure." The malice in her tone was undisguised.

Keziah snapped her eyes to her belligerent cousin's, but Jennie was studiously avoiding her gaze. Why the venom?

Before she could ask, the front door flew open, banging against the wall with a sharp crack. The glass knickknacks adorning the mantel rattled. A masculine voice gave a harsh rebuke to Elizabeth's urge for calm. A lone figure stomped through the house, bypassing the parlor. Lyman Hill.

Keziah took in Mr. Hill's enraged profile as he made haste toward Father's study. Elizabeth followed but stopped at the parlor door.

"Elizabeth, why is he here? What's going on?"

The house servant stammered, clearly befuddled at his irate behavior. "Said he must speak with your brother post-haste. I can't say why, missy."

Keziah's heart pricked and she swung her gaze to Jennie, who was looking out the curtained windows as if the disturbance were normal . . . or, perhaps, expected.

Fissures of fear snaked down Keziah's back at the sound of masculine shouts thinly concealed behind the study doors. The crash of some fragile frippery caused her to jump in fright.

Mother appeared, her eyes wide in her pale face. "Heavens, what is happening, Keziah?"

"I—I have no idea. Elizabeth says Mr. Hill urgently demanded to speak to Nathaniel. They are in Father's study."

At that moment, the study door flew open, and a slew of curses blistered the air. Mother gasped, two bright-crimson spots of mortification staining her cheeks. Nathaniel limped into the parlor, blazing fire as he approached Keziah.

"Tell me it's not true. Tell me." He spoke through his teeth, and she took an involuntary step back. She'd never seen her brother so enraged.

Mother rushed to his side and took his arm. "Nathaniel, stop this at once. Your sister has done nothing to merit this kind of reaction."

He yanked away from her grip, his face and neck mottled red with anger. "Are you a spy, Sister?"

She trembled but glared back. "Of course not! Whatever put such an idea into your head?"

"Mr. Hill saw you."

She blinked, her mind groping for any semblance of rational thought. "Saw me what?"

Lyman Hill stepped into the combustible room, straightening his cuffs, his lip curled into a sneer. "Don't play us for fools, Miss Montgomery. I saw you myself. You visited the Chatham County Jail only just this morning."

Exhaling a shaky sigh, she fumbled for a response. Perhaps the right words would calm her brother's fury. "Yes, I did. I've not withheld my desire for doing the Lord's work, showing charity to the needy souls there."

Mr. Hill stepped close to Nathaniel's side, and Keziah felt as if a pack of wolves were encircling her for the kill. Her fingers brushed behind her, grazing the embossed wallpaper at her back.

"Is that what you call it? Doing the Lord's work?" Mr. Hill gave a mirthless laugh. "I suspect you were only there to visit a Dr. Micah Greyson."

Mother gasped.

Keziah's heart hammered. He knew. Somehow he knew.

"I—I don't know what you're talking about." Her protest sounded weak to her own ears.

"Don't be coy." Mr. Hill's eyes glinted a cold warning. "We all know he's being held at the jail. Not to mention, your cousin has been watching you. Your behavior is suspect at best. All of us witnessed his forward behavior toward you on several occasions, one of which at your own father's burial."

Keziah shot a scathing glance to her suddenly mute cousin. *Judas.* "Of course I spoke with him. He came to pay his respects. We went to school together. Nothing more."

Mother implored, "Please, you can't possibly think Keziah would be involved in espionage. The very idea is ludicrous! She's a good Confederate girl."

Mr. Hill lowered a dark brow. "Then your good Confederate girl has been traipsing about with a known abolitionist. I've done some checking on the doctor. It appears the Vigilance Committee believes he might even be aiding runaway slaves to gain their freedom."

Nathaniel speared her with a dark glare that turned her stomach into jelly. "No sister of mine would dare be involved in something so insidious—would she, Keziah?"

Mother lurched to her side. "Stop this slander immediately! Of course your sister would never dream of disgracing our family in such a way. And consider her illness—she's not capable of carrying out such a thing."

Keziah opened her mouth but realized arguing with Mother would only prove her guilt. Clamping her lips shut, she met Nathaniel's eyes with steely determination.

His clenched jaw could barely form words, but he managed nonetheless. "What say you, Keziah? You can speak for yourself, can't you? Are you an abolitionist?"

She longed to deny it, to spare herself their cruel condemnation. But all was lost now. Even if she denied it, her brother would keep her as a captive at home. Her ability to pass freely had come to an abrupt halt.

Something hot and strong rose up inside her, begging for release. She was tired of being spoken for and ignored. Tired of being told she was too fragile to matter. Tired of living under the weight of shame and embarrassment.

Memories of little Solomon's mangled hand flashed before her and she lifted her chin, resolved, and stared deeply at her brother. "I am."

Mother's tearful wails. Jennie's glare. Lyman Hill's smirk of triumph and Nathaniel's hardened features. She saw them all, yet a peace unlike anything she'd experienced flooded her with calm that was nearly tangible.

A muscle ticked in Nathaniel's jaw as he studied her. Sadness flickered across his face for the span of a breath before a coldness washed it away. "You're a traitor. A worthless, Negro-loving, weak-minded piece of trash."

Keziah stood straight under the verbal barbs, but they stung. Deeply. Blinking back tears, she forced her gaze to Mother's, watching the distraught woman sob into her handkerchief.

"Why? Why should the hue of one's skin be the difference between bond and free? Why should possessions and money be the difference between oppressor and oppressed? The Almighty says he made man in his image. Not just white man, but all men."

The room was thick with silence, save Mother's soft

sniffles, when the back of Nathaniel's hand cracked against her cheek, knocking her into the wall. Pain exploded in her skull and she tasted blood as spots danced before her eyes. Mother screamed.

He loomed over her, the veins in his neck bulging as he shouted. "Are you transporting fugitives? Are you?"

She licked her lips but said nothing, too shaken to form a reply. He'd never laid a hand on her before. Panic clawed at her throat. God forgive him, he was going to kill her.

Mr. Hill's smooth voice attempted to soothe Nathaniel's rage. "Come now. Be reasonable. It's not the girl's fault. She's addled. Not right in the head. Haven't we seen enough of her ghastly episodes to confirm that fact? Punishing her would serve no purpose."

Nathaniel gritted his teeth. "I can't stand to look at her."

She bowed her head, her cheek and heart throbbing. Her throat ached.

Mr. Hill nodded. "Of course, of course. The only reasonable course of action is the one your father balked at carrying out. But I see the time has come. Keziah must go to an asylum."

No! Would her brother truly agree to lock her up and treat her like a lunatic? His bitter words of hate lashed her over and over.

*"Traitor."*

*"Weak-minded."*

*"I can't stand to look at her."*

She tasted the saltiness of her own tears but did not wipe them away.

*"Trash."*

*"Addled."*

*"Treasure."*

The last voice was different. Soft. Kind.

*"You are a treasure, Kizzie Montgomery."*

Micah's gentle words from a lifetime ago pierced her heart afresh as Mother, Nathaniel, Jennie, and Mr. Hill argued about her fate.

*"Worthless."*

*"But we have this treasure in earthen vessels, that the excellency of the power may be of God, and not of us."*

Dropping her head in her hands, Keziah murmured the name of the One calling to her beyond the screaming taunts of madness. "Jesus . . ."

*I make you worthy, little one. You are loved. You are valued. You are my treasure, whom I purchased for a beautiful purpose. I am the God who sees you.*

She raised her head, no longer feeling the sting of barbs flung at her.

*I have this treasure. I have Jesus.*

She picked up her skirts and fled the parlor before the arguing group realized she'd gone.

# CHAPTER 29

KEZIAH FOUGHT BACK TEARS as she stumbled past the ram-shackle buildings lining the Savannah River pier. Ma Linnie's pub had to be nearby. The sun would soon be setting, and the leers of ill-mannered dockworkers would only grow bolder and more dangerous as day slipped into night.

Thankfully, she'd attracted far less attention than she'd feared. The pounding of Yankee cannons had engaged most of the sailors, fishermen, and brawny freight loaders, luring them into the fight. Some had responded to the chivalrous call of duty. Others out of mere curiosity. Either way, she was thankful for the scarcity of prying eyes.

Her head ached but hurt far less than her bruised heart.

Her eyes felt puffy from crying, her legs sore. Every time she considered returning home, the whisper called to her again.

*I love you. You're my treasure. I am the God who sees you. . . .*

Stepping past a slew of dilapidated crates, she winced when the shards of a broken bottle crunched underfoot.

"You're a pretty little filly."

The masculine voice taunting her from behind turned to laughter when she quickened her pace into a run. Footsteps pounded closer. Wiry fingers clamped down on her wrist and spun her around. The foul stench of liquor and body odor nearly gagged her.

A large man with stringy hair snickered in delight as his lust-filled gaze roved over her body. Terror sank its claws in her.

From nowhere, a broom handle hammered her attacker's head with a sharp crack.

Howling in agony, he dropped his hold and gripped his head. "Ow! What did ya do that for?"

A feminine voice scolded, "This girl ain't none of your affair. Get your sorry hide away from my pub."

The man slunk away, grousing and still clutching his head. Keziah turned to see Ma Linnie standing on the curb, broom in hand and a worried look darkening her wide face.

"I thought that was you. Land's sakes! What in all of God's earth are you doing in this part of town, girlie?"

Forcing down sobs of relief, Keziah flung herself into the soft pillow of Ma's arms. Pudgy fingers stroked her back.

"There, there."

Keziah could no longer restrain the tears and sobbed

softly. Somehow Ma ushered her into the pub's kitchen and seated her in a spindly chair, pressing a cup of weak tea into her hands as she spilled out the disaster that had befallen both her and Micah.

Ma plunked next to her at the scarred worktable. "I wondered why I hadn't seen Doc lately. I figured he was holed up, stitching up men for the Relief Commission."

Tears pooled once more and Keziah swiped them away, angry she couldn't stem the well of emotion. "His time is running out. The judge is due soon. Micah will hang if he doesn't escape. I sent Brothers a note. The plan is to smuggle Micah out tonight through the jail's dead house, but what will happen if he can't find a way to get there?"

Ma's eyes twinkled like firecrackers on Independence Day. "Who says we can't give him a hand?"

She blinked. "You can't sneak around the Chatham County Jail! You could be hurt. Or worse yet, arrested!"

Ma chuckled heartily and Keziah frowned. "I don't think it's funny."

The woman shook her head, graying curls springing free from her stained mobcap. "Ain't that. You sound just like Doc only a few months ago. He come in moping something fierce because you were bound and determined to help those poor runaways."

"Micah talked to you? About me?"

Ma took a sip of her tea and grinned. "Ain't never seen a man so besotted over a woman in my life."

Taking a slow breath, Keziah sat still. Micah besotted—over

her? "You must be mistaken. Micah only considers me a friend."

"Ha!" The loud bark of laughter nearly made Keziah jump from the chair. Ma pounded her hands on the table as if it were the best joke she'd ever heard. "Girlie, you need to open your eyes. That man is head over heels in love with you."

Keziah's heart thudded. Warmth spread from her chest, radiating out until it consumed every part of her. Her breath hitched. "But he's never said so."

"Can't. He's got some fool notion in his head that he's bad for you. He thinks if you're with him, your life is in danger. He's made himself nearly sick trying to keep you safe. Meanwhile you're trying to keep him safe, and now you're bossing me, afraid I'll get hurt too." She leaned forward. "When are you two gonna let almighty God do the protecting and get on with your life?"

All this time . . . If Ma Linnie was correct, Micah loved her after all. Heat bloomed on her face.

Ma murmured, "Poor lamb, ain't much we can do about your family. Not tonight, anyways. You can stay with me for as long as you like. But the doc? We can do something for him. Are you up for it?"

Keziah stood. "I'll do anything."

Micah tried not to groan as the prison lackeys dropped him unceremoniously in the packed earth of the jail's dead house.

Faking his own death had been easier than he'd thought.

Early in the afternoon, he'd complained of a pounding head-ache to the guard on duty, requesting a visit to the sick bay.

The guard, one Micah hadn't seen before, had smirked, stating medicinal powders were only for patriots, not traitors. He'd muttered that Micah would be doing them all a favor if he just died.

So he did.

When the evening guard had discovered him unresponsive in his cell, their examination had been a kick in the middle to see if he moved. He took the blow with quiet limpness. He had held his breath while they checked him, thankful the growth of his beard would hide the thrum of life pulsing in his neck. They wasted little time loading him on a litter and dumping him in the dead house. No wonder coffin alarms were all the rage. If the average fellow was buried after an examination similar to the one he received, graveyards were filled with more living than dead.

Once he heard the slam of the outside door and the heavy footfalls die away, he relaxed a fraction, trying not to shiver in the icy darkness. Slitting one eye open, he looked straight up, seeing nothing but blackness. He turned his head and spied a shaft of pewter from a single window high overhead, illuminating the vacant eyes of a corpse staring back at him.

Micah steeled his jaw, tried to force himself to breathe in and out slowly. He would have to wait several more hours in the cold tomb, completely silent and unmoving. When Brothers had brought bread late in the afternoon, he'd whispered terse commands. Failure to stay utterly still might mean capture, especially if the prison lackeys were required to bring in another dead body during their watch.

He had to remain like this until midnight. No movement. No sound. Only breathing.

Judging by the odor seeping through the air, they would be shallow breaths at that.

⸻ ◈ ⸻

"Are you sure about this?" Keziah glanced around the darkened streets as Ma handled the reins of the horses jerkily dragging the hack behind them. Her nerves were stretched thin, but next to her, Ma sat perched atop the driver's bench as if she were doing nothing more than visiting a friend for supper. Could anyone hear them approaching?

Keziah couldn't repress another leery whisper. "I feel like everyone is watching us."

"Pshaw! You worry too much. We're not trying to hide, remember? We approach our enemies with bravado. They'll be less suspicious that way. Besides, I took care of Washington's and Jefferson's hooves, didn't I?"

The older woman certainly had. Wrapping burlap around the horses' hooves and legs had been nothing short of genius. It dulled the clip-clops against Savannah's stony roads. Still, marching up to the prison bold as brass edged on insanity. Keziah shot Ma a sideways glance and clutched the driver's bench with white-knuckle fingers as the monstrosity dipped and swayed side to side.

Ma Linnie was crazier than a loon. She must be to have come up with such a plan.

It was well past midnight and Keziah was nearly sick with fear that something had happened to delay Mr. Brothers. Was it her own terrified concern or Providence trying to warn her?

Peering through the streets, she sucked in a sharp breath. A cluster of dark shapes scattered around the square. The watery moonlight illuminated long shadows. Weapons. And soldiers. A whole passel of them.

Breath freezing in her lungs, she shook Ma Linnie's elbow and hissed, "Turn around."

Ma frowned. "Why?"

"Soldiers. Just up ahead."

Ma chuckled. "I see them. Let me do the talking."

But the woman made no motion to turn Washington and Jefferson around. Keziah nearly retched.

Another minute passed before a harsh voice barked a command. "Halt there!"

Ma jerked on the reins. "Whoa, boys. Hold up a spell." The cranky horses made no protests and immediately stopped as if disgruntled that they were out at such an hour to begin with.

A soldier approached, his steps forbidding. Even in the faint moonlight, Keziah could see the suspicion in his hard face.

"What are you doing out in the dead of night?"

"Heading over to the Chatham County Jail. Funny you

should word it like that. We're the pickup wagon for the dead."

He narrowed his eyes. "In the middle of the night?"

"Not usually. Most times the undertaker has us wait till morning, but there was some poor feller that died day afore yesterday and his family is wanting him buried at home, all proper-like. Gonna be a long drive, and time's a-wasting."

The soldier shifted his firearm. "Lady, don't you know Yankee devils are at our doorstep?"

Ma sniffed as if insulted. "'Course I do! That's why I'm in a hurry to get the job done. I don't figure the Yankees are gonna bury him all proper-like, do you?"

The man fell silent. Keziah held her breath.

He nodded in her direction. "And who is she?"

Keziah dropped her gaze to her lap and prayed her trembling didn't show.

Ma patted her knee. "This here's my daughter. She's a good girl. Always helps me with the pickups and whatnot."

The soldier studied Keziah, and she resisted the urge to squirm. "Can't you speak for yourself, girl?"

Ma clucked her tongue. "Ah, poor girl won't be able to answer you nary a peep. She's a mute. Swallowed a brick of lye soap when she was just a wee thing. I don't know if you can tell, dark as it is, but she's real pretty. Good cook too. Say—" her voice rose as if a brilliant idea had just struck— "you lookin' for a wife? My girl would do you proud."

Flustered, the soldier stepped back, clearly uncomfortable with how the conversation was proceeding. "I—uh—"

"Give it a think. With your comeliness and her being so pretty, you'd have a pack of good-looking young'uns."

Keziah's body flushed hot with mortification. Ma was insane, plain and simple.

Even in the moonlight, it was evident the soldier paled as he pulled at his collar. "She's a beauty to be sure, ma'am, but I—"

Ma slumped as if disappointed. "I understand. Bad time to be takin' a wife, I reckon, what with you brave boys fighting off Yanks."

He heaved a sigh of relief. "Yes, ma'am." With a tip of his gray kepi, he took another step away, ready to flee her matchmaking noose. "You ladies be careful. If our men don't hold Fort Pulaski, Yankee vermin will be crawling everywhere."

Ma batted her eyes. "We're in good hands with you fighting for us."

The soldier cleared his throat and moved aside, letting them resume their rickety journey. Ma snapped the reins with a "Giddyap," and the old horses sluggishly obeyed.

Once they were past the square, Keziah shook her head slowly. "I don't know whether you're touched or brilliant."

Ma cackled. "Sorry for giving you such a start. But it worked, didn't it?"

A smile curved Keziah's lips. The older woman wasn't a loon after all. She was a wily fox. "Still, did you have to go on about what our potential children would look like? It was humiliating."

Ma snapped the reins again, snickering. "Reckon so. But

then again, it got him so flustered, he didn't even think to ask why the horses' hooves are wrapped up."

Keziah's angst unwound a slight degree as she sagged against the bobbing seat. "I shall never underestimate you again." Laughing softly, she murmured, "And I'm relieved you're on my side."

Ma stopped the horses just before they reached the corner of the jail. "We can't go any farther than this. The warden will know I'm not a regular lackey for the undertaker. He'll smell the lie a mile off."

"So what do we do?"

"You need to find some place to hide. I'll divert the guards' attention someway while you sneak past. Find the dead house. If Micah is gone, well and good. If he's not, you drag his sorry hide with you. We'll drive like we're heading out of the city and then circle back. The trees are so thick behind the prison no one will see either of you. There's a secret cargo hold in the bottom of the hack. Micah can hide back there until it's safe. He's transported dozens of passengers the same way. He'll know what to do."

Her heart fluttered like a dozen hummingbirds had taken hold inside. *God above, help me.*

At least the dress she'd been wearing when she left home was black. No risk of detection from bright colors. With a thick gulp, she lifted the hem of her hoopless skirt and ducked into the tall bushes lining the road in front of the fortressed jail. She settled and waited.

She could hear the wagon squeak back into motion and

Ma's none-too-quiet commands to the horses. She must have approached the front walkway, for the creaking wagon stopped and Keziah could hear her loud huff of impatience.

"Foul horseflesh. Just when I need to be in a hurry . . ."

Masculine voices drifted closer. The guards.

"Something wrong, ma'am?"

Keziah could almost see Ma's glare at the horses as she fabricated her story. "Indeed. It's this horse of mine. Washington here is in a foul mood tonight. He keeps stopping. Barn-sour old fellow."

She heard one of the men's low chuckle. "He may have a bit more mule in him than horse, eh?"

Ma snorted. "I should've named him Benedict Arnold instead."

Their laughter burst, then died away. "Why are their hooves tied up?"

Keziah cringed, holding her breath as she crouched in the bramble. The perfumed scent of jonquils tickled her nose. *Don't sneeze . . .*

"Washington here has sensitive feet. Smithy told me that for light travel I should try wrapping his feet in burlap. Says it cushions the strain on his back legs."

"But why are the other one's wrapped too?"

Ma scoffed. "Well, you wouldn't want Jefferson to be jealous of Washington's new shoes, now would you?"

The men laughed and asked her where she was headed. As she spun a wild yarn about getting ready to go to her daughter's house the next county over because she was "scared of them cursed Yanks," Keziah took a deep breath and crept across the black expanse of lawn, focused on the stone wall surrounding the property. With a final glance over her shoulder to ensure she wasn't being watched, she jumped. Her fingers scraped against rough rock.

She gasped for air, every muscle straining. The stones were uneven, providing plenty of places for her toes and fingers to grip. Even with that, stinging cuts broke across her fingers as she clawed for the top of the wall.

There. Her hands curled around the cold rock as she pulled herself up and over the wall. She slid to the ground on the other side with a soft grunt, backside smarting from the impact, muscles burning from the exertion. Taking a moment to catch her breath, she squinted into the darkness, searching for the outbuildings behind the prison.

Where would the dead house be? She crept past small buildings dotting the back property. That one? No. Tool shed. One structure lay directly behind the enormous jail, squatting in its massive shadow. Her pulse quickened.

Keziah brushed her fingertips against the brick, moving slowly in the deep darkness. Feeling her way along the edges, she stopped when her hands rested on a cold iron handle. The door. Uttering a prayer it would be unlocked, she fought down her tremors and pulled the heavy door open.

She slipped inside and set her jaw. Whatever this building was, it was cold. Very cold. The blackness was scattered only minimally by a thin shaft of moonlight from a window high above.

With her hands held out before her, she crept through the building, groping for anything that might tell her where she was. Her hands brushed something that stung. She yanked her fingers back. Something fiery. And wet?

Feeling again, she grazed the solid object before her. Not fiery. That snap of shock was from a huge block of ice packed in wet sawdust. With a groan, she turned back toward the door. It was the icehouse. Not the dead house.

A strong arm encircled her waist, dragging her backward toward the opposite wall as a hand clamped over her mouth, cutting off her scream. She grasped at the hand muting her cries for help, but to no avail. Solid warmth held her tight. So similar to that night long ago outside the church. The same arms . . .

"Who are you?" The soft, masculine whisper held no malice, only urgency. The voice was familiar. Warmth spread through her. It wasn't too late. Praise God, they weren't too late.

Keziah sucked in a cold whoosh of air as the fingers over her mouth slowly loosened. "A friend of a friend." He would know the code words used by both escaping slaves and conductors alike.

She heard his soft inhale. "Kizzie?"

"Yes, it's me."

"What are you doing here?" His voice sounded angry. Afraid.

"Getting you away from here."

She pulled out of his hold and lowered her hand until she

gripped his cold—no, icy—fingers. How long had he been waiting?

"Why didn't Brothers come for you?"

"I don't know. He told me to be in the dead house before midnight and he would arrive soon after."

Unease came over her. "We're in the dead house? I thought this was for ice."

She could hear the humor tinging his tone. "Corpses don't smell as bad if the air is cold."

Shivering in revulsion, she drew him toward the door.

He resisted. "Wait. Where are we going? Who's helping you?"

"Ma Linnie. She'll soon be driving around the back. We must hurry."

He muttered something under his breath and she frowned. "She was my only option."

Covering her warm hand with his own, he moved forward, in the lead. "If that woman doesn't get us shot, it'll be a miracle."

Micah swayed unevenly on his feet but kept a tight grip on Kizzie's slim fingers as they darted across the expanse of yard behind Chatham County Jail. The weeks of malnourishment had taken their toll.

His heart pounded wildly, but he dared not stop. They were close. So very close.

He caught Kizzie when she lurched forward unexpectedly,

her boot snared by a rock or gnarled tree root. Slipping his arm around her waist, he heard her deep pulls of air as she kept pace with him.

Her warm breath fanned his cheek in the night's inky darkness. "Don't—let me—slow—you down. Keep going."

"Not without you." He half propelled her forward toward the stone wall. If she thought he could run and leave her abandoned, she didn't know him at all.

He tightened his grip on her slim waist, a lump of gratitude wedged in his throat. He owed her his life.

The wall lay just ahead. Before she could protest, he hoisted her up, sure she had a good grip, and watched as she disappeared over the top. Glancing around for guards, he gritted his teeth and began climbing, his breath strained. Only when he dropped to the dirt safely on the other side did he dare inhale a full breath.

Free.

They plunged into the blanketed protection of the trees, both of them panting heavily. He braced his hands on his knees and breathed deeply. His legs burned. The sprint across the yard had been the only exercise he'd been afforded in weeks.

Her soft whisper broke the silence. "Ma—should be coming—down this back road—any moment."

He nodded, though he knew she couldn't see the motion. "With what?"

"Two horses—and a wagon."

He frowned. "Won't somebody hear the noise?"

"Ma wrapped the horses' hooves in burlap." He heard the grin shaping her mouth and bit back a chuckle. Only Ma Linnie would have come up with such a tactic.

A sudden rolling sound approached. He peered through the foliage and sighed with relief to see a wagon coming, its warped form outlined by faint traces of moonlight. A robust person sat on the driver's seat. The horses' hooves made little sound.

The wagon slowed to a stop and he reached for Kizzie's hand again. "That her?"

"Yes."

"Let's go."

Emerging from the trees, they darted to the waiting conveyance. He lifted Kizzie into the driver's seat, settling her next to Ma. He then climbed over the wagon's edge and dropped into the bottom of the bed. Ma's round face turned toward him with a sassy smirk.

"Nice night for a drive."

Keeping silent, he smiled in return. As she clicked her tongue, the wagon lurched into motion. He shoved aside a roll of burlap and some scant supplies hiding the cargo hold. If he could find the latch, he'd drop inside and be safe from any surprises.

Before he lifted the latch, he heard Kizzie's sharp gasp. Ma yanked the horses to a sudden halt.

Shuffling sounds. Men's footsteps and a dark-throated warning.

"Hello, Sister."

# CHAPTER 30

KEZIAH SAT MOTIONLESS, unable to comprehend why Nathaniel had stepped in front of the wagon in the dark of night, nor how he could have known they would pass this way.

"Nathaniel? What are you doing here?"

Though only the moon illuminated his features, she could see the smirk. "Trying to find my wayward sister, of course." He shot a glare at Ma Linnie. "Is this another of your riffraff friends?"

Ma cut him a scathing glower. "Boy, you're so wet behind the ears, I've got a good mind to pull you over my knee and give you a thrashing. Haven't you got better sense than to scare two defenseless women in the middle of the night?"

Keziah caught the glimmer of warning brewing in his eyes, and a cold brick settled at the bottom of her stomach. Nathaniel was not himself. Unpredictable as a spring cyclone.

"Wet behind the ears?" He laughed a mirthless sound. "Hardly. Deceived by my lying, Negro-loving sister? Yes."

He was completely unhinged and far too smart to be fooled.

She swallowed. "How did you find me?"

"Where else would you be but trying to free the Yankee scum you're apparently so devoted to? I had a hunch you'd return here. Where is he?"

She lifted her chin but didn't respond.

"Don't toy with me. Tell me where the doctor is."

"Why would I know his whereabouts?"

He smirked. "Stubborn to a fault, I see. Perhaps this gentleman knows more than you do."

A scuffling sound split the air, and Keziah nearly cried out when two more men emerged from the darkness, dragging a bloodied Mr. Brothers with them. Pulling him into the middle of the road, they dropped him in front of the wagon. The burly man rocked on his knees before lifting his gaze to hers. The moonlight turned the bloody mess staining his face into black splatters.

"Do you know this man?"

Before she could reply, Brothers barked a laugh and interrupted, his words slurred from his split lip. "I don't know this lady. Ain't you got better things to do than harassing innocent people?"

One of the men kicked him in the ribs and he collapsed onto the cobblestone road with a grunt.

Taking her cue from Brothers, she looked at her brother with stern disapproval, praying he didn't see her dismay. "I've never seen this man before in my life."

"Really? Because my friends with the Vigilance Committee believe he was on the way to free the doctor."

She remained silent, stretching the tension between them like taffy.

Nathaniel stepped close and, before she could protest, grabbed her roughly by the wrist and jerked her from the driver's bench. Ma protested until the deadly sound of a firearm's hammer clicked through the air.

Keziah grimaced at the pain shooting through her arm. She yanked away from her brother's clawlike grip but stalled when she realized it was he who'd brandished the pistol. Its barrel glinted like ice in the moonlight.

His voice was hard, cold. "Who is this doctor of yours, Keziah? A friend? An acquaintance?"

Her pulse galloped. "I already told you. The man Mr. Hill was speaking of was a friend from childhood. A schoolmate. That's all."

"I don't believe you." He cocked his head to one side and studied her. Her mouth went dry. "What is he really?" He arched a brow. "Maybe your lover." He grinned, his eyes glassy. "Are you a whore as well as a traitor?"

"Enough!"

Micah's commanding voice caused her to whirl in panic.

Jumping from the back of the wagon, he strode toward Nathaniel with measured steps before placing himself between her enraged brother and her. "You'll not speak another word of slander against her."

"Micah Greyson. I should have known you'd be with her." Nathaniel's eyes narrowed. "Your father was ever singing the merits of that demon John Brown, and he raised a son just like him." He sneered. "You always were overly fond of my sister. Tell me, did she come to be a traitor all on her own, or did you woo her to it with sweet words and caresses?"

Growling, Micah smashed his fist into Nathaniel's nose with a sickening crack. The pistol flew from his hands, landing with a thud on the cobblestones. Mr. Brothers suddenly roared and turned on his two captors. Flesh pounded flesh, and she covered her mouth with trembling fingers.

Ma Linnie's harsh whisper sliced through the air. "Keziah, get up here!"

"No, I won't leave him!"

She launched herself at Nathaniel and pulled on his arm, begging him to stop as the two men locked in a fight like angry bucks.

With a grunt, Nathaniel shoved her away and she fell on her backside, pain exploding through her hips. Micah grabbed Nathaniel by his shirt collar and landed another blow to his jaw. Hunching down, her brother slammed his fist into Micah's stomach. His breath left in a whoosh as he doubled over.

The horses pawed the ground nervously as Ma struggled to keep them from darting away. Keziah rose to her feet, wincing against the pain. Brothers had knocked out one of his attackers and was about to finish off the other. Micah and Nathaniel were now on the ground, wrestling over something . . .

The pistol.

With a roar, Nathaniel shoved Micah off him, his eyes wild. The pulse thudded slowly in Keziah's ears when he rose unsteadily and turned toward her, weapon in hand.

His voice shook. "You've disgraced the family, Keziah. You've disgraced Father and all who know you. I'll not let you continue."

He raised the pistol, aiming directly for her heart, and she heard Micah's shout as he scrambled for the outstretched weapon.

*God, forgive him.*

An explosion rent the air as a solid presence flung itself in front of her. A cry of pain. The person blocking her collapsed to the ground. Fists pounding flesh again. Brothers shouted, "I'll deal with him . . ."

Feeling numb, slow, she looked down at the person crumpled in a heap before her. She heard a scream of anguish and suddenly realized it was her own.

Hiriam lay at her feet, crimson blossoming across his chest.

Keziah cringed as she clung to Hiriam's hand in the back of the wobbling wagon. One look at Micah's grim face and she knew the man she'd loved all her life was slipping away.

Somehow they'd managed to get him into the wagon, and now Ma urged the horses toward the Negro church. Micah stayed at Hiriam's other side, continually checking his pulse and pressing his hand to the bleeding wound.

Keziah gripped Hiriam's limp hand and felt her throat constrict. "Why did he jump in front of me?"

Micah squeezed her shoulder. "Because he loves you."

Gulping down a sob, she kissed the old slave's knuckles.

Time blurred as they arrived and carried his limp form into the church and down the tunnel, lowering him onto a lumpy cot.

Rose rushed into the room, carrying a flickering lantern, a thin robe wrapped around her nightdress. She stared at Micah. "Doc? Is that you?"

Keziah realized how different Micah must look to Rose. He'd lost weight, and a dark beard covered his jaw.

Rolling up his sleeves, he answered tersely. "It's me."

Keziah moved to Hiriam's side and gripped his limp fingers again. His eyelids twitched.

Micah hastily began unbuttoning the blood-soaked shirt, muttering to Rose. "Gunshot. Near the heart. Still alive but barely."

The woman moved to bring Micah clean water and towels as Keziah stroked Hiriam's gray-whiskered cheek. After a moment, his dark eyes peeked open. He grimaced but, upon seeing her, softened.

As Micah leaned over to assess the damage, she wiped her blurry eyes.

"Hiriam, why?"

The old man rasped, choking on the words. "I heard Master Nathaniel. He went crazy. Threatening to kill you." He wheezed and she tightened her grip on his fingers. "So I followed him."

She kissed his hand but never let her gaze leave his face as he struggled.

"I—I was wrong. Should have helped you more with the runaways. The Almighty's plan may not always be the path of least resistance. Fact is, his way is where the old devil throws us the most trouble." Hiriam flinched and shifted. "I lost sight of that. What you—you and the doc do . . . it's important. Freedom . . . it's worth fighting for. Worth dying for." His eyes misted as his lips tugged upward. "That's my gift—to you."

Tears streamed down her face as Micah pressed a cloth to Hiriam's wound. Crimson life soaked the rags. She pressed another kiss in his palm and sobbed when his rough hand cupped her face.

"I'm—proud—of you, missy. You're—the daughter—of my heart."

With trembling lips, she whispered, "I love you."

He smiled and then winced. "Love you too."

Micah's movements grew more hurried and Keziah felt a niggling awareness that Hiriam was losing ground. Anguish swelled in her chest.

Micah's eyes met hers over Hiriam's chest and she could see it—the sorrow, the certainty this sweet man would not live much longer.

Something gurgled in the old man's chest, and Micah grasped his hand. "Stay with me."

Hiriam shook his head, his expression serene. "Jesus done called me to go home. I saved Missy Keziah. It is enough."

His eyelids slowly drifted shut.

"Hiriam!"

But it was too late. He was in the presence of Jesus, leaving behind the most beautiful smile she had ever seen.

⤙⧫⤚

Ma Linnie frowned and propped her hands on her hips. "You got to eat something."

Tucked in the back of the pub's greasy kitchen, Keziah pushed away the grits growing cool in the dented tin plate. A knot had wedged in her throat and refused to leave.

She toyed with the spoon. "I can't. My stomach is in a jumble. Since last night . . ." Tears blurred and she hastened to wipe them away before Ma's probing gaze could witness her volatile emotions.

After Micah had seen to Hiriam's burial arrangements, Ma had led them back to her pub in the wee hours of the morning. She'd given them each a room, and Micah had shuffled into his, likely asleep before his head hit the pillow. Keziah had lain awake, squirming against the iron-framed cot, but sleep refused to come. Every time she closed her eyes, Hiriam's face shuttered in death rose up, and tears she thought she had exhausted squeezed out. After two hours of tossing and turning, she'd given up and risen to help Ma prepare breakfast.

She stared at the congealing grits. "What will happen to Nathaniel?"

Ma plunked down into a chair, cupping her steaming mug of chicory coffee. "Likely not much."

"But he killed Hiriam!"

Ma sipped and knit her brows. "The authorities won't care."

"But . . . the circumstances . . ."

"Ain't no jury in the South gonna convict a slaveholder of doing what he wants with his own property. You know that well as anyone."

Keziah rubbed her temples. "What Hiriam did . . . I don't deserve it. I—" Choking on a fresh sob, she kneaded the tight skin over her eyes.

Ma's soft hand patted Keziah's arm. "You got to stop beating yourself up. He knew what he was doing. He sacrificed so you could live. Make the most of his gift."

Schooling her emotion, Keziah nodded and straightened her spine. Ma was right. Still, the weight of all of it—Mother's heartbreak, Micah's escape, Nathaniel's wrath, and Hiriam's death—it was too much.

She grabbed a semiclean rag and wiped spilled splotches of grits from the worktable. "I don't know what to do with myself. I don't even have a place to go."

Ma waved a hand. "You can stay here, of course. Don't think another thing of it."

"Only if you allow me to earn my keep."

"Fair enough."

Keziah tossed her a grateful smile. "Thank you. Your kindness—"

"Is nothing more than God telling me to love you, child." Ma finished her thought with a grin. "It's no hardship."

Dropping the soiled rag in the wash bucket, Keziah teased, "No wonder Micah thinks so much of you. Speaking of which, I need to talk with him. See what he plans to do next."

"When you come back, we'll tackle meal preparations."

"Yes, ma'am."

Keziah pushed her way through the overly warm kitchen, walked down the quiet corridor toward his room, and knocked. No answer.

The poor man was exhausted. She rapped again, harder this time. Ma had said the pub had few guests currently, so she need not worry about waking anyone. No stirring or sound of footfalls reached past the closed door.

She fought a sudden unease. "Micah?"

A swell of panic burst in her chest, and she twisted the tarnished knob, opening the door with a soft squeak. She stepped in and stopped, her heart crashing.

The bed was made, sheets tucked neatly in place. The room was swept free of any personal items save for a single envelope propped on the nightstand, Keziah's name scrawled across its front.

Micah was gone.

# CHAPTER 31

JUNE 14, 1862

"Come on, miss. How many times are you going to break my heart?"

Keziah shot the grizzled man an amused look as she gathered his empty plate. "When will you cease asking?"

The other fellows gathered in the pub chuckled as Old Man Brubaker smiled widely beneath his wiry beard. "I'll stop when you finally say yes."

Ma Linnie cackled from the corner. "George Brubaker, you're old enough to be her great-grandpappy. Stop teasing her so."

"Aw, you never let me have any fun." The men laughed

and went back to their war chatter, newspapers, and cups of switchel.

"Think Lee can take Virginia?"

"Likely so. We've been beating back those blue-bellied Yanks for months now. Kept them out of Savannah."

Another voice spoke up. "They did take Fort Pulaski, though."

"Sure enough. Then they turned tail and ran. Lincoln's puppets are a spineless lot."

"Don't know about that. You hear of this Yankee fellow Ulysses Grant? Jeff Davis better keep his eye on that one. . . ."

The never-ending cycle of war talk usually intrigued Keziah, even more so since she'd been living with Ma Linnie, who actually encouraged her to read as much of the paper as she wanted—a luxury rarely afforded back home. Mother had always discouraged her in "using her mind overly much." But the news didn't capture her fancy today. The sameness of everyday life had grown gray and bland.

She trudged into the kitchen with the soiled dishes and dropped them into the washtub. Staring into the dancing water, she allowed the steam to warm her skin, despite the sticky humidity gluing her bodice to her back.

She just wanted to feel something. Anything. Anything but this longing ache for Micah.

She shoved the memory of his smile away. He had left her with no warning, but she didn't blame him. Not really. Had he been recaptured after escaping jail, the sheriff would have hanged him first and asked questions later. Micah did what was necessary. Still, his abrupt departure and meager note had stung, leaving only a painful void behind.

She'd read his good-bye letter so many times, the seams of the hastily folded note were beginning to crumble.

*Dearest Kizzie,*
*I leave you, for the time, in Ma's capable hands.*
*Never lose heart, hope, or faith, and never forget you are treasured.*

*Ever your friend,*
*Micah*

The note was etched in her mind. It sounded like a final farewell, save for the use of "for the time" and the boldness of "ever your friend"—a letter closure usually reserved for betrothed couples. She was flummoxed. But mostly she feared for his safety. And she missed him. Dreadfully so.

It had been two months and no word, each day stretching longer than the last.

With a fortifying breath, she closed her eyes and did the only thing she knew to do with her troubles. Pray.

*Heavenly Father, you know where Micah is. Keep him safe. May he sense your comfort and peace with him. Lord, bring us together again, if it be your will. If not, help my heart to accept it.*

*Your will be done.* She'd never before realized how difficult a prayer that was.

Keziah added the other soiled dishes scattered around the kitchen to the wash pot. She ought not be glum. Ma had been so good to her, taking her in when she had no place to go and no skills to claim.

Despite the strain of physical work, she felt well. Rested. She'd had no illness or episodes since living above the pub. And Ma had sheltered her like a mother bear, constantly wary of anyone who might be curious about the new girl staying in her lodge.

Ma entered the kitchen, huffing against her girth and carrying a tray piled high with more dirty dishes. "Land's sakes, those men leave more messes. So glad I'm not a man."

Keziah took the loaded tray from her outstretched arms. "That makes two of us."

Ma plunked into a chair and fanned her flushed cheeks with her apron. "Mercy, it's warm today. Doesn't help that half those fellows in there are smoking like chimneys."

Keziah grinned. "I heard Ironside Stewart tell Old Man Brubaker that smoking would send him into eternal punishment."

Ma snorted. "Smoking won't send a feller to hell. It only makes him smell like he's already been there."

Giggling, Keziah dropped the last of the dishes into the steaming water and went to work cutting up curls of lye soap to add to the brimming pot.

"You feeling all right?"

She squirmed. The older woman was far too wise and observant. "I'm fine."

"Humph. Never took you for the lying sort."

She whirled around and opened her mouth to defend

herself but, upon seeing Ma's eyes soft with sympathy, cut off the protest. "I don't know what's wrong with me."

"Feeling at loose ends?"

"I suppose so."

Ma continued to fan her red cheeks. "Understandable, considering all you've been through. You missing home?"

Was she? Not much. "No, not really. Not with Nathaniel's rage or Jennie's betrayal. I don't miss Mother's constant worrying, but I hate that I hurt her so deeply." Her shoulders sagged.

"Things may be different between you all one day. Perhaps after the war is over."

"Perhaps." Keziah turned back to shaving soap into the washtub. Maybe she was missing the thrill of conducting, an activity that had been at a standstill for the past two months. Brothers had warned them he was being watched and would have to suspend all Railroad work for the time being. Eventually, he promised, the smuggling of slaves would resume. Maybe she was searching for some kind of excitement besides cooking meals, washing dishes and linen, and cleaning dingy rooms.

No, it wasn't excitement. She longed to matter. To make a difference in someone's life. She *needed* to matter.

"You miss Doc, don't you?"

Her throat tightened, and she could do little more than nod. She couldn't even explain her feelings. How could she describe what she hardly understood herself?

She was weary. That was all. Numb from too many

changes. Listless from the halt of excitement. She would never give voice to such thoughts to Ma Linnie when the woman had been nothing but kind to her, but in some ways, the pub felt not much freer than her home. She couldn't leave, fearing she'd be recognized by Nathaniel or one of his cronies.

The customers didn't even know her real name, only calling her Ann, a precaution employed by Ma to ensure her identity remained a secret.

She had simply traded one prison for another.

Prison or free, any of it would be easy to bear if Micah were by her side.

# CHAPTER 32

Keziah breathed in autumn's distinct spice as she walked through crunching leaves and snapped twigs littering the yard of the old schoolhouse.

She had braved leaving the pub more of late, though rarely had she gained the courage to travel this far. Perhaps it was the passing of time, or maybe the recent knowledge that her brother had married, giving him something to occupy himself other than ranting over his wayward sister and the evil abolitionists slithering through his city.

Upon hearing the news of his nuptials, she lifted a prayer for his heart to soften and for his mind to heal, not only for his sake but the sake of his new bride as well.

She was not foolish enough to think she would be welcomed back home with open arms. Someday, if Providence ordained, but not during the hot, pulsing emotions of war. The country continued to rip further apart. The Union was finally beginning to win their skirmishes, but the worst was far from over.

Word had gotten back to her that Mother had begun telling friends Keziah was ill and living in a sanitarium. Whether it was a lie she had concocted or a lie spun by Nathaniel's lips, Keziah didn't know, but it likely saved Mother from societal repercussions after Keziah left home.

*You just want it to be you and me right now, don't you, Father?* She'd reached a point where she stopped looking for Micah's return. She thought of him every day—in truth, every hour—but God had shown her that he was not simply overseeing her journey. He *was* her journey. The realization had not taken away the pain but had brought her a tremendous measure of peace.

She walked slowly, savoring the rare quiet, pausing to admire a flaming red maple as she tucked herself deeper into her shawl. The faintest nip in the air boded that the days were steadily shortening.

As she passed the old clapboard schoolhouse with its peeling whitewash, Keziah meandered to the grove of trees just behind, relishing the scent of dying leaves. Absently running her fingertips over prickly bark, she smiled. Memories found her at every turn, but they were no longer painful. Only sweet.

Laughing children in trousers and pinafores. Lunch pails. Ribbons and primers. Slates and pencils. Aggies and skipping games. Childish infatuations and innocent heartbreak.

Keziah paused before the Kissing Tree and let her eyes travel over the carved initials, the deep grooves of hastily scraped hearts. *B loves L. Darcie loves Jim.* So many names and stories.

"Are you still searching for your name?"

Heart in her throat, she gasped and turned. She knew that voice. . . .

She pressed her back against the Kissing Tree, and her pulse skittered when she found a pair of blue eyes staring at her with unrestrained intensity.

Micah.

He stepped away from the tree in front of him, moving slowly toward her, holding her captive with his gaze. She heard the tremor in her own voice, feeling as shaken as the crimson leaves rattled by the soft breeze. "Am I dreaming?"

"I was about to ask the same. You're even more beautiful than when I left."

Heat flushed up her neck, but she could think of nothing other than that he was standing before her, his countenance brimming with something indefinable. Something that unearthed sensations she thought she'd buried. He was alive. Clean-shaven, healthy, strong, handsome, and blessedly alive.

She bit her lip, suddenly uneasy, feeling undone as he moved closer.

"How did you know I was here?"

"I stopped by the pub. Ma told me."

She felt her voice crack. "I was so afraid . . ."

He stopped short and smiled wistfully. "I know. And I'm so sorry I had to leave when I did."

She stared absently at the thick-trunked trees surrounding them, toying lightly with a low-hanging limb at her fingertips. "Where have you been?"

"Philadelphia."

"Working at the hospitals?"

"No." He shifted his weight. "The Pennsylvania Abolition Society."

She took a moment to absorb the news. She'd heard of the pioneering antislavery organization. It had become a major advocate and driving force behind the Underground Railroad.

She looked everywhere but his face. What was wrong with her?

"I made it there, half-starved and exhausted. William Still gave me a steady job, allowing me to treat the malnourished and sick who came to their door."

She didn't want to ask—knowing might be too painful. But she couldn't stop the question nagging her. "Why did you come back?"

"Look at me."

Slowly she lifted her eyes to meet his.

"You know why I came back."

Did she? Her mouth felt dry as rolled lint. Before she could protest, he slipped his fingers into hers and tugged her deeper into the grove of trees. "Come with me. There's something I want to show you."

Confusion swirled through her as he led her to a large oak tucked deeper into the thicket behind the school. He looked into her upturned face and his grin turned tender.

"I never found the courage to show you this before. I wanted to, but . . ." He swallowed. "Look."

Blinking rapidly, she focused on the rough bark as Micah removed his free hand hovering over the tree trunk.

*Micah loves Kizzie.*

Amazement and warmth flooded her like crashing waves against rock.

He pulled her to him and cupped her face in his warm hand, his touch achingly gentle. "I've loved you for as long as I can remember. Deep in your heart, you know why I returned. I cannot live one more moment without you."

Tears burned her eyes as her spirits soared. "I love you too, Micah."

He nuzzled her forehead and temple with his lips. "I was always too shy to tell you. Even when we were nothing but children, I longed to carve our names on that old Kissing Tree, but fear held me back. What if you didn't feel the same way? So one day I snuck out here and carved our names on this tree instead. I determined to make you mine from that moment on."

Prickles of delight rose on her skin at his low voice and gentle caresses. "Micah, it's you. It's really you."

He leaned in and claimed her lips, sweeping her toward

him with his fevered embrace. Long moments of tender desire were broken by his shaky breath as he reluctantly pulled away and placed his forehead against hers.

"I know what I said before about societal obstacles, but it's not the same in Philadelphia. If we were to move north, things could be so different. Better. For us and our children." He paused. "What I'm trying to ask is, will you marry me?"

She threw her arms around him and laughed with joy. "Oh yes! I'll marry you. God could give me no greater gift."

With a whoop of elation, he picked her up and twirled her through the air, only stopping when she gasped with laughter. She traced the line of his jaw and wrapped her arms around his neck, knowing she was grinning like a lovesick girl. She didn't care. God was giving her the desire of her heart.

"But you're still a wanted man. And I—"

He kissed the tip of her nose. "Not in Philadelphia. I already have a home picked out up there. In fact, Mr. Still was quite adamant I return quickly with my bride. He's eagerly anticipating your arrival. It appears they are in great need of women willing to see to the needs of other women and children who arrive at their door. And of course—" he winked—"I've been searching for a nurse to aid my work as well."

She giggled as he smothered her face in light kisses. "I'm not a nurse. I have no qualifications."

His voice husky as he feathered his lips across hers, he murmured, "Mm, the primary qualifications are unrivaled courage, blonde hair with tints of red, cinnamon eyes, and that the applicant be in love with the physician."

Her stomach flipped as she melted into his embrace. "In that case, I'm more than qualified." She pulled away and led him back toward the schoolhouse.

Tucking her close to his side, he laughed. "Where are we going?"

"To tell Ma Linnie, of course."

"Something tells me she already knows. From the moment I brought you into her world, she's teased me mercilessly."

Her brows rose in surprise. "Really? What did she say?"

"'It's plain as plain can be, Doc. That pretty little thing has engraved her name on your heart.'"

# ACKNOWLEDGMENTS

THANK YOU for taking this journey with me. The adventure began as a family vacation to the beautiful city of Savannah, Georgia, and blossomed into a deep love for the charming Southern town. Many of the buildings and businesses in this story are fictitious, though I attempted to remain true to Savannah's historical layout. Some of the details of the First African Baptist Church of Savannah are also fictitious, but this historic building really was used in the Underground Railroad, and the congregation continues to meet today. You can learn more about this amazing place of worship, the people who served there, and other fascinating points of interest by visiting http://firstafricanbc.com/history.asp or http://www.savannah.com.

From the moment I stepped foot on the city's cobblestone walk, I was entranced. God slowly unfurled a story in my heart—the tale of a girl who battled epilepsy as a child, just as I did, but grew to understand her worth in the eyes of a loving God. That story flowed from heart to pen, and I'll ever be grateful for the many who helped bring this novel to your hands.

Jesus, thank you for being the One who sees me. Your love is unfathomable.

To my supportive husband, Todd: thank you for giving me the freedom to be me. I love you. Bethany, Callie, and Nate: laughing, learning, and loving with you three is one of the greatest gifts God has given me. Being your mom is a joy. (Bethany, I attempted to "do in" as many characters as I could, but I'm not a suspense writer. I'll have to leave that to you, my dear.)

Morgan and Taylor, I can't wait to meet you and hold you in my arms. Mommy loves you.

To Dad and Mom, Ron and Linda, my brothers and sisters, nieces and nephews, Grandma Gladys and Grandma Joyce, cousins, uncles and aunts, dear friends and adopted family: you are treasures. My life would be incomplete without you.

To Janet Grant, my incredible agent, who shows grace at every turn yet pushes me to give my best: thank you. There is no one else I would want to have with me on this journey.

My deepest thanks and appreciation to Jan Stob and my phenomenal editors Shaina Turner and Danika King, as well as the entire Tyndale team. Shaina, thank you for seeing the potential in this story and for your unrelenting encouragement. You have blessed me beyond measure. Danika, your fingerprints on the edits made it blossom into something far greater than I could have done alone. I stand in awe of your talent.

To all the Bookie authors and my writing peeps at ACFW Arkansas: thank you for being the best cheering squad ever! Your laughter and wisdom are gifts that keep me pressing forward on the hard days. To my wonderful church family at Pilgrim Rest and my faithful Vision Team supporters: a thank-you seems inadequate for all the prayers and love you've offered up over the years. May God bless you as you have blessed me and countless others. Special thanks go out to Nate and Tami Sakany, as well as Allen Arnold, whose mentorship in teaching me to "write with God" has transformed the way I approach each moment.

I can never thank you enough, dear reader, for sharing your time, your thoughts, and your heart with me. As I wrote *Engraved on the Heart*, God continually brought you to mind. You were prayed over as I struggled to find each word, each thought, and weave it into something that might settle down deep. If you've struggled with feeling ignored or rejected, may Keziah and Micah's story be your own. You are loved. You are treasured. There is a God who sees you, and he has engraved your name upon his heart.

## ABOUT THE AUTHOR

A PASSIONATE LOVER OF STORIES, Tara Johnson uses fiction, nonfiction, song, and laughter to share her testimony of how God led her into freedom after spending years living shackled to the expectations of others. She is a member of American Christian Fiction Writers and makes her home in Arkansas with her husband and three children. Visit her online at www.tarajohnsonstories.com.

# DISCUSSION QUESTIONS

1. Keziah and her family often worry about the social stigma associated with epilepsy. Though we now live in the era of modern medicine, can you think of any illnesses that are still widely stigmatized or feared? Why is that the case? What can you do to avoid shaming and instead support people who have these conditions?

2. When Micah returns to Savannah after five years in Philadelphia, he realizes that he no longer fits in. Why not? Have you ever gone back to a place you once lived and felt the same way? What was that experience like?

3. After Keziah hears Amos speak and learns about the brutality of slavery, she prays, *Forgive me for my apathy.*

*I've never truly seen the horrors inflicted upon your children,*
*have been content to turn away as long as my own home*
*was happy. . . . Help me make a difference.* How does God
answer her prayer? Have you ever been awakened from
apathy in a similar way? What was your response?

4. Micah tells Ma Linnie that he wants to prevent Keziah
   from involving herself in the Underground Railroad.
   In response, Ma Linnie says, "Love doesn't manipulate.
   And it doesn't control. Love gives, even if it costs the
   giver everything." Is there a relationship in your life
   where you've seen Ma Linnie's definition of love in
   action? What happens when love does try to control
   and manipulate, rather than give?

5. Though Hiriam is a slave himself, he initially opposes
   Keziah's desire to help fugitive slaves. Why does he
   react this way? Did you sympathize with his reasoning?
   What eventually changes his mind?

6. Throughout the story, various characters voice their
   belief that God is on the side of the Confederacy. Why
   do they think so? What causes Keziah to disagree with
   them? Why is it dangerous to believe that God is just
   on the side of your group—politically, socially, or
   otherwise?

7. Were you as surprised as Keziah when she answers the
   door to an unexpected arrival in chapter 24? In what

ways does this person upset the balance of peace in the Montgomery family? What changed him so drastically?

8. Keziah faces opposition to her abolitionist convictions from her entire family. What enables her to stand up for what she knows is right? Have you dealt with similar opposition from people you loved? How did you react?

9. Near the end of the book, Keziah finds peace in the midst of Micah's absence: "God had shown her that he was not simply overseeing her journey. He *was* her journey. The realization had not taken away the pain but had brought her a tremendous measure of peace." Have you ever waited a long time for something you weren't sure would ever happen—or are you in a period of waiting right now? Why is it so difficult to trust God during these times? What does it mean that God *was* Keziah's journey, rather than the overseer of her journey?

10. If the story were to continue beyond the last page, how do you imagine Keziah's and Micah's lives playing out? Would Keziah's mother ever change her mind? What would become of Jennie? Of Nathaniel?

Look for the next novel
by Tara Johnson

COMING SUMMER
2019

# TYNDALE HOUSE PUBLISHERS IS CRAZY4FICTION!

### Fiction that entertains and inspires

Get to know us! Become a member of the Crazy4Fiction community. Whether you read our blog, like us on Facebook, follow us on Twitter, or receive our e-newsletter, you're sure to get the latest news on the best in Christian fiction. You might even win something along the way!

## JOIN IN THE FUN TODAY.

 www.crazy4fiction.com

 Crazy4Fiction

 @Crazy4Fiction